The Champion's Test

By M. Francis Lamont

For Uncle Ed

Dragons Never Die

"Holding Up the Whole Damn Line"

First thanks go, as always, to my daughter Morgan. Keep on dreaming and don't stop dancing. Tanya, my beloved cousin, wine, and cheese in the mountains sounds good soon. Wendy, Analyn and my good luck girls, Amber and Emily, I know you're always there to help. Amanda, Dillon and Laurel and the crew at Longriders, I'll never forget how you encouraged me. To my fellow Captains, Barbossa and Jack, your prayers held me up, and your laughter kept me sane, thank you.

To my cast of heroes; Barry, Craig, Dan, Dustin, Gwen, Liam, Manu, Simon, Todd, and Viva. You all inspire me with your words and works. I'll never forget your advice and will be forever in your debt. Eternal gratitude to you all. Special thanks to Viva for plugging the series on Patreon, I love you!

A special shout out to the man, the face of the series, Will Taylor. You're a dear friend and superstar in the making. I can't wait to see what your future holds.

A huge and unforgettable thank you to everyone who bought a copy, shared a post, or posted a review. Each of those things make such a difference for any author, especially a new one like me.

Last but never least, to the people I wouldn't have made it through the drama without, my 'team': Erin, Heather, Karla, Steff, Lila. Thank you for the 'red pen' opinions.

M. FRANCIS LAMONT

CHAPTER 1

Violetta was unmistakably terrified of the way that the gladiators were staring at her. How could she be so foolish as to forget that the other gladiators trained in the same space as Cassian. She knew that they shared cell space but the sudden reality that they could reach out to touch her just as easily as her lover could was unnerving. The rain fell on her shoulders, a heavy weight on a body already cold and weary, but the light in the doorway was a welcoming beacon in the dark that held the promise of warmth and respite from the downpour.

She leaned into Cassian's embrace. His arm holding her tight against his chest, the heat radiating from him helping to stop her shivers.

"Come, let me show you the way." The medicus said with a welcoming smile that eased a touch of her trepidation.

Once they were within the torch lit corridor, she watched Cassian brush a strand of his long sun-streaked hair behind his ear so that it fell over his shoulder and exposed the bruise darkening on his jawline. She could only imagine the pain that he was in and with a glance at the head of the medicus, his jet black hair bound in a single tail down the middle of his back, she decided that she could no longer hold back words simply because she was a woman in the domain of men.

"Medicus? The injury was sustained to his jaw. Vitus Census applied his fist with a violent rage. The son of Felix was utterly bent upon destruction. I pray that the damage is such that you can repair it."

Waiting for his response filled her mind with concern for Cassian and the weariness of the night started to make itself known throughout her body. The druid turned his head to smile at her he leaned his head to inspect the injury she was explaining, nodding in understanding of her words. It felt as though he understood that she had lived a life in constant fear, hiding in the shadows but now was finding her voice with newfound confidence.

"We shall see better in greater light. Follow to the infirmary." He said, turning to unlock the door.

While he tried the key Violetta let her dripping head rest against Cassian's chest, closing her eyes for a moment. A second arm wrapped around her, holding her tight against him so that they could savor the contact for every second before the next stage in the night's adventure began.

Cassian led her inside, grinning at his friend for a second before his lips fell in a wince of pain. "Arturo," His hand gripped the druid's shoulder as he continued. "Before you break a single word let me say that I stand aware of the need for surgery and that you would say that your drugs are needed to make such a thing happen. You should know that I would prefer you to bring the German with a hammer to knock me the world of dreams."

The druid laughed and Cassian looked back down at Violetta to murmur through the painful swelling. "Arturo stands the only man who hold a love for blades that rivals my own. Though his are of a different sort I pray you do not develop a similar taste." His eyes twinkled with laughter despite the pain that he had to be in, making her smile in return.

"I do not think that is a worry you need carry." She replied, glancing at Arturo who was looking at the tools he must have prepared in anticipation for operating on the man that stood as his dearest friend. The looks passing between them reminded her of that between brothers even more than friends. "Still it does seem like the skills I am intended to learn here, those that Tertius has commanded my efforts towards, are tied to that knowledge. Even if I am not to use them once I am gone from there." She said, the words carrying a note of sadness that she could not hide.

"I do not intend that you will leave these walls to return there Violetta." Cassian said, "I do not yet know how I am to achieve it, but I mean for you to stay with me the rest of our days."

Wordless with relief that his affection for her seemed to have remained constant even upon his time to reflect on the events of the night and her blame in his injury.

"Dominus has instructed that I am to assist you in any way that I am able. I have had no formal training, but I am quick to learn." Violetta smiled "I am hopeful that you do not find what skills I have to be lacking."

"I am certain that your skills will be adequate enough for this night." He said with a warm smile "There is one talent you possess that no one else upon this earth does. I would put it to use and get the needed surgery underway as soon as our patient is prepared properly."

She watched the look of protest wash across Cassian's face, but Arturo's voice and demeanor left no room for it, from either of them.

"What skill is it that you think I have that will aid in the preparing for a surgery that I cannot being to know how to accomplish?" She looked back and forth between the two men, hoping that the medicus did not hold some illusion that she had knowledge of drugs besides the vial he had prepared and sent to her. "Did…did Dominus say that I held knowledge of medicines? Apologies if he did, I do not possess that kind of knowledge."

"All that Tertius said to me was your name, Violetta." Arturo said. "The skill I refer to is that of enthralling the god of death and convincing him to let me, pardon, let us use some drugs to send Cassian to sleep so that I can do this surgery the way it needs to be done. If he is awake, you will spend more time soothing him than you will learning."

He had begun to open vials that were resting upon the table and lighting candles at an alter against the wall. Wrinkling her nose at the smells assaulting her senses Violetta tried to take in what he was saying and what it meant. "Enthralling a god? You wish for me to pray while you work? After convincing him to take your drugs, the same that almost led to his death in the arena the day I was upon the pulvinus?"

"There will be no drugs and I will not be asleep for hours after this is done." Cassian growled, shaking his head at the table and its contents. "Arturo, no. You knew my answer before I set foot upon the sand and you would have my woman attempt to convince me otherwise? To think, I told her that you were a wise man. You stand a greater fool than the Romans she left behind in the house of her Dominus."

Sharing a glance with Cassian Violetta knew that part of his protest was worry for her. He did not want to leave her unprotected against the curiosity of his brothers. Each man had a different story of how they came to be a gladiator; some were prisoners of war some were attempting to work off debt but a great many of them were criminals. Everything from theft to rape and murder was represented on the sands just feet away from where she could be alone in an hour or so. Was she safe or was his concern well founded?

"You will take the drugs and there will be surgery." Arturo said in a calm voice despite Cassian's anger. "You need the rest and will need it even more so after the task I must do. You will not be required to train tomorrow or the day after. No matter what the lanista says I am not going to risk you rebreaking bones or having the incision become infected."

"I said I will not submit and that is where I still stand. Arturo, I told you that day, after the games, that I will not take such again, willingly." He pushed past both the medic and Violetta, heading towards the door. Near the exit, whether from pain or weariness, Cassian stumbled, losing his balance, and almost upsetting the torch from it's sconce in the wall. Violetta rushed to his catching him around the torso.

"You have caught the very god I referred to Violetta. I pray enough for any two men, but all my prayers are useless when it comes to the one you now hold." Arturo chuckled and continued to prepare his instruments.

"Steady self and see reason in words from beloved friend. You fight the inevitable." Violetta said, easing her champion back to sit upon the table. She attempted to sound firm and resolute like Arturo but internally she was trembling with fear that he would make for the door a second time, forcing her attempt a more intense resistance to his departure. That alternative would surely see one or both to the ground and she wished to avoid that if possible.

The uninjured corner of his mouth tightened downward as she continued despite his protesting glare. "If you wish to take to the sands as you say, to train for the upcoming games in Rome, then this surgery is as critical to that even as any other element of training. There is no avoiding it Cassian."

He studied her face momentarily then looked away, frustration written on his brow as he battled his training and knowledge against his own wishes. "The games of Romans" His voice was slightly bitter in the tone, trying to hide a fear she could well understand. The break was not lethal, but surgery was always a thing that would carry the risk of death. The gods alone knew what would happen to any man beneath the power of the medicus' drugs.

Violetta pleaded silently that her words would be enough to persuade him to allow the procedure. This was what she had been brought to the infirmary for instead of the house. Would Tertius rethink his decision if she were not helpful tonight? Sinking dread replaced hope the moment he spoke, his voice made rougher by the pain that must be growing with each word.

"No. I know too much of these poisons and the effects they cause on a man. Their potential for harm is to great, as is the price." He shook his head, firm in his refusal but still not meeting her eyes. "I stand with my refusal."

"The price is just as high if you refuse Arturo. Dominus will know. If he thinks you are incapable of fighting he will refuse you your training and withhold you from the games in Rome." She countered, taking a step towards the door, and closing it. Turning to face him she sighed. "That would remove the purpose of my being here in the eyes of Tertius and Census both. I will be returned to his house as soon as he hears of this."

Stepping closer she reached to touch his hand "Give voice to fears and see them answered." Looking at Arturo she hoped that he would join her in trying to convince Cassian to break words regarding what was bothering him about the surgery. She had always thought him to be fearless, but this reaction could not be explained with any other word than fear.

"I have no fear of this or the man that wields the blades." Cassian said. The anger in his voice startling her. He glanced at the druid behind her then sighed. Reaching to take her hand and thread his fingers through hers, Violetta shivered when his other hand touched her cheek. "If you wish it so then I will allow it. I would not be why you are sent back to that place. I will not be the cause of your return to fear and torment."

"Gratitude. Gratitude Cassian." She smiled and brought his hand to her lips to press a kiss to his fingers. "I do not want to leave your side and I swear to stay by you through this. Mine will be the face you see when you wake. I will be here."

"The girl accomplishes more with a few words and a soft touch than I could with an hour of argument." Arturo stepped up to them both and clasped his hands around theirs, which felt, to Violetta, like his blessing given to their union. "He may be the gladiator, but you are my personal champion. Help me prepare the wine for this foolish, stubborn, 'god' Violetta."

She smiled and joined him at the table near the wall. "I can follow directions if you are able to explain what is needed."

CHAPTER 2

Cassian watched the man that was as dear as a blood brother to him instruct the woman that held his heart on how to mix the drugs that would put him into a sleep deep enough that they could mend the injury to his jaw. He hated the need for the drug as much as he hated that he would be unable to be here for her on her first night in the ludus he called home. Would she be harassed? Would Tertius truly leave her to sleep in the cell down the hall from the room they now stood in? Perhaps Arturo would return to stay with her after his prayers, but how could he know? How could a sleeping man protect anyone? Especially a woman who was as lovely as a goddess situated among men who, if they were lucky, the women they saw were nothing but whores sent to pleasure them for coin in their master's palm. Especially a woman who was as lovely as a goddess, here among men who, if they were lucky, saw nothing but cheap whores sent to pleasure them for the coin in their master's palm.

"Do you two mean to conspire against me in all such matters or will you allow me the allegiance of my woman in some things Arturo?" He said, wincing, wishing that he had not tried to make the joke. The pain was dizzying and the tension from it was starting to cause his entire body to hurt.

"I assure you that I will not coerce her loyalties unless absolutely needed. She is yours and yours alone." Arturo said, trying to reassure him with a glance over his shoulder while he guided Violetta's hands to blend the oils needed for the vial he would consume in moments.

He had faced dozens of men in the arena, he was told it was near a hundred matches, less than five of them had lived and only three of them had defeated him yet he was nervous about the next few hours. Had love made him a coward now?

"You would have my gratitude for this Arturo, but I will wait until this is finished to offer it." Cassian growled.

Watching Violetta slowly stir the vial made him want to smile. She was so focused and serious that she was not looking at him, but he was mesmerized by the calmness that she had about her. Perhaps this was what she was meant to do? He had never seen a woman medicus before, could Violetta be the first? "What say you Violetta? Are you the loveliest medicus I have ever seen?"

Looking up at him with a smile that sent his blood racing, the vial held out like an offering to the gods instead of to an injured fool of a man too proud to admit the fear of the unknown.

"I will do my best to learn, to become one." She said quietly.

Her hands were steady, but he could tell her voice was nervous. Slinging an arm around her waist, pulling her close while taking the vial into grasp. "Then I shall toast to love and friendship and the hope that they are enough to guide me back after this." Without another word he tipped the clay vessel back, swallowing the sweet brown liquid with a grimace at the unwelcome taste.

She pressed against him and kissed the corner of his mouth before both she and the druid eased him down on the table. Cassian could not help but stare at the steel and copper tools on the tray beside him. Arturo had handcrafted most of them, designing them in tandem with Cirandon to suit the medical needs of the men in the ludus and their, unique injuries. The tools of regular medicine had been declared inadequate by the druid years ago and even now there was still need for more, new tools. He often heard Arturo lament the fact that he was now forbidden to use the works of the blacksmith because of his refusal to acknowledge the lanista as any sort of superior to him, as a man or master.

The drugs were beginning to do their job, Cassian's vision blurred and his breathing relaxed, he would sleep soon, and no one could know if he would wake later. "Goddess, little priestess, swear to me that you will stay within these walls until I wake. I…it is not safe, there, while I sleep." He looked to Arturo. "Lock the door brother. Lock it when you go to prayer and I give oath that I will wake, no matter the pleading of the gods for my eternal company."

He felt Violetta slipping her hand into his "I am here with you and I will stay, at your side. Your hand will be in mine until you awake." Her voice said, the last thing he heard before falling into oblivion.

"Put his hand down and wash your own." Arturo said, his eyes never leaving the tray of instruments he was preparing. There was no time for gentle words or coddling, the length of time since the injury was already increasing the danger and risk of infection. He did not want to comment on the fact that the continued talking between the lovers did nothing except to cause Cassian more pain, more swelling, complicating the surgery that would already be dangerous enough.

"You will need to listen and do exactly as I instruct. If you deviate or hesitate, it could cause a bleed to worsen or, if you make a grievous error, it could kill him. I will not lie to you and say that this is easy. You do not, really, know what you are doing so if there is any chance that you are unable to do what is needed you must tell me that now. I can find other hands to assist me if required but you were brought here for this purpose." The druid met her gaze, his dark eyes probing to see if she was afraid or doubting herself. "I know you love him, but can you treat him?"

"I would see him whole once again, able to do what he loves; fighting upon the sands of any arena, standing victorious champion once again in the eyes of all." Violetta said, with an amusing note of defiance in heir voice.

Arturo wondered if it was possible that the child did not know who he was in the ludus and in the life of the man on the table before them. "You leave the question unanswered Violetta." He said, bringing the prepared instruments back to the stand beside his operating table. "I need to know, now, this instant, if you are capable of setting love aside for medicine. If not then go sit down, pray if you hold any faith, and leave me to get my work done."

The firmness in his tone frightened her, perhaps bringing to the surface some memory of a fearful encounter in her former house. He felt angry for her that this had been her life until this moment, but there was no time for pity if they were to save not only Cassian but the other men under his care. If they were going to be a team and save not only Cassian but the other men that were under his care. There was not a day that did not see someone within the walls in need of aid and she had to be able to handle them without fear and with the confidence of a medicus that would see them calmed and ensure that they did not, always, see her as a beautiful girl but as the one who would mend their injuries.

"Yes medicus." She said, letting go of Cassian's hand with a visible reluctance that he could sympathize with but for now he had to be firm.

When she returned to the table, he handed her the tray of tools. "They are arranged, specifically in the order they are going to be needed. Pay attention and be quick in your response. I will have no delays in this. He means as much to me as he does to you, though in a vastly different way."

When she looked up at him from the tray, he was almost certain that there were traces of tears in her eyes, though she might be curious at his words it was obvious that her emotions were getting the better of her. "Violetta," He began washing the injured area to prepare it for the first cuts. "I know that you are scared, just as Cassian is. You need to put that aside for the time being. I can promise you that you will have the time you need to shed tears and pray to your gods for…whatever things a girl like yourself offers prayers for. In this moment, however, you must brush aside tears, thoughts of the night's events, no matter the pain of them, and ignore your fear. Trust in me as Cassian does, as Tertius and the gladiators do. I am well skilled, and this operation should be a success. I will need your aid, now, for that to happen. Focus on the task and it will be over soon. Hand me the first blade and bring the candle closer but do not tilt it and cause the wax to pour on his flesh."

She held the candle still, and he watched her eyes flicker between Cassian and himself. "Blade and pay close attention while I find the shift in the jaw that will show us where the break is. If we are blessed by the gods it will not be as bad as it seems. The swelling and bruising can hide many things.”

He pressed his fingers along the line of the gladiator's jawbone, whispering prayers that the damage was not the dangerous break he feared. Closing his eyes at the subtle shift beneath his press Arturo took the blade in hand and brought it to the edge of the swelling. “I am going to cut though the swelling to see if the break is complete or if it is merely a fracture partially through the bone. One will require more cutting and the setting of the bone, the other merely a protective covering and a few days rest. Which will be as hard to convince him to do as it was to take the drug needed to examine him.”

He was rewarded with a nod that almost spilled the pooled wax. “Careful girl. I do not want to see him burned.” He said, slicing the delicate flesh slowly, easing it aside to expose the bone. “Look here. Do you see what I see Violetta?”

Arturo thought that she might gag when she saw the red oozing around his fingers. The bone finally showing itself after he sponged away enough blood had a crack across it, he could not tell at this angle how deep the crack went an if it was a break or just a crack.

“I see, Medicus, but what does it mean?” Violetta asked, bringing Arturo from his thoughts of simple medicine and back to the need for teaching this young girl. Explaining how to do what he was about to do and why, ensuring that the man under their joint care was able to wake in the early hours of the morning when the drugs would wear off.

"It means that there needs to be a deeper cut to discover if the jaw is broken or cracked. The difference could be life and death, it could be the difference between the sands or mines."

He glanced up at his student, as he suspected she was even paler than she had been when she arrived, but he was thrown by the determination in her eyes. Perhaps there was more to this slip of a girl than he thought. Certainly, there had to be more than her beauty, fear, and the need to be protected to make Cassian want her for more than a night.

"Then hand me the next blade and bring the light closer. We continue. Steady hands and do not look away." Arturo said, refocusing himself as well as his student with his words.

Executing his commands precisely Violetta responded, "Your words, my will, Medicus."

CHAPTER 3

Hours later, Violetta sat holding Cassian's hand while she prayed that he would wake. The druid had been gone for two hours if his candle time piece was accurate. He had locked the door behind him, whether it was trapping her inside the room or keeping any man in the halls, Roman or gladiator, from being able to enter, she was not sure. Whatever his reason for it she knew that she was safe enough for the moment. While she was safe from further trauma it left her mind to focus upon the disaster that was her participation in the surgery and how she had almost cost the man she loved his life.

It was just after Arturo had made the deeper cut when more blood poured down Cassian's jaw to the table. She had leaned forward, trying to give him more light and see the damaged bonc for herself, but the wax from the candles had dripped onto the druid's hand. She had screamed in horror as the blade in his hand had slipped to cut downwards.

There had been no time then for apologies, it was a rushed, instinctual, reaction to the cut. He had sworn in a language she did not understand, barking commands for cloth and stitching, heated blades to stop the bleeding and prayers that it had not been too deep. She had been terrified that Cassian was going to bleed to death in front of her and it would have been her fault.

There had been tears on her cheeks when, at last, Arturo looked up at her. "I told you not to lean the candle, I told you that was going to happen." His tone had made her jump, when he stood up setting down the blade and pointing at the other tools. "You will cease tears and do as you are told, handing me tools. If you cannot do that then go weep in a corner and be useless to me for the rest of the night. I will have a guard take you to your cell when I am done."

His voice was so full of anger that she had almost burst into tears once again. Glancing down at Cassian, laying on the table with his life in the balance Violetta dug deep to find the courage to face the angry druid. "My apologies Medicus. Which do you need next?" Setting the candle down next to her lover's head while Arturo ignored her words and stitched the new wound closed. The druid seemed to be muttering to himself, whether in prayer or annoyance she could not tell, so she gathered several more candles from around the room so that the light was concentrated in the area around the surgery. "Perhaps this shall eliminate the need for my hands to be occupied with anything other than fulfilling your commands."

Her words and the increased light made the dark-haired man raise his eyes to meet hers with a little less anger than had been there before. "A wise idea woman. Now, hand me both those tools near your left hand and then tilt his head towards you, slightly. Move him gently so as not to jar him or the injury."

His voice was calmer, gentler, with the new light. She hoped that, perhaps, she was going to be forgiven for the accident now that she had corrected it without needing him to tell her how. Perhaps he was like Meridius, the body slave of her proper master who was like a father to her, and respected actions more than words. Doing as she was told, with a slow, calm, pace they finished the surgery as a team. When it was done Violetta attempted to start a conversation once again.

"Apologies one again medicus. I do not, I did not, know how to stop the bleeding. I did not intend to burn your hand." She looked down at the risen blister on his hand "Can I tend that for you? I may not know much of surgery but burns I know. The son of my Dominus enjoyed burning some slaves. I have much more experience with injuries born of abuse than I do with weapons of the sands."

"There is no need to offer more apology Violetta." Arturo replied. Holding out his hand to her "You treat a burn with… what?" He asked as she applied a wash of cool water to clean the blood of surgery away and expose the burn.

"I am treating you with cool water to cleanse, and then I will apply the juice from inside this plant." She brought a small plant in a clay pot from the bag of things she had packed in the final minutes in her former house. "I do not know if you are familiar with it but there was a slave from a region of Africa where the skin of man is as black as night, he used this, the juice inside the leaves, to treat the burns of a brand."

She carefully sliced the tip of a leaf and squeezed a few drops of the greenish glossy fluid onto the burn, coating the entire area before looking up at him for his reaction.

"What is it that your friend calls it?" Arturo asked, picking up the pot with his other, still bloodied hand.

"He is no longer of this world. Aloe Vera is what he called, though." She smiled at him "The juice can be drunk as well as used on many other injuries." Looking around the room at the windows. "I could grow it here, in this room. By the windows would be good. Do you think it would be allowed? Would you allow it?"

His face was dishearteningly neutral, the dark brows even and brown eyes staring at her as though she were mute. His full lips twitching to one side were the only indication that he had even heard her.

"Arturo? Do I have your permission to grow more aloe?" Violetta asked again, with a clear voice. Would he be able to see the use of the plant or was he going to ignore it because he had little faith in her use inside his structured world of the infirmary?

"I grow most of my herbs, the ones that I can, in the sanctuary garden I use for my prayers." Before she could ask to see it he held up a hand to silence her "I will not allow another in my garden, so I will allow you to grow it here, as long as you are an infirmary attendant. Keep it out of my way and do not let it distract from your learning what I am commanded to teach by the fool upstairs." He said then turned to finish washing the unburned hand free of blood.

"Gratitude Arturo." She replied, almost to herself since he did not seem to care for her presence. His tone at the mention of the lanista's orders worried her more than she wanted to admit. Cassian had said that he would welcome her, for his sake at least, but it seemed as though he already begrudged her the space in his work. Even though she was to assist him with the heavy workload Tertius had said that he carried the druid did not seem to want help. Perhaps he feared that she would not be able to face the other gladiators, making her less useful than he needed her to be. Remembering the looks from the men in the yard she wondered if perhaps he was right.

"I respect that this is your world medicus. You did not want an assistant and, I am sure that after tonight's mistake, you certainly do not want it to be me." Her voice was not as confident as she wanted it to be. "Cassian trusts you, so that means that I am supposed to trust you. For that to happen, sir,

I need you to be honest with me, even if it is unpleasant, even if you hate me. I need to know who to trust."

"I would have to know you if I was going to hate you Violetta." Arturo said with shake of his head. "You can trust that I would keep you safe from the dangers of the ludus even without the request of Cassian. You can trust that I will do what I can to teach you what you need so that you can stay close to him. He cares about you. I think he loves you more than he has loved anyone in his life. Those things do not equate to trust for either of us."

He was dodging the answer to her question. He was a decent man was all that his words said. "What would it matter to you if I trust you? Your actions say that you do not want me here and I caused an accident that. I will find a way to be helpful to you, I will learn to do what you need from me."

"If you are to learn, if you are to become a medicus, then you will need to trust me." He made his way to the door, unlocked it before stepping out into the hall that was now as dark as the midnight sky outside the window beside her. "Perhaps in the morning we will find a way to start building towards that. He should wake soon. Give him water when he does."

She had no chance to answer before he left her with Cassian and her thoughts with the door locked between her and the rest of the house filled with men that would see her as prey to their desires, at least until the man asleep on the table was able to establish his protection over her, if he still wanted to.

Looking around the room Violetta sighed in relief to see a tray of food being kept warm beside the fire. She could not remember the last time she had eaten and standing up from beside the table she felt faint, near to falling. Sitting back down on the hearth she turned to keep her eyes on Cassian in case he moved or woke from the drugged sleep, she forced herself to eat slowly, savoring the simple fare in the quiet peace of the infirmary.

With all the candles still beside the operating table most of the light was concentrated there but the glow was enough to finally give her a chance to take in her surroundings. There were shelves along two of the walls. The looked as though they were carved right into stone. Once her meal was finished, Violetta rose to her feet to inspect the contents of the shelves and the herbs that were hanging from the rafters.

"So many different things. How does he use these for medicine when they're cooking herbs?" She asked the sleeping gladiator, knowing that he would not answer.

Taking a candle with her to glance over the shelves she was immediately frustrated to find that not only was every bottle labeled in writing instead of symbols. She was fairly certain that it was the language that the druid used in his homeland. It was unlike anything she had seen before.

She put the bottle back on the shelf, twisting it so the label was visible. She could not read in her own language, or even that of Greece where her mother had been from. It was an impossible thing to even consider reading in such a strange tongue. Walking around the edge of the room further it was a surprise to find an alter in the darkest corner.

The top was a mess of former offerings and ashes from candles and incense. "No wonder there was a mistake in the surgery. The gods must be displeased because of the state of their alter.

Setting down the candle and taking a few more from beside Cassian Violetta drew more hot water from the pot by the fire. Washing the surface of the alter and each icon and idol carefully before putting them down in the proper places, not knocked over or backwards. Once she had all the pieces, including candles, properly in place to honor the gods of medicine in any country, she prayed and lit the incense to go along with the words. She hoped that though the druid's gods were different from her own, that Cassian's gods were different than her own, that they were hear her plea regardless.

Prayers offered and the alter restored Violetta made her way back to her lover's side and sat, determined to be with him when he woke, so that he saw her face as soon as his eyes opened. Her persistence was no match for the weariness of the night in the house of Census, added to the stress of the day combined with the surgery. In a matter of minutes her head was upon the table and her eyes were closed in the deep dream filled sleep of a mind at ease.

CHAPTER 4

Deep in the ludus Argus sat, staring through the bars at the empty cell beside him, the one that should be occupied by Cassian. It had stood empty for weeks while Cassian was gone. He had thought that the man had been sold or died, Cirandon had not told him if either was true. Whether it was due to lack of knowledge or instruction from their Dominus the German had not been willing to speculate. Now the man had returned, with what was either a child or a small woman pressed to his side, but his cell remained empty though it was well past midnight.

All the other men were asleep, he had seen the druid pass by on his way to pray to the gods of his homeland in the villa garden where herbs and vegetables were grown for the house and infirmary, even the lights of the villa had been extinguished for the night. Still Cassian did not appear. Had the man died in the infirmary or been removed to the villa once again?

Since that girl had been 'gifted' to him months ago his friend, his brother in arms, had not been the same. He had been a more driven force in the arena but at night, when they were face to face with each other in their cells there was less talk, less banter regarding the other gladiators and the Romans commanding them all. He had talked about the girl; things she had said, things he had said and what she mean to him.

Argus was almost certain that the woman would lead Cassian to his death or at least cost him the newly regained title. If the small being pressed to his said was Violetta, then the world of the ludus was about to change. Would the champion of the house be distracted by the knowledge that his woman was within the villa? Would it lead to his injury or make him fight harder? How in Hades the Celt had managed it he was afraid to ask. The woman did not belong in this house, in the ludus or anywhere near gladiators. Someone like that would be nothing but a distraction to anyone attracted to her. He thanked the gods that he did not suffer such from such. just then he heard bare footfalls coming down the hallway.

"Who comes?" He called, his voice a dangerous growl.

"You would if there were not bars between us gladiator." Replied a soft but masculine voice in the shadows.

"Jovian?" He said, almost laughing at the response. "How is it that you come here? Did Dominus forget you before locking the gate?" Argus wondered if the youth were afraid of the other gladiators and that was why Jovian had come looking for him, safe in the knowledge that he would be as safe as possible here.

Stepping into the light of the nearest torch Jovian's dark eyes met his own and Argus could not help the smile that spread across his lips at the welcome sight. "I stand more than glad to see you boy. Do you risk the wrath of Dominus by being here?"

He watched the answering smile falter and knew that Jovian was thinking the same thing that he was the anger of the lanista was a thing to be feared by even the great among the gladiators. It did not take more than the wrong look or word and the whim of the Roman to see a man sent from the house to the fighting pits in the heart of the city's underbelly.

If Tertius were particularly offended the slave in question might be sent to the mines west of the city.

Coming to his feet Argus considered briefly if that was what had happened to his training partner. Had Cassian been sent somewhere for displeasing Tertius? Was that why he had been gone and had returned with an injury that had taken him…to the medicus. The realization hit him hard. The champion, wherever he had been sent, had been injured. The way he held the girl with a protective tenderness and the way that she jumped, flinched, and cringed at every loud noise spoke to a lifetime of abuse. Cassian, a man who was always aware of his surroundings, had become even more vigilant. He watched every man, even his own brothers-in-arms, as though they were a threat to the woman he so obviously cherished.

He was still without the man that would help him get to the greater part of the games, without the training he needed to stay alive because of that girl. If she were anything more than a child, she would have to answer to him and more than a few others among the brotherhood. The Celt was well liked, and the woman was disposable, they all were. Every woman in the bed of a gladiator was just like the one before, nothing special. Not like the wild-eyed youth in front of him.

"Jovian? You stare with wild eyes but speak no words. Are you in danger by being here or are you here because you are in danger from someone else?" He asked, suddenly needing to know the answer immediately, before anything else was said.

"I am in no danger from Dominus tonight. He is in bed with his wife."

His lips curled at the last word making Argus wonder if Jovian felt the same way about women as he did? "What sent him there with such certainty that he will not be looking for you? I do not want you to be hunted and hurt because you are here with me. Why are you here so late with bars between us?"

"I took Dominus' robes when he joined Domina in their bed. I do not think he realized that he left one of his sets of keys linked on his belt." The boy had a wicked grin on his face when he added. "With the wine they have there is little chance of them leaving that room before the sun is high in the sky."

"Then it is fortunate for me." Argus said with a lazy grin spreading across his lips. "Where did you go tonight Jovian? Where did Dominus take you tonight that brought Cassian and the little viper back with you?"

"Viper?" Jovian tilted his head, sending the dark curls of his hair sliding over his shoulder and making Argus want to play with the dark ringlet. "Violetta? She is…sweet." He said with a strange smile. "She loves Cassian, even though she knows he used to bed every whore brought to him. She knows that and still claims to love him. Is that not a strange thing?"

Argus simply shook his head, he wondered if it was a lie to get the man to risk his life to save her from whatever troubled her at the house of her Dominus. Who could forgive, ignore, such a past at Cassian had? Argus wonder, if faced with the choice, could he overlook the same past? He looked down into the deep dark eyes and knew, he could forgive nearly anything. "Maybe not so strange if you believe in love. Perhaps she does?"

He wondered if Jovian had ever thought that what he did with their Dominus was wrong? For many it would be something that could not be overlooked, even if the lanista put him aside, stopped calling him to his bed for sexual gratification. There were many men that did not see body slaves, those that served the bed and bodily needs of their masters, as anything more than whorish toys. He had never seen or heard of one that had been treated as anything else even after their position was changed, except the Doctore's wife Nala and even she had been used by the Romans up until her death.

"Do you think she does?" He asked, reaching a hand through the bars to trace a finger down Jovian's cheek. "Do you think she loves him?"

Jovian shrugged his slender shoulders. "I did not come to talk about them. I came to see you and," he brought forward the hand that had been behind his back. "I brought you a gift of your own from the house of Census."

Argus looked down to see a square wrapped in silk held out on the open palm. "Jovian? What did you do?" He reached down to lift the silk "Tell me you did not take something valuable from that house. Dominus will see you whipped for such a thing if he does not allow then to cut off your hand for theft." Not only would it see the boy disgraced but permanently disabled and unable to do most things, he would be turned out and starve or worse in the back alleys of the city.

"I promise it is nothing that will be missed." He giggled and finished lifting the silk to reveal fruit candied with honey so heavily that it sparkled in the dim light of the torch. "I simply thought that you might like something sweet. It is was given to me, but I thought of you."

Argus leaned against the bars, his jaw slack in amazement that in the midst of the finery and attention Jovian must have gotten, dressed as he was in embroidered silk with painted eyes and jewelry decorating his perfect compact frame, he had considered Argus.

"You thought of me? There? Tonight?" He asked, slowly reaching to take a piece of the fruit. The sugar melted on his tongue, letting the flavor of the berry slowly coat his tongue. He could not remember the last time something so sweet had passed his lips. Pressing his eyes closed, Argus savored the long-forgotten flavor remembering when his mother had made such treats for him and his brother.

Opening his eyes, he met the eager and expectant gaze on the other side of the bars. "I cannot recall such a taste. It has been that long since I enjoyed a luxury like this. Gratitude Jovian."

His gratitude was rewarded with the sight of Jovian's eagerly clasped hands, coupled with a bright smile. "I think of you in all places. You are most welcome for the fruit Argus. You must keep it secret from the others or they will question how you received such things. I hope, when you taste them, you will think of me. Perhaps?"

"You can hold trust in that knowledge Jovian." Argus said, tucking the remaining pieces away in the small box of his private properties. There was not much in the box as he had not been able to keep many trinkets from his home when he was taken to be a slave in his youth. Carefully closing the lid, he knew that once the candied treat was gone, he would keep the silk as a memento of the rare gift.

"You are often in my thoughts in recent times. Tell me again why Dominus does not permit your attendance of the games. Does he fear your desire to join us upon the sands or just that you want to join us in the ludus?"

He had been teasing, but the instant change in Jovian's demeanor; the hesitation in his smile and how his eyes cast immediately to the ground, told Argus that he had hit closer to the mark than he had ever intended.

"He fears all that. Even more than that he claims that he made a promise to my mother that he would never allow me to break her heart by becoming a gladiator."

"Your mother?" Argus asked, wishing that he could ease the pain in the dark eyes that had been beaming moments ago. "Who is she that Tertius would make a promise to that would see a perfectly capable man kept from the sands?"

"You see me as a man?" He asked, his eyes lighting once again.

He had ignored the other question though it was not important in the glow of his smile. "Of course, I see you as a man. You are no longer a child Jovian. You have not been for some time." Argus' voice was almost a whisper. "You have been in the villa too long if you have not been able to see that. Dominus…I think he likes to see you that way, as a child, so he can abuse you however he likes."

"You do not know!" Jovian became suddenly angry, glaring darkly where there had been a delighted smile a breath ago. He stepped back from the bars, the slight frame shaking with the surprising rage that had taken over.

"You are nothing but a gladiator. How could you understand the love of a Roman?" He hissed as Argus' heart clenched to hear the agony in the other voice. "Dominus LOVES ME!"

CHAPTER 5

Waking with a groan Cassian blinked at the ceiling. The stiffness in his back from the bed and his jaw from whatever it was that Arturo had done to his jaw to fix the damage of Vitus's angry fists. He fought the instinct to touch his jaw but there would be stitches and the medicus would remind him that there was a risk of infection, so he watched the ceiling instead.

He had stared up at the cracked plaster more times than he could count over the years but only once before had he woken to the sight. It had been the first day he was training as a gladiator and the small German known as Lugo had clipped him with the flat side of his hammer. The next thing that he knew was the chuckle of Arturo and the sight of the ceiling before his friend joined him to ensure his brain was still functioning as it should.

That was many years and even more injuries ago. The ceiling still looked the same, but he had not woken up alone then as he was now. Or was he? Slowly he became aware of a warmth at his side. Looking down his right side he saw the pale face and dark hair of Violetta. Her eyes were closed, the dark fans of her lashes lay on cheeks flushed with the heat of the room. Arturo must have stoked the fire before he left with her in mind as it was unusual for the infirmary to be this warm, even during a storm like the one they had arrived in. He would try to remember to thank the druid later for allowing his woman the luxury on her first night in the ludus, especially when the night of their arrival had been so traumatic.

The ludus was a different world from the villa of a wealthy silk merchant, so different than what she was used to. Even though they were monsters, Felix and Vitus Census made sure that their 'property' was well maintained so that they could do the job that they had been purchased for. While Violetta was the worst treated body slave he had ever seen, she did have more than one dress, a blanket of her own and the cell in the basement of the villa was not too cold. Separate from the abuse of Vitus she was better treated than many slaves here, in the house of Tertius that she was now a part of, the house he had brought her to. He had brought his little priestess out of a pan only to sit her at the edge of an inferno that could consume her. This warm night might be the last kindness allowed for some time.

Thunder rumbled outside the walls and brought Cassian back to the present. The violent deluge had soaked every man on the sands. Their misery in the water was not lost on him even though he saw them only in the brief moment before he had helped Violetta down to put her feet upon the holy grounds of the ludus training sands. She had been dripping wet just from the small walk from the wagon to the covering of the ludus dining hall, they had been in the rain from the moment it had started and had stayed there until Cirandon had decided that they had done enough. Violetta was not to be under the command of the Doctore like he and his brothers were. Was it to be Arturo that oversaw her care? Or would Tertius involve himself in her daily life?

He remembered the look in the lanista's eyes when they had left the wagon, with his guard Julius Lucius, to put the roof onto the wagon. Tertius had not blinked when Violetta had fallen in the mud; tripping on the plank and filling Cassian with a worry that now seemed almost laughable.

She had survived years of trauma and assaults of various kinds in the house of Census and he had worried about this? A trip over a piece of wood in the rain, into mud, had caused him to worry nearly as much as seeing her walk into a room with Felix on the other side of the door. If he told her this, that he had laid awake thinking about the bruising on her hand with as much concern as the ones on other parts of her body, put there by angry hands, would she laugh at him?

The thought made Cassian smile. The brief lift of his lips sent a small flash of pain through him to remind him why he was in the silence of the infirmary. The stillness and quiet was so encompassing that Cassian guessed that it must be close to dawn. Soon the earliest risers in the villa would begin to stir, beginning their work of the day hours before anyone else. Determined to take advantage of the rare moment of privacy before Tertius made his champion accountable for the lanista's ambitious desire for advancement that he could not earn himself within the city of Rome.

Cassian rolled to his side to be better able enjoy watching his woman sleep. Propping his head on his hand he reached to touch the softness of Violetta's hair. The silken texture played through his fingers as he stroked her cheek that was as pale as the marble used to carve statues of the gods, except for the bruise that we could just barely see without moving. The mark was almost as dark as a plum and nearly the same size. Even though the hand that had made the mark would never be raised against her while he lived, the painful imperfection on her flesh filled him with fury and a deep sense of failure in himself.

With a sigh he traced her hairline and wondered if she would forgive him. She was his to keep safe and he had not done so. "Never again priestess. I will not fail you like that again until the day the gods take me." Releasing her hair, he pressed a pair of fingers to his lips and then to hers. "Let this seal my vow. I will never fail in your protection again Violetta."

"Do not swear vows the gods will not let you keep, my friend. You doom yourself before your feet touch the floor." A familiar voce said quietly from the doorway.

"If the gods would prove me wrong they would have to exist. So, my vow will stand, you religious bastard." Cassian replied, mumbling around the pain of moving his injured jaw. His fingers found Violetta's hair again as naturally as they took grasp of his swords.

"As always Cassian, you force me to pray that your unholy words meet your ears alone. If your mother could hear the lack of faith from her son, she would…"

"She would break no words from her grave or living that would condemn me. A fact you know better than I do." Cassian said, cutting off further admonishment about the faith of their homeland.

"Indeed, I do. She was a good woman." Arturo said, circling the room to light a few of the candles to replace those that had burned out.

Cassian balked inwardly at the way the druid's eyes lingered on Violetta5 at his side, silently saying that she was not of the same quality of woman as his deceased mother. He did not know the strength of the seemingly child-like girl at his side.

"So is she, Arturo." He said, emphasising carefully so that his friend knew that there was no room for discussion. "She is the greatest woman I have ever met, without exception Arturo." He slowly sat up, taking care not to wake Violetta. "You will see it soon enough, if you have not already."

The pride in his voice was audible while he met the questioning gaze of his oldest friend. How could he explain the strength and indomitable spirit of the woman beside him to a man that had never found the company of women to have any use outside time spent with the priestesses that served the same gods as they did, as he did, when they were in their homeland. Cassian could not recall Arturo breaking words with any woman for more than a few moments in all the years they had been slaves together.

"You will train her to assist you, as Tertius commanded?" He asked, mumbling around the swelling that was as irritating as it was painful. "She needs this Arturo. Needs you to teach her so she can stay safely down here."

"How can you see down here, in the ludus, as safety for a woman?" Arturo said, a hint of agitation in his usually calm voice. "You do not think that the second she is left alone that one of your 'brothers' or one of the guards will take advantage of her vulnerability."

He stormed to the table so that Cassian could not look anywhere else but his friend's eyes, but the Celt was not put off by the challenging glare. "If any man among them is foolish enough to touch that which is mine, they won't live to see the next sunrise."

"You speak as though she is property and not a person. Cassian!" The druid put his hands onto Cassian's shoulders which made the champion want to shrug them off. "That girl is in danger here. You must know that and accept it. She is not a medicus. I do not think that she has that in her."

He did not want to hear this, did not want to hear what was coming next, there was no way to stop the flow of words or the note of truth in them.

"If I train her, she might learn the skills and might even be able to use them, but she does not have the heart for this. She will never innovate and create new tools and medicines as I have. I'll admit that the plant she brought with her from that house is interesting, but she will never, truly, be a medicus"

"That is not…Arturo you will doom her to be returned to that house if you tell this to Tertius. You do not know her as I do. She can do what is needed. Tonight, how afraid she is, there is so much more to her than this."

He knew that it sounded as though he was pleading for her, making excuses when faced with undeniable information. He could not let this be what happened to his priestess. She was better than the druid could know from just a few hours during surgery after the night she had been through.

"Trust me Arturo. I beg that you trust my instincts and give her a chance, give her a chance for the sake of the bond between us."

Watching the decision weighing in the mind of his friend Cassian looked around the room, noticing the way she had cleaned up after the surgery and after what must have been her meal. Finally, his eyes landed on the alter. Usually the infirmary alter was a jumble of offerings from many of the men and more than once the holy figures had been arranged in a gladiator's idea of strategy for upcoming games. Now it was pristine, and it did not take a genius to see who took care of it.

"Arturo? Before you say another word about how she is unfit for your world, how she does not belong in the ludus, look at the alter. Look what she did for you." Cassian pointed. "I doubt your attitude deserved such a kindness. If I know you at all you yelled at her at least once."

The druid paused his pacing to stand looking down at the alter. "She did this? She washed the icons and the alter surface?"

He stooped to look at something Cassian could not see. The Celt smiled when Arturo murmured "By Airmid, she has oiled the wood, all of it." He turned his head to meet his gaze. "My brother, the girl is a trained acolyte and you did not tell me? You have brought me a priestess? You have taken a priestess of the gods to your blaspheming heart?"

They shared a gaze for a few moments before both of them burst into laughter at the absurdity of that truth.

"I swear to you, Arturo, if that is the truth. If that is her training, I was not privy to the knowledge. She did not tell me." He rubbed his jaw, wincing at the pain brought by the laughter. "I have called her 'my priestess' and she did not say a word about its truth."

He caught the look in Arturo's eyes as he nodded "She will tell you, and me, in her own time. Time I will give her as I teach her what the gods have directed. She can stay."

CHAPTER 6

The chill of the morning woke Violetta on the floor before the hot coals of the fire. Barely awake she blinked, looking around in confusion. Where was this place? How did she come to be here? Where was Cassian?

Pulling her blanket tight around her shoulders she looked around, taking stock of the room as she tried to recall the night before. The table where Cassian had lain while under the power of the medicus' drug was empty a few feet from the hearth where she sat.

She had been at his side, holding his hand as she had promised but he was nowhere in the room and the door was still closed. Who had moved her while she slept? Had Cassian woken and moved her so they could lay together in greater comfort? The blanket carried his scent of cedar and sandalwood, but it was faint, and it seemed colder than it should have been if he had been at her side recently. What if he had died in the night and the medicus had moved her only to remove the body?

"Surely someone would have woken me if he were gone? Even if it were to return me to the house of Census. They cannot be so cruel as to leave me with no chance at farewell." Sitting int silence Violetta thought she heard the faint sounds of men's laugher. "Surely if the champion of the house was dead there would not be laughter this morning."

Standing she tightened the blanket around her shoulders and bit her lip as she tentatively tried the handle of the door. With a sigh of relief, she found it unlocked and stepped out into the hall, dimly lit by the glow of the rising sun off the sands. The latrina was on the far side of the covered platform facing the sands that the gladiators used as a dining hall. If the other gladiators were the brutes she had been led to believe she might not have another chance without having to worry about them harassing her.

They would, she hoped, get used to her presence given the chance but until they did, she would have to exercise even greater caution than she had in the house of Census. Finding the chamber that she needed, thankfully as vacant as the training grounds, Violetta was shocked at the etchings and graffiti on the walls. The smell of the room said that it was never cleaned and obviously was given no thought beyond it's most basic uses. The overwhelming odor rushed her from the room before she could see if any of the markings were related to Cassian.

"He may simply stand a man to those that train with him however he will always be a hero to me. If he yet lives, I will make sure that he knows it everyday,"

"You had best pray that he lives or there will be consequences that you cannot pay, girl." A deep voice growled suddenly at her back.

Spinning, Violetta's shoulder hit the broad, unmoving, body of a man, obviously a gladiator. The impact threw her off balance hard enough to knock her to the ground. Staring up at him she had to swallow a small cry of fear as she took in the angry expression on the face towering above her. His fists were clenched at his side as though he was holding back the urge to use them against her. "I did…I did my best. He lived and breathed when I saw him last."

Her chest tightened and her limbs were trembling when she scrambled to her feet. The gladiator watched her in a way that made her think that at any moment he would reach out to take hold of her. She had faced angry men more times than she could count but this was different. Often when the Romans were in a fit of rage she had taken the brunt of their wrath so that it did not fall on the more elderly slaves who would not easily recover from the bruises and worse that the men of the house of Census rained down in their fits of temper. Argus was more terrifying.

Even at his worst, like the night before, Vitus was not half as fearsome as the man towering about her now. The green eyes were like emerald daggers, the muscles in his neck twitched with each step that he took to follow her retreat across the platform towards the hall to the infirmary.

"When you saw him last?" he snarled, "What kind of medicus does not know the location of such an important patient? Especially when you are known to share his bed."

His lip curled as if her very presence in the ludus offended his senses, but just as she was about to turn and run, he continued. "How do you not know he lives? Did you leave him along in the infirmary to sell yourself to his brethren while he lays dreaming of you?"

She had backed as far away from him and his anger as she could. Her back now pressed against the wall she was unable to retreat further and when he planted his hands on either side of her shoulders all chance of escape disappeared.

"I would not, ever. Cassian is my heart and when I fell asleep his hand was in mine. I woke next to the fire to find a blanket over me and him gone from my side. I would not have left the room at all had it not been from need and the hope to find…"

Her attacker shook his head "Hope to find the next man who you would seduce at the command of your master? We will not have such a whore here again."

His hands slid down the wall to grip her shoulder and Violetta had started to struggle. This man was more dangerous than she had thought and there was no way to reason with him.

"Please, let me go. I will just return to the infirmary and leave you to the sands." She pleaded, but his grip tightened painfully.

"No. You will just do as the other whore. He deserves better than you both."

"And she deserves better than your abuse." Cassian snarled, his fist flying through the air between them. When it connected with the other man's jaw the attacker released his hold on her shoulders and Violetta ducked clear of the skirmish.

She watched in amazement as her injured lover delivered blow after blow against the other gladiator. Though the other man was larger, Cassian delivered a beating, fists striking with a fury that was breathtaking in its intensity.

When the other man lay bleeding on the platform Cassian straightened to speak. "Lay a hand upon my woman again and I will not be so gently. You know nothing of what you speak or who you dishonor with vile words."

When Cassian turned to take her hands and raise her to her feet the fallen man muttered; "She is just a woman. Easily replaced."

Before he could turn to return to the beating Violetta caught his arm. "Enough. Please. His words meant nothing me now that I know you still live."

Watching him weigh his decision she gently stroked the tip of her fingers down his arm. "Cassian? Let us depart. Leave him be."

With a nod he followed the tug of her hand. "If I catch you with hands upon her again, Argus, I swear to her gods that you will choke on your own blood before I finish with you."

Argus nodded in acknowledgment of the threat and Violetta led Cassian down the hall back to the safety of the infirmary. She noticed that the only other door in the hall, the one that the lanista had said was to be hers was no unlocked. The reality of the isolation of her new position, how far away from the cell were Cassian would be secured at the end of each day she would be, sank in with a nervous shudder. What if one of the other men made the same kind of attempt? Would the door even lock to offer a moment's frustration to an attacker?

Once they were back inside the infirmary Violetta let loose a sigh of relief. "Where did you go? I woke alone with no knowledge if you lived or not. The medicus was gone as well." She fidgeted with a few of the bottled on one of the tables that she had cleaned the night before. "I do not think he wants me here. He is not likely to teach me willingly. Will Tertius send me back if Arturo refuses or says that I cannot be taught? I swear that I can learn this. I was nervous last night and hurting after…" Her voice choked on the words but before she could continue Cassian pressed a calloused finger to her lips, silencing her fearful rambling.

"He will teach you. Arturo assures me that he will not hold the mistakes of frightened hands against you." He pulled her close to his chest where she inhaled deeply, letting his strength soothe her terrorizing memories.

"Why did you not tell him what you suffered, Violetta? He would have shown compassion for your pain. The man is closer to me than any other. I promise you can trust him to be honorable above all else." His voice was soft, and she could tell his question was in earnest but how could she have told a man that he held so dear the atrocious thing he had been forced to do? She could not even think about it without tears stinging her eyes.

"Apologies, champion, I could not speak of it with someone else for I cannot bear to think of it myself."

His arms tightened around her, a cheek resting on the top of her head as he held her in silent agony. The quiet filled the room for a few moments before she heard him whisper; "Gods forgive me, for I will never forgive myself." She could not tell if he were talking to her or the heaven and could not ask. She stroked a circle in the center of his back, trying to ease the torment in his voice and body.

"Where was it that you went? Why did you not wake me before you left? I was…I though you had died, and I was left alone in this place."

His body tensed in a way that made her think that he had worried about the same thing as she had. That was why he had protested the druid's drug in his system before their work on his jaw.

He stroked her cheek with the tips of his finger, bringing a smile to her lips before he spoke. "I thought to be back in the room before you woke. I was breaking words with my Doctore, Cirandon. He stands as close to heart as Arturo since the days that we trained together as brothers. He prepared me to face the test to earn the mark of the brotherhood as gladiator. He wished to know if I stand capable of rejoining the men today." He paused and pressed a kiss to her temple. "Apologies for causing concern. I thought that the druid would have invited you to join him in morning prayer so that you would not be alone and vulnerable to the men. Never did I think that Argus would be the man to threaten you."

"That is the man you told me that wants to train with you? What cause does he have to bear such hatred towards me? Does he blame me for the time you have been gone?" She shook her head, stepping out of his arms to fold the blanket and rekindle the fire for the day. "I doubt that Arturo would wish my company for prayers. I do hope that he might grant me time for my own this morning."

"I will not only permit it, but I will encourage your prayers, apprentice." Said the druid, surprising them both from the doorway as if her thoughts had summoned him to appear at just that moment.

"You have spoken to Doctore, Cassian? I fear that he and I will not agree on your return to the sands this morning. I would have you rest another day, under supervision if needed. I want to ensure that you do not train alone in your cell and undo the work we both did in the late hours of the night."

Violetta looked at her lover, smiling at the idea of spending the day with Cassian. She was surprised to see that he did not share her joy. Instead his eyes were narrowed in an angry glare at the man he had just told her was his dearest friend.

"Cassian? What is wrong?" She asked, standing up from the hearth with a nod to acknowledge her instructor and his words.

CHAPTER 7

Cassian met the calm gaze of Arturo with unbridled rage. Once again, his friend refused to understand his need for the sands beneath his feet and the feel of his swords in his hands the eagerness in Violetta's eyes was tempting, so much so that it hurt to have to disappoint her. That had to be Arturo's plan.

"Violetta? Now would be an ideal time for your prayers. I would have words with your instructor before I take to the sands." He took her by the arm and guided her to the door with a smile. "Close the door and you will not be bothered. No one yet knows that is your cell and I will speak to my guard, Julius Lucius, who you must call Lucius only, and ensure that there is a solid lock put on your door as soon as it is possible."

She looked first and him and then towards Arturo who nodded with a resigned sigh. "May I borrow candles until I can find my own to build an alter with?"

He was relieved that Arturo not only nodded but gave her several of his own pure white candles. "Take what you need from here and I will see it replaced so that you do not have to worry about dealing with those in the villa."

He was showing her a kindness that even Cassian had not expected by gifting her items to make the alter that she needed to pray to her gods in the way she felt necessary.

Walking her to the door of the cell, he waited until the door was closed and her could hear her arranging things to make it the way that she wanted. There was a smile on his face when he returned to the infirmary. It quickly fell to the previous scowl when the druid shook his head in response to the question he had not yet asked.

"I am going to the sands Arturo. I will share the morning meal with Violetta after her prayers, then I will train with my brothers. You can break words against it, with Tertius if you must, but I will not be denied the sands another dawn."

Arturo set aside the container in his hand and turned to face him with a look that was infuriatingly calm, almost patronizing in the boredom in his eyes. "Cassian. You were submitted to my care last night by Tertius because the fool of a Roman knows that I will not let you reinjure yourself simply because you are not able to wait to heal. You are not training. Not today though perhaps in a day or two. If you rest and do not strain yourself too much with…other activities."

His eyes flicked towards the door in a suggestion that was not lost on the gladiator. "I remember last night, with great clarity, Arturo. There was nothing special said regarding my inability to train. I am not going to injure my jaw at the pallus, just as I am not going to sit idle for days while a title match in Rome itself is in the balance."

"Not even in the arms of your lover? When did Cassian begin to choose glory before the arms of a woman?" Arturo replied, scathing judgement in his voice while he returned to the herbs and oils before him on the table.

"When the life and safety of my woman hang in the balance. Title be damned to nothing without her at my side. Arturo? I need to be a god on the sands of Rome, and I will not wait."

The idea of sitting idle in a cell was unbearable, even the knowledge that it would be with Violetta did not tempt him as it once would have. "I will not let her go back to that place while I still live. I need you to let me train, to get back to what I do best." He leaned close to the druid. "Arturo, do not try to stop me, not this time brother."

He met the dark eyes of Arturo and held them in a glare for several minutes. He was hoping that there were no more words he needed to break in order to convince the only man in this house who knew who he really was and why he was here that this was what he needed to do.

"You will not be moved from this choice? She is not just a passing fancy or a hope for redemption for Nala?"

His voice was soft and full of understanding, yet Cassian still wanted to put his fist through his brother's throat for the suggestion. "She has my heart, Arturo. No reservation or regret."

"Then I will make you this bargain; join me for prayers every day until you leave for Rome and I will offer no objection to your return to the sands this very morning."

Cassian stared at him in utter disbelief. He had never though that the druid was serious about his requests to return to the devotions he had offered the gods as a child. "You want me to wake and pray with you? In return for being allowed to train as I am meant to? As you, yourself, have told me that the gods intended for me to do when they saw me to this cursed place and life of slavery? You are going to bargain with me?"

He shared a long, unflinching stare with Arturo before they both burst into a round of laughter that ended with the Celt flinching with a small hiss of pain when he touched his jaw near the stitching. "You are certain that it is not broken?"

When the druid nodded with a smile; "Quite certain. Violetta and I both inspected it very carefully. It could break with another hard blow. I hate to use the word 'luck' regarding injuries but if you took one or two more blows as hard as those Vitus delivered, then I might be telling you something different." The dark eyes narrowed slightly; "that does not mean that I will allow you to train without agreeing to the offer."

"I have no time for such thing. If it is company at prayer that you want, then ask Violetta to join you. After the attack by Argus this morning it may take more time than I thought for them to accept her. It is not safe for her to be alone, not yet."

"She will be safe soon enough, once you return to the sands and make it known that you are capable of defending her." Arturo replied, shrugging. "That will happen sooner if you agree and join me for prayers."

"It will happen just as soon if I defy your foolish attempt at bargaining and simply join the men as they train. You are not going to attend Tertius and tell him that I am unable to fight."

Arturo shook his head. "No. I would not do that by choice. I have already been summoned by the lanista to answer to your condition."

"If that happens then, if you tell him that I am unable to train, Violetta goes back to that place and I will not let that happen. Damn you for this druid." He growled, pacing the floor. "A week of prayer, no longer than that."

He sighed with relief when his demand was met with a nod.

"A week of prayer. Starting tonight." Arturo said with a smile that bordered on sarcastic. "Go. Train. I can see the eagerness in your eyes. I will see to the girl's training."

Cassian grinned and almost bolted from the room. He considered pausing to tell Violetta that he had gotten his way, but he heard the voice of his brothers in the dining hall calling his name. He would speak to her later in the day, when Arturo attended the sands, he was likely to bring his new assistant to observe the men. He hoped that act and the fact that he would find ways to make sure that every man upon the sands understood Violetta's position as medicus just as well as they would understand that he would hold the title of champion until the day the gods claimed him.

Slowing his jog to the confident swagger that every man upon the sands would be familiar with Cassian strode out of the hall into the sunlight with a broad grin. "It seems that you have been crying for me like the little girls I have always known you to be? Your champion has returned. What man among you would raise weapon to challenge my health and ability this morning?"

His grin broadened, despite the pain in his jaw, when the sands erupted with calls and jokes from each of the men. He was surprised to see even Argus joining in the calls. Perhaps the younger man had learned his lesson, or he simply knew that if he wanted to reach the zenith of his potential there was no one else that could teach him what he needed to know.

Proximus stepped away from a table, the same one Cassian and Violetta had made love on weeks earlier the Celt noted with a smirk before the large German spoke. "Once you have food in your belly, Champion, I would be happy to test where your skills rest after weeks away from proper contest."

"You think yourself capable, without the protection of Tertius's desired outcome of the test to keep you safe, Proximus?" His tone sounded as though he had almost forgotten the name of the man before him when Cassian knew that it was part of a night that he would never forget.

"Fill your belly then join me so that we can find out together." He teased with a grin before Cassian took a pair of bowls to the ancient cook, a man who had his back broken in the arena years ago but now served the ludus as the cook.

"There is a stomach other than my own that needs nourishment before I return to schooling your ass, German." He called to Proximus.

Moving quickly Cassian took a bowl and one of the small loaves made for the gladiators to the door of Violetta's cell. He eased the door open and peered around it, expecting to see Violetta settling her meager belongings around the room. He was surprised to see her kneeling before an alter she must have spent all her time building since he had sent her here. He could not hear the words she was whispering but instead of lingering he simply set the food on the floor and closed the door behind him when he left to eat in the company of his brothers.

The minutes of brotherhood while they ate, before falling to the command of the whip wielded by Cirandon, were like a drink of cool, fresh water. He laughed without a care in the world and when he stood to join the men upon the sands he felt as though he had never, truly, left it.

The starting exercises to the day had been the same for all the years he had been a gladiator and he was sure that they had not changed in many years before that. Today he felt like a new man with a drive he could not remember since the very first day his feet had touched the ground he had come to know as sacred.

"Come Proximus, show me what skill you possess. If Argus and I are indeed to stand upon the sands of Rome's Circus Maximus, then both of us need to be able to defeat the city's fallen champion."

When both Germans gave him the same confused look he added; "My woman's master, along with our own, arranges a fight upon the sands of the greatest arena in the Republic. Argus, if you train at my side, will join me in that fight and Proximus, as a member of our brotherhood now, will show us both what we need to know in order to send his former opponents to a glorious death and the afterlife."

He looked at Cirandon who nodded his agreement before cracking the whip in his hand and calling loudly; "Gladiators! Take position."

CHAPTER 8

"Medicus?" Violetta called from the doorway. She was not sure if she was to be permitted to call him by his given name or if, as his student, she was simply to call him by his title. Cassian was close to the man and so, she guessed, he was granted special privilege. Would such familiarity ever be extended to her?

"Ah, Violetta. Your prayers are done, and you have broken the night's fast?" Arturo answered, barely looking up from his work on the table.

"I am ready to learn. Gratitude for the food that you brought me. I cannot recall the last time I had bread still warm from the oven." She said with a smile.

Sitting down across from her instructor she began to sort through the herbs that Arturo had already discarded. "If I remove the wiltcd leaves and there is clean water, perhaps with a touch of honey in it to sweeten the drink, then the plant will refresh a little so that they can be useful?"

The druid picked up one of the discarded bunches to inspect it, his face seemed to be considering her words as carefully as he considered the plant. "I do not know if such will work for these. Astrix has no eye for herbs and he is, unfortunately, the one that Tertius sends to the market to select them."

He sighed then paused with a strange smile before he took her hands in his "Perhaps though, in time, he will allow me to send you to accompany him? You would be able to select finer plants for us to work with, I hope. For all my skill I cannot seem to keep a decent garden green and growing, is that something you can do?"

Violetta felt a strange calm at the touch of the druid. Whether it was his faith in her or the fact that he had agreed to teach her, which would keep her safe from being returned to the house of pain and horror, it was a soothing touch. She gave him a small smile, "Yes. I think I can make a few things grow if there is a space with some light that I might plant." She took a thoughtful breath "There are some things though, that I do not believe can be grown in a climate like ours here. There will always be a need for those things that cannot be grown here and when they are not in season."

Arturo nodded his agreement and to Violetta's surprise simply stated "Then a garden you shall have, as soon as possible. For now, though, it is time to tend to our slightly more living charges." He stood and waited for her to join him. "We shall go to the sands and observe the training until the lanista sends word to speak to me about Cassian. You will join me in that meeting and represent yourself well under his questions. Understood?"

She nodded quickly, taking the basket of bandages her handed her. "They will not hurt me, will they?" Her voice was more nervous than she had meant it to be, but he answered without a moment's pause.

"Hurt you? Not with actions though there is not a man among them that will not make a remark. I advise you to mask your shock or upset well or they will make a target of you even more than I expect them to. They have to get used to you too Violetta, do not forget that this is their world and not yours."

Once they arrived at the sands it took a moment for Violetta to take in all the action around her. Only an hour earlier all had been still, but now every inch of the yard was churning with the activity of more than a dozen gladiators. The men were of varying sizes, some were large like Argus and the giant Proximus that Cassian had faced in the match in the hall just above them and others were small like Jovian, who's whereabouts she suddenly found herself wondering about for a moment. Was he safe and happy upstairs in the villa? What did he think of her being down among the men?

Spotting Cassian on the far side of the yard, defending himself against the two men who towered above every other man on the sands. Even the man with the whip that stood like a dark tower of analytical judgement was not a comparable size to the pair of men her lover faced simultaneously. He was not even close to being one of the larger men in the ludus, but the skill he was exhibiting was unmatched by all the other gladiators.

He was incredible, drawing her to the edge of the platform like a moth is drawn to a deadly flame. She could see that there were several other gladiators that were as interested in what the trio was doing across the yard as she was.

"Violetta!" Arturo called from behind her. "Do not set your foot upon the sand. Come. Sit here by me. I would have you prepare the linen for bandages. You need to observe all the men, not just the one you favor most. If you can see how the physical damage is done, you will learn to undo it. Since I cannot send you to practice with them, even the recruits, I must find new ways to teach you what you need to know."

Looking down at her feet, on the edge of the stone platform, Violetta realized the need for Arturo's admonishment and turned to join him. As she sat in the shade near his feet, she heard a chuckle from the few men nearby who had been watching the matches, while waiting for their own chance to prove themselves. One of the gladiators, a tall man with bright blue eyes and hair the color of golden wheat, caught her gaze and held it while he joked to those around him.

"Come medicus, let the woman train. I am sure every man here has a lesson or two in mind for her."

"She does not need your words between her ears, Tarconus." Arturo replied, his voice a flat warning that even Violetta could recognize.

"It was not words that he thought to use, and it was between her thighs he would provide the training." One of the other gladiators called, making Violetta blush deeply with embarrassment.

"Tarconus would soon find his ability to teach any woman removed if he, or any man, thinks to lay hand upon the assistant of the medicus." Cassian's voice rumbled across the sands bringing an abrupt stop to the laughter of the waiting men.

Raising her eyes from the basket to Cassian's face she was relieved to see the scowl he had given the gladiators was quickly replaced with an encouraging smile with a swift and playful wink when he saw her face.

She could not help the smile that spread across her face that grew when the man who had joined Tarconus' teasing said to the other men. "What did I tell you? She is not for the likes of us lowly men. Your eyes are better turned to the sands so you might dream of the likes of her…in the afterlife where you'll be soon enough, you fool."

"That is Barrius. He is not a man you need to fear. Tarconus is not a danger either though he speaks the part to gain popularity among the men." Arturo said quietly while he made notes with a stick of charcoal. "You are fortunate that Tertius is not yet upon the balcony. Though they would not risk his anger by being so jovial when they are meant to be at work, the lanista would not be amused at the distraction that you presented by being so near to the sands. If steel were in the hands of the men there could have been grievous injury, even a death, caused by just one distracted gladiator. You had the attention of every man in the ludus from where you stood."

"I did?" She asked in surprise. In the house of Census there was little attention paid to her outside the needs of Felix and, at times, his son Vitus. The idea that she would be a distraction to the gladiators was one that she had not considered. She knew that she would be unwelcome in this world of violent men, but, other than Cassian and Arturo, she had thought that she would be ignored more than anything else. "Apologies medicus. I was distracted myself and did not see the danger."

Her words were met with a silent nod from her instructor as he returned to his notes, so Violetta sorted the linens for bandages; tearing them into strips and setting aside pieces too small to bind a wound but usable for padding when needed. It was not hard work when compared to the fine silks she had worked with for years, so she was able to take in more of her surroundings and the activities of the gladiators while safely far from their immediate sight.

The men that had been watching were now involved in their own matches, some with the deliberate slowness of learning new actions but others attacked one another as though their lives depended upon it, like the wooden weapons in their hands were steel that could take a life at any strike. Flinching when she saw Cassian take the flat of a blade to his arm that was strong enough to throw him off balance with a laugh from Proximus.

She needed a distraction from the worry she would have to grow used to, something to take her mind off everything else. She wanted to know more about the man beside her, a druidic priest of a country she had been taught was as primitive as it was barbaric. He was not likely to answer her questions about himself, but what would he tell of the others that were now in her world. "What is he like?" She asked, looking up towards the villa above their heads.

"Cassian? I would hope that you know him well enough that you do not need to ask me about him." Was the skeptical reply.

"No. Apologies. I was asking about the lanista, Tiberius Tertius. What manner of man is he?" She asked, keeping her voice low enough that it could not be overheard. "I have little experience with him and have never met any other lanistas. Is he a difficult man to please?"

The frown that met her question was so sudden and severe that Violetta almost wished she had not asked it. Had she brought offence again?

A few moments later her instructor chose answered in a clipped tone, carefully choosing words that spoke more of his personal feelings about the lanista then he would admit to her.

"Tertius is a Roman, Violetta. Make no mistake of his soft words and what may seem to be kind actions of bringing you here away from what you lived through in the house of Census. It was not for your benefit, but for Cassian's which means it is for his own use that you are here." He set aside the writing to give her his full attention. "There is little kindness in him, and I would not advise putting trust in him for anything unnecessary. I will do my best to ensure that you have little need to meet with him alone. I will keep that responsibility to myself and, if he wishes words with you then Cassian or I will be at your side."

He must have seen the concern in her eyes because he crouched to put a hand on her shoulder. "Things will settle soon enough, and the men will get used to you. Between myself and Cassian there will be little doubt of your position within these walls." Arturo smiled at her with a strange look in his eyes. "He loves you. I have never seen this kind of devotion from him that he has for you. For good or ill, he trusts you."

Feeling as though he was about to join Argus in his warning against breaking the heart of the man he cared for like a brother, Violetta replied; "I hope that you know that I would never hurt him and that I am not using him to escape the pain of my past." Her voice was defensive and angry, even though she knew it was disrespectful she could not help voicing her argument against the accusation.

"You misunderstand my intention, child." His dark eyes sparkled with amusement and warmth. "I was going to suggest that you let him in, past your own defences. Give him some trust in return."

How could he know that what he asked of her was the hardest of all things? That every man to have crossed her path, from her father to those in her former house, had broken trust with her in a way that had led to her pain.

"He has my heart, Arturo." She dared to try his given name due to the intimate nature of their talk. "I would be a fool to deny my trust when he has all else that I am."

His eyes flashed with a sudden sadness that brought a question to her lips before she could stop to think. "Do you know what it feels like? To not feel complete if you are not with one another. What it feels like to love?"

He sighed and the look he gave her was that of a broken heart. "Oh yes, young one. I have known love and loss unlike anything you can yet imagine."

CHAPTER 9

The joy Cassian felt with his swords back in his hands was unmatched by all thoughts save that of Violetta sitting at the feet of his friend who would teach her what she needed to know in order to stay within the ludus walls. She was safe now and he could focus on the future, the one they would share together once he found a way to convince the lanista to purchase her from Felix. The thought of her being returned to the house of Census sent a surge of hate fuelled rage through him and with a spin of his wrists he delivered a blow to the back of the knees of both Argus and Tartarus that sent them to the sand with cries of pain that echoed in his ears.

"Cassian!" Cirandon called loudly from a few feet away. "Tell me what instruction was in that blow? Or was it just a fit of temper that should not have been displayed by a champion?"

He knew that the Doctore was right but who among them would understand what he was feeling. Had any of them been helpless to stop the one that they loved from being brutally assaulted? Perhaps, but he did not imagine that any of them had been forced to be not only a witness to the assault but an accomplice to the barbarous act. There had been little choice but still his hatred for the act and the man behind it was sitting like a rock in his gut.

He glanced towards Violetta and wondered if she would ever let him touch her again? Even standing across the yard he could see the purple bruises on her arms and the cautious look in her eyes each time she surveyed the men. When her gaze met his own her lips smiled but her beautiful blue eyes did not match the sentiment, instead they held what looked like fear. The Thracian was next to her, laughing, as were the men around him waiting for their turn to train but neither Arturo nor Violetta joined in the laughter. He knew that he had to let her find her own way among the gladiators, for good or ill, but he wanted to help her develop the confidence she would need, if she would let him.

As soon as possible he would find a moment to be alone with her. If it was true that she held some fear or trepidation of him because of what had happened with Vitus then he would begin the work of courting her, winning her trust and affection back with the gentle touches and soft words, perhaps a gift.

He smiled at the thought of how her face might light up if he were able to come up with some coin to put in the hand of Arturo or Astrix if needed, to spend at the market on some pendant or trinket, perhaps an ornament for her hair. Surely all women liked such things. He would take the gift and some wine to her cell. They would talk and drink while he seduced the woman he loved back to his arms where she belonged. He would present her with the gift and, he hoped, find himself the hero in her eyes once again. He would be back where he belonged before the trip to Rome and the next great battle; in her heart as she was in his.

He was determined that Rome would be a shining high point in the legend of his life, not the first and certainly not the last. It would be the first with Violetta at his side and he was determined to convince Tertius and Census that she belonged there, permanently. Once she was purchased, he would put all his will towards convincing the lanista to let him marry her. He would call her his wife, not only under his breath to make her smile, but under the laws of Rome and his own people as well.

Suddenly, from the balcony, came a voice that wiped the smile from his lips and froze his blood; Lycithia.

"Arturo! Attend the villa. Now and bring that," She paused as though struggling to find the word to describe Violetta. "girl, with you. I would have words."

Tension filled his body and his eyes flew to meet Violetta's. He had not had time to prepare her for the lanista's wife and Arturo would not have thought it to be necessary. She would have no idea how to protect herself from the manipulations of the silver-tongued viper. He watched as she gathered the fabric she had been sorting and joined Arturo on his feet, taking a step towards the dark hall that would lead them to the steps to the villa, out of his world and into that of the Romans.

"Cassian! Return to training." Cirandon called, nodding towards where Proximus waited beside Argus with training weapons in hand.

"I ask but a moment Doctore, for a drink of water?" He was certain that his friend and every man upon the sands knew that it was not a drink that he needed.

"Water you may have but there is no time for anything else. There is much work to be done still if Proximus is to prepare both of you to face the gladiators of Rome. Finnicius has a reputation of deliberate savagery and if you want to survive then you must give these lessons your complete focus."

"Cirandon, I need to…"

"Cassian, you need to focus on the sands. Now."

There was no room for negotiation in his voice as they stared at each other with only a few feet between them. Part of him wanted to step past his trainer, his friend, damn the consequences, and whisper hushed words of warning in Violetta's ear, but the consequences were too great, and he knew it.

"Yes Doctore." He said his eyes following Violetta until Arturo led her from sight. "Proximus you had best make my lesson worth not being able to prepare her for hers."

Cassian forced himself to chuckle as though his words were merely a jest, then spun the twin blades in his hands and stalked back to the pair that waited for him. Without another word he burst into a melee of intense swordplay that disarmed Argus, leaving him with only his shield to stop the blows.

Proximus joined his laughter but the sound died as blade met blade. The ferocity of the German's frustration in each blow sent vibrations down the wooden shafts so intense that they made the Celt growl with the pain of them.

"Is that all you have Proximus?" Cassian called, stepping back to let the sting in his hand subside. "I thought a champion of Rome would have so much more in him than this."

The champion knew that his words had the desired affect when Proximus changed the grip on his weapons. He spun the gladius in his left hand to lay flat along his forearm, acting more like a shield than a sword while the other swung like an axe, short and heavy blows that forced the Celt into a defensive stance. Cassian was unable to use his usual tactics and finessed footwork while studying his opponent and so he acted on pure instinct alone, the instinct to survive.

The pair of champion's faced off again, after a swift disconnect of their weapons and Proximus, despite the loss of his title through whatever scandal had every other man in the ludus whispering whenever the German left the room, had obviously not lost any of his skill despite the fall. It was only moments until he had backed Cassian more than a dozen feet across the yard and his back was pressed against the pallus. The touch of the wood against his back prompted the Celt to spin around the thick column and bring his wooden blade in a slice across Proximus' exposed back as he backed away. The force pushed him into the wood and gave Cassian time to gain some distance and perspective on how the German responded to the taunting. The usual threats of the underworld that he had tried during the test of the Brotherhood weeks ago had not phased Proximus, but the challenge of his worthiness of the title of champion sent him into a savage rage truly worthy of the arena.

The guttural cry from the pallus brought Cassian's focus back to one thing and one thing alone, victory.

"Tell me, Champion," He mocked, "Did your former Dominus send you from Rome for acts of savagery or was it simply because even his body slave gave greater sport in the arena than you?"

The taunt over the disgrace he suffered seemed to cause a loss in whatever control Proximus had and he charged Cassian with a roar.

There was only a split second to make the choice of action but he lowered one blade in a sweep to trip the German and, as he landed on his chest in the sand, Cassian pressed the tip of the opposite gladius between his shoulder blades.

He rolled over and their eyes met with an angry glare from the German into the amused gaze of the triumphant Celt. "Temper, temper. A champion should have better control."

"Cassian. Enough." Cirandon called, his whip snapping in the air to catch the attention of every man on the sands.

There was utter silence all around him, every man was still and staring at the pair of men locked in their testing glare. Cassian was certain that if it was steel in their hands that Proximus would be doing all he could to end his life but instead, since they were only the wooden practice swords, he was trying to calm the anger that had been brought to the surface by the teasing.

Straightening, he offered his hand to help his fallen brother in arms to his feet. The wordless stare continued as they each assessed the intent of the other man. Cassian did not break into his usual grin. This was more important than his practiced joviality could mend. He would wait for the German to break words first, but he held no ill feelings towards him.

Softly the silence broke from above them, not with the voice of a Roman but the barely audible sound of the stifled tears of Jovian. Cassian stepped back from Proximus so that he could see the young man that he was so familiar with weeping shamelessly on the balcony, his eyes locked on Argus alone in a pleading, pain filled gaze.

He wondered if there had been something between them while he had been away and that he had not yet been told about the obvious secret.

"Jovian? What troubles you boy?" Cassian called up to him, attempting to sooth his young friend so that the sands could once again be a place of training for both he and Argus. Proximus had stalked to the water barrel among the other men leaving the two alone to face each other.

Blinking, Jovian turned to look at Cassian, the sorrow on the face painted with streaks of kole marking the trail of tears on his cheeks. "Cassian? Why do you get all you can dream of and the rest of us have to wait and hope for the gods to hear our prayers to even give up a glimpse of our joy? Why is it always you?"

"Jovian, I did not ask for this. What dream do I have that you want?" He held his arms wide, turning slowly. "Do you want to stand upon the sands now? Face Argus in mortal combat? Step food upon the sands and stand a gladiator? Is THIS what you want?" He cried, pointing to the lash mark on his back and the stitches on his jaw. "Tell me boy, is it?"

CHAPTER 10

Violetta followed Arturo up the rough stone steps and into the villa where slaves were busy washing the walls and polishing the marble floors. She glanced around at those doing the tasks so familiar to her and wondered what it was like to not fear the sound of the master of the house in the hall. Not a single slave around her seemed fearful, some even seemed to be happy at their tasks, talking to their friends and sharing quiet laughter at secret jokes.

"Violetta? Come." The medicus called from the far end of the hall. She had not noticed that she had stopped and that he had gotten so far ahead. "It is not wise to keep Lycithia waiting."

"Apologies." She said, walking quickly to join him. "You call our Domina by her given name and not her title? Is this permitted or is it your special privilege? I have never heard of such before but your status…"

"My status in the past means nothing here." He interrupted sharply, a note of bitterness in his tone. "I do it because there is little they can do to me and they both know the consequence of violence towards me." He paused and softened his expression "No matter how comfortable they may try to make you feel in their presence you must never mimic my attitude towards them. They are dangerous in ways Census never understood."

She nodded her understanding, wondering why Felix had never bothered to investigate the nature of the people he was involved with. If he had Violetta was certain that she would not be in this house now, or ever, and that thought was all but unbearable. Her inner thoughts about how different her life would be from the one she lived now, fully of possibilities and hope, were interrupted by the sound of an angry, commanding female voice.

"I do not want to spend days on the road to Rome with your little pet preening beside you like a little peacock!" Lycithia shouted into the face of her husband as the pair of slaves entered the room.

"He is not my pet. He is my body slave and as yours will be at your side." Tertius countered, pointing to the auburn-haired woman beside his wife. "I would have mine as well. I will need his help to prepare myself to stand among the elite of the city. The invited guests of Titus Claudius, with the challenger of their city's champion mine to command. We will be the toast of the city. Jovian is needed to help prepare me for such company."

"I am sure that our host, wealthy as he is, will have more than enough slaves on hand to help you get dressed Tiberius, without the need for Jovian's company in our wagon." Lycithia scoffed, rolling her eyes, and finally seeing the pair of medicus' from the sands waiting in obedience to her command.

Violetta made brief eye contact with Jovian. He looked near to tears at the insults from Lycithia, whether from hurt or anger she could not tell. Bowing her head, she dared to interrupt the tirade. "Domina. You summoned us?"

Her eyes stayed pointed to the floor, waiting for the Roman woman to finish her approach. She could hear the brush of silk across the floor and the soft chime of metal as her earrings knocked against each other. Violetta wondered if she was like Selenia or one of the other Roman women she had met on the pulvinus the day she had been dressed as one of them.

"So, this is Felix's little flower that has stolen the heart of the great Cassian. I admit I was expecting more of a temptress. I suppose after the whipping at the villa the spirit of one so young could be broken but perhaps some time away from such things will bring color to pale cheeks and fire to your heart, making a suitable mate for our…stallion."

"You talk about them as if they are horses for breeding instead of people with hearts and souls." Arturo growled, not quite under his breath but not loudly either.

"Their hearts and souls are not my concern, medicus." Lycithia snapped at him. "Nor are they yours. If I want to breed slaves like racehorses, then I will do so. You will stay out of it."

Violetta watched as they glared at each other and wondered at the simmering hatred. Why did the lanista not stop it? Speak to the insolence of her instructor or the rudeness of his wife? She looked up briefly to see that the lanista was engrossed in staring out the window at the sands instead of dealing with the conflict in the room.

"They are incredible. If only Claudius would allow Proximus to return to the sands of Rome. What an amazing day of games it would be. I have yet to choose the man to join us in Rome Jovian." He said to the boy at his side who was watching the fight in the room instead of the yard. "Who would you choose if not Proximus?"

"I would choose Argus, Dominus." Jovian replied. "He trains with Cassian and would make a great addition."

Before Tiberius could reply Arturo raised his voice to Lycithia, making all three other occupants of the room stare in surprise at the outburst.

"I do my job and do it well. I will not help you turn that girl into a breeding mare for your amusement. You would simply steal the babe to raise as your own, you conniving…"

"Arturo! Cease!" Tertius finally spoke up. "Get out!" He yelled, stalking towards the pair of medicus' "If I could, I would whip you to within an inch of your miserable life. Be gone from my sight."

Arturo spun on his heel and left the room, but when Violetta started to follow Lycithia spoke "Stop girl. You were not dismissed yet. I would still break words with you."

"Of course, Domina. As you say." She stopped and turned back, standing demurely while she waited for further instructions, silently pleading for Arturo to return to stand at her side.

"I still do not see why it is that he is so taken with her Tiberius." Lycithia stated, her voice bored as she circled Violetta. "She is small, almost delicate. How can she handle the brutality of life in the ludus?"

She felt a hand beneath her chin, raising her eyes until they met. Forcing her face to remain blank, neutral despite the condescending insults from the woman before her, Violetta wondered how someone with so much privilege had lost her empathy and the ability to see the humanity in other people. The brown eyes staring back at her could have been warm, maternal, and friendly but instead they were hard and calculating in their appraisal.

"I am stronger than I might appear Domina." She said carefully, trying not to agitate her or appear argumentative as Arturo had done. "Was there a specific need that I might see answered?" Perhaps forcing herself to sound helpful might make things easier between them. Even if Arturo was right about her darkness there was no need to make an enemy of this woman.

Lycithia smiled, a devious turn of her lips that sent a shiver through Violetta at the sight.

"What I want, young medicus, is a child and Arturo has failed to help me conceive. This is now your charge as well." She stated, crossing her arms with a look of appraisal in her eyes.

"I will do my best, of course, Domina, though Arturo is much more schooled in such things than I am. I have just begun to learn the ways of medicus." Violetta said. She could not take on such an important task as the heir to the household, not while she was learning the basics of medicine. It did not seem as though Lycithia was going to give her a choice in matter.

The Roman woman shook her head at Violetta's protest, looked towards the window to ensure that her husband was still engrossed in watching the gladiators before hissing in her ear. "You will see that I have a child in my arms within the year. If not from my womb then it will be from your own. If you do not find a way to quicken my husband's seed in my womb, I will see to it that it is your body that carries the heir to the house of Tertius."

"Domina…I have not thought to carrying any child. I am gifted bodily to Cassian and if I denied him then I would surely be returned to the house of my master." She could not imagine this monstrous woman understanding the love between two slaves that she did not see as humans. The terror she felt at the thought of being forced, not only to submit bodily to the lanista but to carry his child solely for the purpose of providing an heir to his household was greater than her disgust at the cruelty of her new mistress.

"I do not care if you fuck Cassian, but if you bear a son before I do then I will claim it as my husband's and take it from your very breast."

She was looming over her, threatening with both words and body. Unable to defend herself, or protest the threat, all she could do was to step backwards to attempt a retreat to the infirmary and as far away from Lycithia as she could get.

"You cannot do that Domina! Take her child?" Jovian cried, appearing at her side, defending her with his outrage.

"Silence, little whore!" Lycithia cried, spinning to slap the young man across the face.

"Domina!" Violetta stepped between them so that Lycithia did not continue to strike her friend. The violence of her temper was startling and even Jovian seemed surprised by the outburst. She wondered if he had ever been struck before today. The way that he wept, cringing from contact, made her think that it was a first, if not ever than at least in a long time.

"What in Hades is this noise?" Tiberius cried, turning from the window. "Stop this drama and break words of explanation. What causes this shrieking and violence in my house? If it does not bring coin or raising of reputation, I will not have it." He looked at the trio, waiting for them to calm down before he continued. "What happened here? Why did you strike Jovian?" He asked his wife as Violetta inspected the cut on his cheek left by a ring on her hand.

"Your pet heard me tell young Violetta that she will be accompanying Cassian on the way to Rome. I want our champion to be pleased and carefully tended on the road and when we are in the city itself." Lycithia said with a serene smile that was as chilling as the vicious one she had worn earlier. "The boy had a fit of temper and I had to slap him to bring him back to his senses."

She shrugged as though the answer was obvious and put her hand to Violetta's shoulder, with a subtle but painful squeeze was a warning not to correct her lie.

"I am both grateful and honored, Dominus." Violetta said, releasing her hold on Jovian which allowed him to bolt from the room. "I will do my best to learn all that I can by that time so that I can serve the house of Tertius well and aid my instructor."

The lanista frowned for a moment, when Jovian ran without being dismissed, then switched to a smile. He placed an arm across her shoulders, easing her from his wife and towards the doorway.

"It has not yet been decided if the druid shall go to Rome, nor who will join Cassian on the lists, but I am sure that you will indeed be a valuable addition to the journey." He smiled at her as though they were sharing a personal joke as he added "I am certain that the Celt will be thrilled at the idea of your company in the wagon on the road to Rome. Keep him soothed without making the other men too jealous, eh?"

"Yes, Dominus." Was all Violetta could think to say in response to his crude implication and the swat to her backside as she walked back towards the stairs.

She cringed at Jovian's words to the men on the sands, overheard when she walked past that doorway, his heart must hurt more than. It was a surprise when he ran from the balcony to join her at the door to the ludus when the guard came to unlock the door.

"You would call yourself my friend?" He asked her, breathless and sweating in his emotional state. "Then I will have you mend my cheek and break no words to Argus about this. I will find a way to join the party to Rome if I must throw myself to the top of the wagon to do it. You are going to help me." He stated, leaving her no room for a choice or answer before he dashed down the stairs and towards the doorway that led to the sands and the infirmary.

CHAPTER 11

Cassian could not understand the sudden rage from Jovian and when the boy left the balcony without answering his question, wiping tears that streaked his make-up across his face, he shrugged and turned to face Argus. Instead of his usual eager expression when they sparred the German wore one of rage that matched the level of emotion in Jovian's eyes moments before.

"What is your issue Argus? Do you join the sentiment of the spoiled brat of Tertius? Or are you simply annoyed at my existence?" He said with a smirk that hinted at hopeful that this was not going to be another fit of tempter that he would have to quiet so that the day's work could be done.

"You dismiss him as nothing more than a spoiled child Cassian?" Argus said, taking up his sword and shield again. "Why does everyone treat him as nothing? Why can no one see the potential that is under the paint and preening?"

The Champion watched warily as the younger man started to circle him, aggression in every step. "Argus? Where does this new concern come from? I have not changed the way that I think of Jovian in all the years that I have known him. Nor has he ever given me reason to do so. He is very clever boy, but he is not a warrior."

"Have you ever tried to see him as anything more?" Argus cried, stepping in to swing the sword towards Cassian's shoulder, starting the attack with his hands to follow the one he had started with his words.

The champion was confused at the change in his training companion in the few weeks he had been gone. When he had gone to the marketplace with Tertius that fateful day he had left Argus practicing his well-known side-kick-jump against Tartarus who was holding a shield to block the impact. He had been focused on nothing besides improving his skills so that Tertius would place him prominently in the next games. He had thought that now his goal would be to be considered for the games in Rome when the time came for Tertius to make the choices for who would be included on that great adventure, but now he seemed focused on something else, someone else.

He blocked the blows from the younger man, almost pitying him what seemed to be confusion about the place of the boy from the balcony above them. Perhaps they had begun a friendship of sorts while he was gone. They were close in age, only a few years difference, but what would they have in common that they could have forged a bond over?

"Why would I look for what is not there Argus? Jovian is who and what he is and will never be anything else." Cassian blocked a blow meant for his head and delivered one of his own to the German's ribs. "I do not judge the boy, but I am not looking for the steel of a sword in the soft fruit of a strawberry. I will never find it and would be disappointed if I had expected it."

His response did not calm Argus as he had hoped. Cassian had thought he might see the point that he was trying to make. There was no point in trying to find more in a person who hid who he was with paints and silks. Jovian loved playing at being 'almost roman' and more important than all the other slaves in the house simply because the lanista had chosen him to wait on him hand and foot, cock and ass, to dress him and simper after him with compliments and fawning attentive touches. Jovian was born in the villa and would likely die there too, just as the men of the ludus would die upon the sands of the arena. They all had their fate and it would be foolish to try to cheat it.

He noticed that Arturo had returned, without Violetta, and paused his attack. What had happened that he had been sent back without her? It would have made sense that she was sent to the infirmary with the senior medicus so why was she left alone with the Romans?

"You are as bad as the rest of them." Argus snarled, a rawness in his voice. "There is so much more to him, to any of us, than we show. Why can it not be the same for me? For him?"

Cassian could not understand the sudden emotion from Argus in defence of someone who should not have mattered, not to a gladiator.

"If I did not think that there was more to you than you show when you walk the halls of this place then I would not spend my time preparing you for the arena." He replied, blocking another blow aimed for his head. "If you learn some control you can become deadly, Argus. You may even have the heart of a champion, but the boy is not one of us, he never will be."

Something snapped in the eyes of the other man, something dark and dangerous that made the Celt uncomfortable. Adjusting the grip on his gladius' he shifted his weight to the balls of his feet. Ready to move, to counter the attack he could see coming in Argus' glare, his eyes flicked to the doorway. He had hoped to see Violetta reappear, but still the archway remained empty.

"Waiting for your whore to reappear?" Argus called, getting Cassian's attention as well as his immediate anger. "Perhaps she is too busy tending to Dominus to worry about returning to this place?" He moved in for a quick thrust of his weapon. "Maybe she was dazzled by the finery and chose the ease of serving the Romans over the blood, sweat and death of the ludus you brought her to."

Argus' words hit on the worry that had been needling on his mind since Arturo's return without her.

"Call my woman that again and I will cut off your cock to silence you with." Cassian snarled at the same time he used the edge of his sword to strike the German across the ribs.

"Unlike your little strawberry, Violetta is loyal and if she has not yet returned then there must be a need for her upstairs."

Argus roared with a wordless anger. The sound echoed his upset around the yard and up to the heavens, and the balcony usually occupied by Tertius rang with the sounds of their match which was now a matter of pride, not instruction. Cirandon looked as though he was considering taking the whip to them both, but Cassian was going to ensure that, if nothing else, Argus would learn to keep his temper in check. Changing his tactics with a sudden thought towards success he used his swords to hold Argus' in place while he twisted it until the young man released it, dropping it in the sand.

Once disarmed, leaving Argus holding his shield with a confused expression, Cassian threw the swords to the side and faced off with clenched fists instead.

"Come on then. If you think you are ready, Argus."

His challenger grinned and first smashed the small circular shield into Cassian's ribs and when he grunted at the impact Argus swung hard for his neck. "You are not invincible Cassian. Remember that."

Cassian pulled his head back to avoid the blow that would have connected to his damaged jaw and sent him from the sands for more time than he could afford then threw his own strike that connected to the side of Argus' face.

"Against you I do not need to be, yet." He replied with a dark chuckled before committing fully to the melee. Ducking blows meant for his head and shoulders, he maneuvered in a circle, striking the stomach and back of his trainee. The other men gathered around, watching the fight, and making bets on the winner. Rolling in the sand after a hard shove from Cassian heard Tarcarus and Barrius making bets to which one of them would be on their feet when Cirandon put an end to the match. Standing up he narrowed his eyes, waiting for Argus to get into the position that would allow him to deliver the blow that would guarantee his victory.

"Doctore! Bring them to a halt, now." The lanista's voice called from the balcony, bringing the action to an immediate halt to the fight. Both men straightened and, with a parting glare, joined the other men in waiting for the command from their master.

Tertius was standing at the edge of the balcony, popping what looked like grapes into his mouth. Cassian could not remember the last time he had tasted the sweet fruit and with a brief smile he wondered if, perhaps, Violetta would enjoy them as a surprise along with the gift he intended to see purchased for her delight.

The sound of Cirandon clearing his throat told him that he had let his face show the level of distraction he felt, wondering where his woman was and why she had not yet returned was a new feeling. He refocused on the balcony and the preening man staring down at him and at Argus.

"My gladiators." Tertius called from the railing. "Not only has the champion of the house of Tertius returned to us from his sojourn in the house of our ally, Felix Census, but with him comes a new member of our esteemed household. You will see her soon, if you have not already, at the side of our medicus, Arturo."

The men around him chuckled, Tarcarus made a comment about her purpose among them from the far end of the line. Cassian tensed with annoyance but grinned broadly when Barrius hammered his fist into the Thracian's thigh, causing him to cry out and stop his crude muttering, at least for that moment.

"Now, you men are likely to be wondering what the significance of a mere girl would be to a ludus of gladiators destined to be gods of the sands." Tertius continued with the vain smile he always wore when he had the undivided attention of any group of people, free or not. "I hate to disappoint but, with a singular exception, she is not among you to provide…entertainment."

He waited while the men, other than Cassian and Argus, shared a chuckle. "She is the assistant to Arturo and to be treated with the same regard as you would treat the druid. I will not have the control of my ludus disrupted because there happens to be a skirt in the infirmary. If you can take hold back a death blow at a moment's command in the arena then you can hold any thoughts of desire for another man's woman, for your medicus, to yourself."

The other men nodded as Proximus answered for them. "Yes Dominus. Your will is ours."

"There is also the announcement of the next games featuring the men of the house of Tertius to glorify the gods with blood and death upon the sands."

Every man in the yard, even Arturo, was focused on the Roman's next words.

"The games will not be upon the sands of the arena here in Velletri but upon those of Rome itself!"

Cassian stood a little straighter as the men looked at him. Some of them would be guessing correctly that it was to be his name that would be featured in the Primus of that great city's arena, but he wondered which of his brothers had been chosen to join him on that journey. He hoped that it was not the Thracian Tarcarus. The man was a stubborn fool who spoke at times of following the 'Great Spartacus' in a fight to freedom one day. He was also an arrogant pig who smelled of piss and would not make Violetta's journey with them a time of anything but constant badgering.

"Not a man among you will be surprised to know that it is Cassian who brought this opportunity to our house. It was his skill that impressed Titus Claudius enough to extend the invitation."

Cassian noticed that Proximus' jaw ticked at the mention of Claudius. Perhaps the man wanted to return to Rome after all.

"It is only natural, of course, that he is the first name to be put forward to this fight. Who among you would join him? Tarcarus of Thrace? Proximus of Germania, a former champion of that city? Not this time. For this match, the first of what I pray to Jupiter will be many, the second man to join Cassian on the test that is Rome will be…Argus."

Every head turned to stare at the bloody-nosed gladiator that was not looking at the balcony but the doorway from the ludus where Violetta stood with the teary-eyed form of Jovian at her side as blood dripped from his hand.

"Dominus?" Argus asked, slowly turned to face Cassian, and then look up at the lanista. "Your will is my own."

CHAPTER 12

Jovian watched the joy wash over Argus' face as his name was announced. It was a beautiful thing to behold, his green eyes sparkled in the light of the early afternoon light and the sheen of sweat on his chest from his exertions against Cassian gave him a glow like one of the gods standing among mere mortals. Even the blood on his face made him seem ruggedly handsome. It was only the knowledge that Tertius could see him that kept the boy from running out to throw his arms around the glorious man and kiss his lips.

To share in that moment would have been a joy he would have treasured, almost as much as he would have enjoyed sharing the trip to Rome. How they could have celebrated in secret and stolen moments, kissed, and touched, exploring each other with a sensuality he was certain Argus possessed despite the roughness of his demeanor. The bump of Violetta against his arms brought him back from the euphoric dream of what could have been, and he sighed, letting go of the dream with his breath.

"Is he not the most beautiful man you ever saw Violetta?" He asked, letting her draw him from the doorway and into the hall to the infirmary, past the open door to a storage room that he realized had been set up as a cell for her. "Wait a moment. You…are to sleep here? In the ludus where the gladiators are? Does Domina know? Did Dominus command this?"

"I do not know if she knows, but it is his will and command. It is so that I might learn my tasks at every opportunity. I do not think that my personal safeties were a concern of his at the time of the command nor are they his concern now." She replied.

Her nervous glance towards the sands told him that the confidence in her voice was a cover. She had a real fear that the men would not respect that she was not among them to be used for their bodily needs instead of their medical needs.

"Well, then show them what you are capable of. Can you mend my hand before Dominus sends for me? I would like the proof of bandages to show that I was not hiding like a pouting child." Jovian gave the best smile he could when his heart hurt as deeply as his bleeding hand.

He could not explain it but when Violetta put her hand on his shoulder, he felt a strange sense of comfort. He did not have anyone he could call a true friend. Most of the other slaves in the household avoided him due to the proximity he kept to their Dominus. They thought he would reveal their secret conversations to the Romans if it would suit his purpose or benefit him at all. He had to admit that he was guilty of such things, but only if it were a true necessity or the 'secret' that he exposed was one that Dominus could use for the betterment of the house. They never seemed to see that, when he released a secret, there was, almost, always an improvement in the lives of those under Tertius' care.

"I can easily care for that and, if you would like, I can assist you to repair the damage done by tears to your art." She said with a gentle tone.

He wondered if it was her natural tone or if it was taught to her by Arturo who was as soothing as he was beautiful. "What art do you speak of?" He asked, looking into her eyes while attempting his most charming smile. He hated to think what his paints looked like if she was making a comment like that and the fact that Argus had seen the disaster that his face must look after his tears made him cringe. "You mean my face? You know how to use the beauty paints of the Romans?"

She nodded, easing him onto a stool beside the thick wooden table that Arturo used for all his procedures. "I have no experience putting them on myself, I am better acquainted with silk, but I have put them on several Roman ladies, and they were greatly pleased with the results. I am certain that I can help you return to the glory that you are accustomed to."

He returned the smile, delighted to find someone who might enjoy some of what he did as well. "Your Domina instructed you in the art of make-up? You have a steady hand with a kole brush?" She was like a brand-new delightful gift that did not even realize that she had been given to him. She would be able to help him perfect his appearance, pleasing Tertius and attracting Argus at the same time. Instead of a threat to his position as most beautiful and desired slave in the house she would be able to help him become the only type of champion he ever could be, a beautiful one. "Did you keep any of the silk from the house of Census?"

"If I did not have a steady hand then I would be a poor student for a medicus, would I not?" She replied with a smile, gently cleaning away the blood and preparing to stitch the skin closed. "And yes, I kept a few pieces of silk."

He could not deny the gentleness in her touch and the compassion in her smile while she worked on him. "No, I do not suppose that would be a good flaw to have." He looked at the stitches, small dark lines across his caramel skin. "Violetta? Will it scar? I know that it is not on my face, but I do not want to be scarred if possible. Not even on my hands. It will be hard to make my henna perfect if there is the bump from a scar."

She nodded, examining her own work the same way that he inspected the stitching on his silk robes. "If there is one it will be very fine, a tiny line. Nothing that would be noticeable."

He wondered, since her true Dominus was a silk merchant, if she would help him take care of his treasures. It would be like having a body slave of his own in some ways, as long as Cassian did not find out.

"Thank you, Violetta. You are a goddess with a needle." He batted his eyelashes and smiled up at her. "Are you as good with silk as you are with soft flesh? I have a robe, gifted by Dominus for my last birthday celebration, and I tore a seam. I have no skill for mending such a thing."

"Oh." She gave him a strange, uncertain smile and nodded "I have done that many times in the house of Census. If you can get the garment to me before the lamps are doused tonight, I will do my best to mend it as soon as I am able."

"You are so kind. I think it will be a wonderful thing that you are here now." He made a quick move and embraced her. "I will make sure to reward you for it."

"No rewards are needed between friends, Jovian." She said.

The surprise in her voice matched her face at the unexpected display of affection. Her joy at the friendly contact was even better than he had hoped it would be. If he was going to slowly convince her to help him do things that he was supposed to do, mending his robes and polishing his jewelry to start, he would have to keep surprising her like this so that his requests would not seem so strange.

"What about repairing the damage done to perfection by tears?"

"If you would wait here, I will go and fetch my paints." He said with an impish grin. "Perhaps I should paint your face as well. Cassian would be startled to see the difference I could exact upon you with just a few moments and my brushes. What fun it shall be."

"I am not sure…"

He did not hear the rest of her words. He was rushing from the infirmary towards the stairs so that he could retrieve his precious collection of paints and kohl. It would be a delight to have another person to use his paints on. Sneaking across the cold marble floor he could hear Tertius lecturing the gladiators on what would be expected of those going to Rome, on the journey he was not to be included on. The anger he had felt at Lycithia for his exclusion flooded back to him, along with the memory of the threat against Violetta.

"Perhaps, more than assisting me in such small things, she would lend aid in something greater and help me join the journey to Rome so that I could be with Argus without the eyes of Dominus upon us? Would she take the risk to help me? That is the kind of thing that friends do for each other. I have seen the gladiators take a blow for their brother if it would see him spared. I am sure, if Cassian adore her as he says, she must be one that would lend aid to a friend for something so important."

Jovian took the paint pallet gifted to him, and replenished by, Tertius and slid it into the pocket of his tunic and the robe that had been ripped in a moment of passion with his Dominus. Making his way back to the stairs he considered the night he had received it, the night he had shared his master's bed, and he wondered at Argus' words in the ludus. He had said that Dominus used him and abused him, but that could not be. He had seen how Felix and Vitus had treated Violetta and that was abuse. Surely what was between him and his beloved Dominus was not that. It was love, in a way. Argus did not understand love, not Roman love. How could he? He was a brute from Germania, a beast of a man, but oh what beautiful beast he was.

Carefully finding his way to the stairs and down the dark halls of the ludus Jovian burst through the door of the infirmary with a smile. "Are you prepared to be amazed at my beauty Violetta?" he asked, plunking down on the stool once again with a laugh as it almost toppled on the uneven surface. "I give my promise that you will look like a goddess yourself when I am done."

"Jovian," Her voice now carried a note of uncertainty that made him wonder if he had been wrong. "Are you certain that we should be doing this now? Will Dominus not miss you? What of Arturo? Surely, I should be on the sands at his side, learning how the men receive their injuries. In the house of Census, I would risk the ire of Felix for wasting time on something he would deem as trivial. I had not thought you meant to do this now. I will happily aid you with your own decoration but as for my own…I am unsure."

He laughed again. Her sense of responsibility was a serious as Cassian's own. They were better matched than they knew if this was her way of thinking. "Oh, Violetta. No one will say a word against this. If you are to go with them to Rome, then you must be a vision of loveliness in my stead. If I am not permitted to stand as the jewel of this house, then you must do so in my place." He frowned slightly "It is only a pity that you do not own a silk dress of your own to wear when you attend Lycithia in the villas of Rome's elite."

"You think that she will require that of me? To join the company in the house of Claudius?" She turned to lift a small piece of fabric that was folded into a square and handed it to him. "You might like this. I have no use for it anymore."

The uncertainty in her eyes told Jovian that it would not take much convincing to get her to agree to help him. He had been right about her and the sad lack of confidence in her own ability to charm Romans that were not the monsters that she had be ruled by. It would be the tool that he would used to achieve his desires. Reaching to take the folded square he smiled as he unfurled the sash of golden silk, embroidered with flowers and stars.

"Gratitude for the gift. I shall wear it presently." He declared, wrapping it as a belt around his waist.

"As for Rome and Domina, she is almost certain to make the demand of you." He nodded while she opened the pallet and prepared the brushes. "It is unfortunate that you could not hide me in the wagon with the gladiators. Then I would be able to help you prepare yourself for such things and, if I were not found until we reached the city then I am certain that Dominus would have me attend as well. I would be at your side to help you navigate the finery and elite mannerisms."

He could see the idea swirling in her mind as she began to paint his face carefully. Had he gone too far too soon? Would she see that it was a desperate attempt to be with the gladiators? If he told her how he felt about Argus would it make a difference or simply make her worry that helping him would get her into the bad graces of Tertius? "It would be fun to be there together, would it not?" He added, trying to make it appear as though she was the focus of his thoughts.

"I admit that it would be much less daunting with you at Dominus' side. I know how to prepare our masters for events of elite company, but no one has ever prepared me for such things." Violetta giggled and set down the last brush. "There. You are my masterpiece of the day, Jovian. I do not think I have ever had such freedom with paints, so I hope that you are disappointed."

"I shall do your face and then we can look together. I know where Arturo has a platter of polished silver that will show us our reflection."

She started to protest but he took her head in his hands, gently stilling her. "Shh, sister. Let me play to my contentment and then, when your man sets eyes upon you, he will be so amazed at your beauty that he will be able to speak no words but will take you to that cell of yours and anoint your cot with passion."

"Oh Jovian." She shook her head when he had finished adding a coral pink to her lips. "I do not know if that would enter his mind. After what happened in at the celebration of Felix, what he had to do and bear witness to, I do not think he would desire me in that way. He spoke words of desire towards marriage in a passionate plea afterwards, but since then he has made no advances. I know that the surgery dampens his desire some but…I think he sees me as a case for his charity more than a woman to be desired."

Her words saddened him. Every woman deserved to feel beautiful, even if she was not most men's idea of beauty.

"Sweet sister. You are lovely." Jovian said, leaning closer until the tip of his nose was almost touching hers. "I have known Cassian all my life and never has he looked at anyone the way that he looks at you. Charity is not in his nature and that is not what he wants to give you, I can promise you that."

"But Jovian…"

He stopped her words with the press of his fingertip to her lips, the breadth of it all that lay between their lips.

"Stop words of such doubt or I will kiss you myself to prove your desirability."

"You will do WHAT?!" Cassian's voice raged from the doorway. "What in the name of Hades goes on here?"

CHAPTER 13

"Jovian. Explain this. Now."

Cassian could not believe what he was seeing and hearing. Jovian, the little shit, looked ready to kiss Violetta, not just his usual play with words and teasing, but close enough that he could have done it, would have done it, had he not walked in. Already the boy had gone too far. He looked at Violetta and shook his head, stepping further into the room and trying to hide his distress at what he was imagining.

"Why is your face…what has happened upstairs that you look like a Roman woman instead of my own?"

Violetta rose to her feet, her eyes never leaving his. He hated that there was fear in them. This was not what he had intended, but he had to accept that it might take time for her to not tremble at the sound of anger in a man's voice.

"Cassian. It is not what you think. I promise you." She pointed to the needle and stitching materials. "Jovian hurt his hand and the wound needed stitches. He wanted to return a gesture of kindness with the make-up. Nothing else was meant by it."

She was pleading with him and yet Jovian stood silently, smugly, while he put away the paint that was beginning to offend him as much as the boy's entitled attitude.

"Jovian. Take what is yours and leave. I would have words with Violetta without you listening to each one so that you can report it back to Dominus." He did not look at the boy, the rage on his face would have been relayed to the lanista and used against him when it suited the little peacock.

"But Cassian. I have not yet shown Violetta how she looks after my administration. She should know how beautiful she looks."

The protest was feeble and only annoyed him more with the foolishness of it. As if it were possible that the false blush and painted lips could make her any more lovely than she was when she woke from a sleep in his arms or lay beside him in the afterglow of their passionate lovemaking.

"I will make sure that she knows exactly how beautiful she is, without your help." Cassian did all that he could to ignore Jovian slinking out with a short backwards glance at Violetta who simply shook her head at the boy before looking up at him again with kohled eyes and painted skin.

He waited until the door latch clicked closed before letting out a sigh. "What was in his mind to do this to you? Domina would lose her temper and let her hands fly against you. She will have no rival in this house. Already your youth and delicate allure make you a target of her rage."

He reached his hand to stroke a tendril of hair behind her ear, trying to find the words to tell her that though the decoration painted by Jovian made her beautiful she was even more so without them. His entire thought process stopped when there was a flinch. A moment of panic seized him, and he cupped her cheek, his heart thundering in his chest so loudly he was sure that she would be able to hear it.

"You flinch at my touch? Do the hands that brought bruises to your arms now offend even with soft touch meant to sooth?" He whispered. His voice was hoarse with the emotions that choked him. How could he have thought that what he had done would not bear consequence between them? How could he expect that his touch, no matter how well intended and loving, would not frighten her, reminding her of what he had done, what he had allowed to happen to her? "Apologies. I will not bring you further insult."

He released his hold and, with his head bowed, he stepped back from her with a sinking feeling in his chest. He had never thought to feel defeat this severe, this crippling agony slipping over him. "I was a fool to think it would not be so."

He had turned to leave the room, his heart in pieces as he cursed the name of Census and the monstrous perversion of his son when the soft touch of her hand on his arm stopped his steps and his heart.

"Cassian? I beg for you to stay. Hear my words?"

Her pleading voice halted his heavy feet. He turned to look into her eyes, trying not to laugh at himself when he thought he saw the same adoration there that had been the last day they had awoken in each others arms in the house of her former master. It was not possible, he was a fool to hope, yet he could not hold back the wish that there might still be a chance she did not fear him for what he had done.

"What words does my priestess off from the gods that could sooth my soul more than your touch could, were I permitted such?"

"Cassian, you are…permission? When have I ever turned from you?"

He could hear the distress in her voice, and it was reflected in her eyes, those eyes that held the ocean of her emotions.

"You flinched at my touch. I would never bring you harm, by choice." His voice was firm and agitated, the words disgusted him as much as the memory, but if she were going to reject him then he would steel himself for the death blow.

"It is not your touch, or the memory of the abuse forced upon us both that caused the recoil." She cried defensively before she grabbed a cloth and scrubbed her cheek where his fingers had brushed. Cringing at the rough contact of the cloth until the paint applied by Jovian was washed away to reveal a dark purple bruise. "A blow delivered by Vitus when you were not yet in the room left its mark. That is what your fingers touched."

She clasped his hand while he stared, bemused, and surprised down at her face.

"You do not want me to leave? To stop my pursuit of your heart?" He asked, trying to hold back the rise of his heartbeat. His dream was on the verge of returning to him and he was afraid to ask if she meant it. "Violetta you need to know that you will be protected, that I will protect with my life as long as my heart beats. Even if you not longer hold me close to your heart or wish to have me share your bed, I swear that no man here will hurt you." He straightened, the confident warrior exterior hiding his preparation for her rejective choice. "You are free to make your choice without worry for your safety."

The grip on his hands tightened, drawing his attention back down to the painted face, with the dark bruise exposed that did not belong on her lovely face.

"Cassian. I choose you. Every moment and with every breath, I choose you. If you hold any desire for me at all then I am yours for as long as the gods allow us to be together."

Her words were like a sweet breath of air filling his lungs, using her own grip on his hands he swiftly pulled her against his body and lowered his mouth to meet hers with a hungry growl. The touch of her fingers sliding down his forearms so that her body could press against him sent a thrill through his entire body. She was offering herself to him though her body had to be pained still, she was giving herself to him without the hesitation of her injuries. His tongue parted her lips and for a moment he tasted fruit upon her tongue before he deepened the kiss only to have his tongue meet the bitterness of the paint Jovian had put on her lips.

"Damned paint. Why did you allow him to put the mask of whores and Romans on you? You have no blemish or scar to hide." He growled, his voice husky with the desire building in him.

"I wanted to be beautiful, for you. So that, perhaps, you would not see the victim of a monster instead of the woman who loves you." Was her softly whispered reply, the belief she held in her own words unmistakable in the pulse of the moment.

He cupped her face with his hands. "You are beautiful. You need no paints or falseness to call attention to that." His voice was as soft and tender as he could make it and yet tears still pooled in those lovely eyes that he adored so much. "No tears, little priestess. Please. I would see you smile if I cannot bring a blush to your cheeks."

"There is no sadness in these tears, my heart." Her hands covered his for a moment, the sweet contact savored as she closed her eyes, he could feel her panicked heartbeat slowing and he smiled.

Lowering his hands to her backside Cassian scooped her up to sit on the table behind her. "Let me wash this falseness from your divinity, my little priestess. I want to show you the most beautiful woman I have ever laid eyes upon and then I will show you the effect your beauty has upon the body and will of the man before you."

Her eyes were full of hope locked to his, but with the slightest nod of her head she consented. She consented to everything he wanted to explore, to everything he wished to show her of her beauty and of the strength of their bond. Perhaps this would strengthen them, restore their love to what it had been before the disaster of the house of Census.

"You still hold desire for a priestess defiled?" She asked him softly, when he brought the warm, damp, cloth to her face to begin washing the paint away.

"There is no power on earth or the heavens that could wipe away my desire for you, woman." He replied with a grin. Tapping the tip of her nose with a wet finger, leaving a drop of water that fell to her lip and made her giggle softly.

It was one of the most perfect sounds he could remember hearing and he wanted to hear more of it. He wanted her to smile and laugh, maybe even dance with joy like the women of his long-lost homeland. Could he ever bring her such joy in the ludus? Would their lives ever be simply that of a man and woman in love? Or would every sweet taste of happiness be forever tainted by the will of Romans?

"Woman." She echoed with a shake of her head. "You say the word as though it were a title the same as champion but outside your lips it means so little, even the free Roman women mean nothing more than the worth of their household and the ability to bring heirs to the arms of their husbands." He leaned against her palm when she brought it to his cheek and asked "Why does it sound so different when you say it? What are the women of your homeland capable of that you speak the word with such reverence?"

He regarded her carefully, rinsing the cloth in the bowl of warm water. Her lips, bearing the only remaining paint for him to wash, were as red as the blood dripping from a sword driven through the heart of a man and uttered words that were just as dangerous as a blade. "These fools do not know the value of a woman. In my country they can lead tribes if they prove themselves capable. You are more like them than any woman I have met in all the Republic."

Slowly he wiped away the last of the offending false color and stared down at her barefaced beauty. If he was honest with himself he would have been able to say that she was the most powerful woman that he had ever seen and it had nothing to do with the divine shape of her body or the smile that would have brought Jupiter down from the heaves just to see. Her heart, her soul, were stronger than the darkness around them and he loved her for it.

"Cassian you honor…" He did not let her finish the words, he had to satisfy the need that had been building in him since the moment he had though Jovian was about to kiss her. He needed to be joined to the power that was his lover. He plundered her mouth with his own, her lips that had been parted to speak giving him the immediate access to the sweetness of her mouth. He had dropped the cloth to the table and now, deepening the kiss, he shoved the bowl of water away as well.

Her hands were threaded into his hair and his little priestess was returning his passion stroke for stroke. With her body pressed tight against his he could feel the pearled arousal of her nipples through the thin fabric of her dress and when the pad of his thumb brushed down her throat he could feel her pulse that raced to match his own.

He lifted her from the table and turned, his hands caressing the rounded curves beneath the thin linen before he sat upon the stool often used by Arturo when he worked long hours on some important recipe. Cassian helped to guide her legs around his waist, creating the perfect balance of weight and allowing him to nestle her against the aching hardness beneath his subligaria.

"Fuck honor. I would give you proof of my words and my passion. Here and now, before they come for either of us." One arm around her to keep her tantalizingly close Cassian tugged aside the strap of her dress to ply hot kisses down her neck, shoulder, and the soft mound of her breast. His lips had just found her nipple, the sweet bud tightened and dark, when her moan in response was interrupted by the most unwanted sound.

"Cassian! You are to return to the sands, now. Proximus and Cirandon await you." The deep voice of Julius Lucius called from the other side of the door he was banging on. "Do not make me come in there and…remove you from whatever it is that you do behind a door that should not be closed."

"Damn the man and his timing." Cassian chuckled darkly and set Violetta on her feet.

"He could not have given a few more moments?" Violetta adjusted her dress with a blushing smile. "Perhaps, tonight?" She asked, they both knew what she meant.

"The sunset shall see me from the sands and to your arms if I can make it so, my heart." He whispered, kissing first her forehead, and then taking her lips again. He smiled to himself at the bruising swell of them that would remind her for the rest of the day how much passion he had for her. It would also serve as a reminder of what was to come as soon as they were able to find the time alone.

He left her there, a smile upon her face, and joined his guard on the way to the sands with an undeniable grin across his own lips. Despite the dull ache from his jaw, it was worth it, SHE was worth it, all of it.

CHAPTER 14

Jovian ran from the infirmary as if Cassian chased him though the gladiator was likely to be in Violetta's arms until someone, probably Lucius, pulled him bodily away from her. He had never been the target of that kind of rage from Cassian before and this was not even the worst thing that he had ever done. The list of grievances grew with each moment and the worry that the Celt might decide that he had finally put up with enough from him grew with it. He was panicking and suddenly Jovian realized he was deep within the ludus and no where near the stairs back up to the villa.

"Where am I? How is it that I am within the building and yet have no idea where I am?" Jovian paused and looked around him, trying to get his bearings. The torches cast strange shadows and the silence of the ludus in the hours of training was disorienting.

"If I do not return soon one of them will start to wonder where I am. I do not relish that conversation with paints in hand."

He was wandering back the way that he had come when suddenly he felt an arm snake around his waist and pull him into a darkened cell. His call for help was silenced by a rough hand over his mouth.

"Shh. There is no need to panic Jovian. It is Argus."

The German set him on his feet so he could turn to look at him, both sharing a smile.

"You are a fiend to surprise me in such a way Argus." Jovian declared, brushing hair from his eyes, and watching for Argus' reaction to his perfectly painted face. Some men were immediately put off by the blend of masculine and feminine, but the gladiator barely blinked at it.

"I did not mean to frighten you Jovian." Argus said with a grin. "You know it is not safe down here, especially alone this deep in the ludus. There are any number of crude and monstrous men that might take advantage of such confusion."

"But you would keep me safe from such things?" Jovian asked with an inviting tilt of his head. The strong arm was still looped around his waist and their bodies were pressed together, sending a thrill of arousal through him. Perhaps this was the moment he had been waiting for? The moment that the truth of affections would be revealed between them and he might have a little joy to treasure when they all left him behind to go to Rome.

"I would do all I could to keep you safe. Keeping you with me as long as was needed to make it so."

"What else might you do to keep me safe? To keep me here, with you, in such a small…intimate space?" Jovian purred, angling himself more firmly against the larger man.

"There are many things that I could do, little man." Argus said with a grin. "So many things that have filled dreams would be possible in this space, this time. One more than the others."

"What would you choose Argus? In this moment when you have me to yourself, secreted away from all eyes." Jovian's heart was in his throat with anticipation of what was to come.

The German leaned over him, his green eyes sparkling in the torchlight. The whole world seemed to stop when Argus lowered his face towards him.

"I choose the most forbidden, the most sacred. I choose you."

The next breath was stolen by the press of firm lips against his own.

Argus' kiss was everything that Jovian dreamed it might be, firm, demanding and possessive. He surrendered to the passion he had been imagining and wrapped his arms around the thick shoulders. Pulling Argus even closer so that he could boldly deepen the kiss with a sweep of his tongue and a moan of desperate hunger.

"You do? Choose me?" He asked between kisses, eager for the confirmation of his hope for affection beyond sexual desire.

"Of course, I choose you. You are special, different than everyone else. It is impossible not to notice you. When I fight in the arena, I will fight for you. Even if you are not allowed to attend the games to see it."

The reminder of the pain that brought him to his injury and the infirmary was a splash of water on the smoulder of his lust and ended the magic that was the amazing kiss.

"Your words touch upon the point of sadness that brought me bellow the villa in the first place. You will be going to Rome, but I will not. I am to stay here." He said, taking a step back from the comforting embrace.

"You attend Dominus' every journey, with small exception of the arena here in Velletri. Why are you not attending his needs on the road to that city?" Argus asked, his face full of confusion at the change in years worth of tradition.

"It is not his will but that of Domina. She does not wish my presence in the wagon upon the road. I had hoped to find a way to secret myself in the wagon with you and Cassian, but I would require aid to make that so."

"You would spend days in cramped dark with us?" Argus asked. "What aid is it that you need? I will do what I am able to make it so."

"I do not think it is within your power to aid me in this Argus." He said with a deep sadness in his voice. "I sought help from the woman of the Celt. I know that she is to be in the wagon and that the guards will pay less attention to her actions than to any of yours or even Cassian, if he could be convinced to lend aid."

"The girl? What did she say? Will she aid in this?"

Jovian thrilled at the eagerness in the gladiator's voice and wished that he had the news that would bring joy to them both.

"She has not given answer yet." He said, looking over his shoulder towards the light he could now see from the outside. "I will ask again and see what answer I can persuade from her."

Argus nodded in agreement. "A good plan, just do not let Cassian find you making such attempt, or his wrath will be unstoppable." The German smiled. "Be mindful of what your lips do while pleading for aid. I am not a man to share."

"There is no one I would willingly be with that is not you. Dominus commands me to his side, his bed at times, but you know this." Jovian did not wish to tell Argus that he enjoyed the time in the arms of the Roman lanista. "Please lead me to the stairs so that I may return to duty and consider how I will get Violetta to agree to help me."

Argus chuckled and led Jovian down the hall, around a few bends and to the gate at the bottom of the stairs to the villa where a guard was waiting

"He got lost in the halls of the ludus. See him upstairs. I do not have time for childminding when I must train." He said with a teasing smile that he shot at Jovian before heading back to the sands where Cassian greeted him with a call loud enough that even the young boy could hear.

"I was definitely lost in these depths. Dominus will be waiting for me." Jovian said with a smile, sauntering past the guard and up the stairs to try and settle his racing heart before he found the lanista.

He wanted to wrap his arms around himself and reimagine the arms of the gladiator that had kissed him. Kissed him, Argus had, by choice, kissed him. He had kissed him, held him and for those few moments in the dark cell of the ludus he had known true and genuine affection from a man that had chosen him for himself and not out of boredom or instruction.

He could feel the broad smile on his lips and wondered, briefly, if the paint by Violetta had been destroyed in the passion of the kiss with Argus.

"Oh, what care do I have of such things now." He spun happily on the marble floor, blissful until the silence was viciously cut by the one voice that filled him with dread.

"Why do you have such little care when you have been missing?" Lycithia snarled. "Dominus has been looking for you. Where were you? Sneaking in my silks again you little rat?"

"Domina." He hung his head so that she did not see the smile on his face that even her anger could not dampen. "I was having my hand mended by the new medicus. She took longer that Arturo, but the task is done. I thought that Dominus knew where I was."

He hated this woman more than anyone he had ever met, and she hated him almost as much. There was no reason for it that he had ever given her. He was as polite and charming with her as he was with every other Roman. He had put in such effort, ever since he was a child, to try and earn her affection, but there was no room in her heart for him. It had wounded him when he was younger, that she could not love him or even like him, but he refused to let it hurt him now.

"Then why was he calling for you hmm?" She asked, reaching to snatch at the silk he wore around his hips like a belt. "How did you come by this?"

"It took longer than expected, as I said. Domina." Jovian was losing the battle with his temper and even though it would get him in trouble he was ready to make the woman weep with her own rage and inferiority. "The silk was a gift from Violetta, Census is a silk merchant and so she possessed several scraps of fabric. I like this one and so she gave it to me. Your silks are of a size much too large to fit me but perhaps the material is the same. I cannot imagine that there was enough left after making one of your dresses to be useful for anything else."

The pain and indignation that flashed across her face was exactly what Jovian had intended, her agony an echo of his own at the loss of what could have been motherly affections. His joy was only momentary. Before he could turn to search for Tertius his wife, insult turning to dangerous rage, struck her hand across his cheek for the second time that day.

She seemed as surprised by her own action as he was himself. Never had Tertius allowed him to be struck. The shock of the contact was greater than the pain. His hand raised to his cheek, tenderly stinging from the blow, as tears pooled in his eyes.

"You shameful little brat." Lycithia hissed, straightening with a curled lip to stare down at Jovian's smaller frame. "You will never speak to me with such voice again. Your mother was right to abandon you to become a slave. Even though you were spawned of Rome you are not worthy of her blood."

"You knew my mother?" Jovian asked, feeling the blood drain from his cheeks. "You know who I am? Who I was meant to be? And never broke word upon the subject?"

"I have known and you, slave of Syria, by appearance if not blood, will never know the names of either parent. You are not worthy. Now go appease my husband with your lips upon his cock and the knowledge that neither of your parents wanted you enough to keep you in your heart."

CHAPTER 15

Following Lucius to the sands Cassian could not help the satisfied grin on his face. The only fear he had left, that he had been holding on to, had been dissolved with Violetta's kiss. The sweet taste of her was still upon his tongue just as his annoyance at Jovian was hot and burning upon his mind. That the little shit had painted her like a Roman was bad enough, but it was the act that his own arrival had stopped which had him still enraged.

The boy was about to kiss Violetta and there was no doubt in the Celt's mind that he would have tried more than that. Jovian always wanted what he could not have, and Violetta was now his latest fascination. It might work in her favor if it kept her safe from Lycithia but that did not mean that Cassian had to be alright with how the Syrian boy played his games. His woman was no longer a toy for the amusement of any man. They had both been through enough of such things.

The men at the sidelines, waiting for their turn to train under Cirandon's focused attention, turned to meet his eyes. A few of them shared a knowing smirk, they knew him well enough to know what he had been after even if he had not achieved it.

"The woman, she is yours?" Proximus asked, standing beside him. "I have seen your eyes upon her and more than once I have seen Dominus send her to your company."

"She is, as I am her man. Perhaps you are not the fool I supposed if you can see such obvious things when even Tarcarus does not comprehend." Cassian replied with a smirk, taking up his training weapons from Cicero. The former champion of Rome stood with him as though they were friends instead of men who had tried to kill each other the last time they broke words.

"The Thracian could not smell his own shit if he stepped in it." Proximus said with a chuckled that the Celt could not help but join.

"At least we can agree on that." Cassian said, stepping away from the German and closer to the sands so that he could watch Argus at work. He frowned when Proximus failed to take the hint and followed him.

"You are to fight in my city, my arena." He whispered. "Rome is a place I long to return to. I have things there that are unfinished."

"If you think that I can convince the lanista to bring you over Argus, then you are mistaken. I have no such influence over the man." Cassian shook his head, noting out of the corner of his eye that Violetta had retaken her position next to Arturo. "The company for that journey has already been decided. Besides," He grinned. "I would not subject my woman to days in your company by choice."

Both gladiators shared a laugh and when Cassian took to the sands to fight against Argus the other German stood still, watching the pair for a moment before taking a seat at the table among the others. Putting all else except the match he was engaged in from his mind Cassian slashed, spun with a thrusting sword in hand and dropped low to knock his opponent to the sand with a sweep of his leg.

"Get up." Cassian commanded, taking a step back to allow it. "Guard your lower half better or find yourself upon ass once again."

"What a teacher you are Cassian." Argus said with a smirk, rising to face off against him.

"I would not see Cirandon's time wasted upon simple minds. It is the least that I can do for a friend." Cassian replied.

"The great teacher is otherwise occupied anyway." Argus said, pointing to where Cirandon and Arturo were speaking with each other, their backs turned to the sands so that no man could guess at their words. "So do your best, Celt. Teach me another lesson."

"You will need several, daily, if you are to be ready for Rome. If it is half as magnificent as Proximus tells then both of us will need more skills than we have now." Cassian said, taking the starting position again.

"He likes to spin tales of his glorious life in Rome and yet he is here among us." Argus laughed and pointed towards where the man they were discussing was in deep conversation with Violetta.

Cassian watched the other man carefully, there was no need for jealousy or concern, yet. He began trading blows with Argus but did not engage in the regular rigors of combat as he kept an eye on the pair. He was just about to forget his concern and engage Argus in proper combat when Proximus pressed something into Violetta's hand and leaning close to whisper in her ear. Whatever it was that the German said it made his woman blush and give the big man an uncertain smile before looking across the sands at him.

"I would have contest with him. His arrogance since passing the test requires me to give him the firmest of reminders who it is that stands champion of this house." Cassian said to Argus with a nod.

Ignoring the look of amusement on the younger man's face he bellowed across the yard. "Proximus? Stop your whispers to the woman and step upon the sands. I think it is time for a truer contest between us than we have yet had."

The German stepped away from Violetta with a casual ease. "You would fight me? Are you certain you have rested enough in recent weeks?"

Cassian laughed, spinning his swords with ease. "Rest? Do you stand certain that is what happened? What if my time were spent crossing constant blades with Romans of the Legions and all they could find with balls enough to face me? Do you stand so confident then?"

The men cleared the sand to make room for the battle of the titans. Cassian noted with some pride that Violetta's eyes were upon him, shining with eager anticipation of his victory. Determined to give her eyes the glory they craved from him he stepped towards Proximus who towered above him. This time there would be no command from the lanista to see the German spared from the full strength of his skill.

"Let us see what you can do, little man." Proximus preened as he walked to take position.

His confidence in his own skill was obvious but the Celt knew that with the space afforded by the training yard and the lack of lanista on the balcony he would have a few moves that would surprise the German.

"I stand ready to continue my education of Germans. All day if needed." Cassian grinned and began to circle.

"I shall show you the meaning of the word." Proximus snarled, swinging his sword towards Cassian's head as the other men cheered.

"I do not care what you promised the man Tiberius. It is unseemly to have a woman down there among those brutes. Even if she is just a slave." Lycithia curled her lip in disgust. "It is not right. I will not have it."

The lanista rolled his eyes at his wife, she was being unreasonable and had no concept of the relationship between a gladiator and his master. There were certain bonds, promises, that once given could not be broken. He had given his word to Cassian that the girl would be near him and train with the druid. If he went back on it now the trust between them would be damaged, and it had only just been repaired.

"Lycithia. You do not understand." He groaned. Turning to face her, he was stunned once again at her beauty despite her anger. Her brown eyes were flashing with anger beneath her bright red hair. She was in a light green silk dress that accented the paleness of her skin, without a mole or freckle to be seen. His wife was an ivory skinned goddess that stirred his blood each time he laid eyes upon her. She was the favored daughter of a wealthy family in Rome, he had been lucky to marry her. There had been a man, who she refused to name to this day, that had gotten her with child. He refused to acknowledge her or the child which gave Tiberius, her long-time admirer and friend, the chance that he had been needed to marry above his normal station.

He walked across the room to take her hands in his. "My beloved wife, you, with all your wisdom in many things, do not understand the delicate nature of this situation. If I were to remove the girl then I break faith with our champion, while he trains for the fight that could elevate our house and, perhaps, see us in a position to move to Rome."

"But Tiberius, she is a woman and not a gladiator, down there among them." She said, her voice soothing. "You said yourself that she is a lovely, if broken-spirited, young thing. Why risk damage that would break Cassian's spirit?"

He could tell that she was trying to manipulate him to giving her what she wanted, but he could not figure out why she wanted it, to separate the girl and the Celt, when they had been through so much already.

"Your concern for the girl is as admirable as it is baffling." Tiberius said, pulling his wife into his arms. "What is the true motive behind the demand? My beautiful wife is not jealous of the attention given a slave by her own kind, is she?"

Lycithia laughed. "It is not the beasts in the ludus that I crave the attention of but my own husband."

He gave her a confused look, blinking to hide his worry that his guess would be correct. "You, in my arms, break words of lack of attention from me? What does Violetta have to do with it? I have no interest in bedding a girl when there is a woman in my arms." He pressed a line of kisses to her neck, up to nip at her ear lobe.

"The girl is to distract Jovian. I want to make a child with you Tiberius, to replace the one you married me for. That will not happen if your eye is constantly turned to the boy." She leaned back against his chest, enjoying the touch of his lips.

"Whether through friendship, fascination or fucking I want her to distract that little whore, so your nights are filled with me, our bed, until we welcome a child to this house once more."

He smiled against her skin and pressed a final kiss to the base of her skull. "You are a wicked woman in your schemes. I would hate to be the man out of favor with you." He turned her to face him, their bodies aligned as tightly as their intentions. "I will find some excuse to bring the girl to the villa, at night. I would still have her training with that damned druid. If all goes well in Rome and I am afforded the opportunity I will return Arturo to his captor, our host. That would leave my gladiators without a medicus. She is being trained to replace that annoying, arrogant…" She stopped his words with a kiss.

"If she is a suitable replacement then I would agree. She would make a more bearable choice to look after my needs while carrying your child." Lycithia smiled into his eyes. "Make it so, my husband and find me well pleased."

The lanista nodded, the plan forming in his mind. "The Celt will have his woman; we will have our child at last and be rid of that troublesome druid." His grin became the devious expression that sent Jovian scurrying to ease him with a soft touch or glass of wine. "This bargain grows more advantageous with every passing day. I shall let them have tonight, to remind Cassian what it is that he will be training for. Tomorrow night their world will shift again, for our benefit." He smiled at Lycithia who returned his infectious enthusiasm in her smile.

"Always for us, my love."

CHAPTER 16

The blades in his hands seemed to have a mind of their own as Cassian struck at Proximus. He had never been flooded with jealousy like this before but when Violetta had smiled at the German, he could not help the savage burn of instinct. The pair battled like Titans at the foot of Olympus, equally matched in skill despite their size difference.

"What words do you pour into my woman's ear Proximus? Do you think to earn her favor? Affections?" Cassian asked with a confident smirk. There was nothing the mountain of a man could offer her that she did not already have with him. "It will not work."

"If I wanted a woman, I would not bother to try for one that has eyes for no one but the fool I am facing." Proximus laughed and struck back. "How does young Argus fare in his training? Is he ready for the greatest arena of the age?"

"The pup is growing his teeth but there are many lessons yet to learn that I shall do my best to teach." The trading of blows grew more intense as the reigning champion circled the fallen from Rome. "Too bad that you are not capable of teaching anyone. They will not listen to a man so newly marked."

"You forget that I once stood champion of the city you aspire to grace." Proximus laughed. "I know more about those sands than any man still alive. Argus is not the only one that I could teach."

Cassian grunted in frustration when the German caught his arm at the elbow and held him tight in a position that would force him to drop one of his swords if he wanted the freedom to move.

"What do you think you could teach me? How to displease a Roman so much that I am sold?" Cassian growled as he dropped his sword to the sand to disengage the lock with his opponent. "I know the great circus arena as well as you know this ludus and the house of Claudius even better still. Trust my words when I say there is much I can teach if you but ask."

The men stared at each other for a moment before the German moved to attack and Cassian dove to retrieve the lost blade, rolling in the sand as he grabbed for it and brought it immediately up to block the falling sword of Proximus.

"Why do you think I will need such lessons? What do I care about the halls and cells of your past? I go to fight, to win and return with my woman safe at my side.

"Do you think that you will remain in the wagon while in the city? Allowed to hide away as though you are not in danger of disrupting the balance of wagers scales? You will be paraded before the elite of the city and commanded to perform spectacles. You will want to know where you are and where your friends are."

The words started to sink in, Cassian was beginning to see that the man had a point in how useful it would be to know the lay of the house and cells. It was the next words from his mouth that sealed the need to take Proximus seriously.

"What if your woman is returned to her Dominus in the city? You will wish to know her location in the chance that she needs you."

"Then we will have words, as brothers." Cassian said with a nod. The sound of Cirandon's whip cutting through the air as he called to them both. "Pair up. Cassian with Argus and Proximus with Barrius."

Cassian hid his smirk when Proximus looked at Barrius and then back at him.

"What contest does the little man with his hammer offer?"

Unable to hold back to laughter Cassian crossed the yard to join Argus.

"Do not underestimate him. He is full of surprises."

It was easy to see that Proximus did not believe him so when their match began Cassian and Argus both paused to watch as their friend took the new man to his knees within three blows.

"Did I not warm you German?"

The laughter set the mood for the rest of the training day and the bonds of brotherhood and loyalty began to include the former champion of Rome in a way that Cassian was pleased with. It was important, as slaves and especially as gladiators, that they looked out for one another. The honor that came with the life and death of each man upon the sands was shared by all and so each member of this brotherhood was as valued as a member of the families that they all missed from their previous lives.

The moment that they were released from training for the night, to eat, bathe and rest, Cassian left his weapons with Cicero and made his way directly to Violetta. Sweeping her against his body he brought his mouth down on hers in a kiss that quickly turned passionate. His hunger for her amazed him. There could never be a time when he would have enough of her. The way she smiled against his lips and clasped her fingers behind his neck let him dream of walking the fields and cart paths instead of blood, sands, and the whistles of his brothers.

"Unless you intend to eat Arturo's student for your meal, Cassian, I would suggest that you let her get something to eat before satisfying your more carnal appetite." Cirandon said with a teasing smile, putting his hand of the shoulder of each of the lovers. "There is a time and place, my friend."

"Which is now or was until you interrupted." He replied darkly, unable to stop his smile when Violetta blushed. "But I will heed words as they were well meant, despite being shit for timing."

He took Violetta's hand and led her to the head of the line for the evening meal. Ensuring that the food she was given had not been tampered with, even as a joke from the men. They often added things to the stew that was given to the younger men or new recruits, but if they were wise there would be no such thing done to his woman.

"Come, sit and tell me about your day." Cassian said to her, gently guiding her to the same table they had made love on the night of the test against Proximus. "What did you see and learn of the ways of gladiators, my love?"

"It was..." Her words were cut off by Argus clattering his bowl down on the table across from them.

"I didn't think Barrius could do it, but he took the man down. Who would have believed it?"

"You interrupt sweeter words by braying your stupidity." Cassian growled. He had spent more of the day in the company of the younger man and the last thing he wanted was to share what precious time he had with Violetta with his training partner. Who knew if Tertius might change his mind and part them because of some slight or whim?

"If you paid attention, you would have seen what I did and what Barrius did. Proximus relies on his size to intimidate, he does not see it as a weakness. He may think of himself as a mountain, but he will fall like a tree to any man would sees that he forgets to protect his legs."

Argus nodded his understanding and began to eat as Barrius, and Arturo joined them. The Celt noticed that Proximus had taken his seat with a few other Germanic men across the covered platform that served as their dining hall. Returning his attention to the woman beside him he offered a smiled as an apology for the intrusion.

"What did you think of the training you saw today? Did you learn more about how we become injured or were you overwhelmed by the violence of it all?"

She smiled at his questions, making him wonder if anyone in her life had ever asked for her opinion before? When she paused, looking at the others at the table then back to him, he nodded in encouragement.

"The violence was a little intimidating at first, I am not used to being so close to such things, but it did not take long to become fascinated by it."

"What did you find fascinating? Besides your man?" Argus asked her with a smirk, ducking a swat that Cassian aimed at his head.

"I thought that the variety of weapons was broader than I expected. In the house of…in my former house there was not much except for a whip and swords. The trident was something I would like to see closer. It reminds me of something from my father's house."

"Your father? You have never mentioned him before Violetta." Cassian said, looking at her with renewed curiosity. During all the weeks in the house of Census when they would lay in each others' arms, she had never discussed her life before living in that house. He had even wondered if she had been born under that roof until she had mentioned coming there after an auction in the city when she was thirteen years of age. With the frequency that Tertius attended such auctions it was even possible that the lanista had seen her there, though it was not a thing that he would remember now. "What country does he hail from?"

"He and my mother were from Greece. They fled here and I was born on the voyage." She said with a dismissive shrug before taking a bite of the evening bread.

"You are a child of Neptune then? With no nation that you call your own?" Arturo asked, setting his cup down with a flash of interest in his eyes that Cassian knew meant that he was either plotting something new or trying to remember something that he believed the gods had said to him in his meditative prayers.

"I know no home but Roman soil, Arturo." She said with a smile.

Her voice was full of discomfort that belied the smile and Cassian shook his head at the druid, trying to discourage him from more questions.

"I would see you to another home this night." Cassian said softly in her ear.

"Another? You whisper of dreams or escape?" She replied with the special smile that he loved.

"I speak of my arms. My home is within yours and I would give you one within mine." He stood and offered her his hand. "Let us retire to more privacy."

His arm slid across her shoulders as they walked from the dining hall but the call of Tarcarus stopped him.

"Cassian? You forget to share the entertainment. Do not hog her all night. I would have a turn."

"You would have…" His voice dropped to a growl and he turned to glare at the Thracian. "I will sever your cock if you touch her."

"You and what army?" He said, standing with a wicked grin that reminded the Celt of the same that Vitus wore.

Barrius, Argus and Proximus all rose to their feet as the gathered company quieted.

Cassian gestured for Violetta to back away down the hall.

"It seems the question has been answered for you. Now I will go and spend the night with my woman and give you no further thought."

He headed towards where Violetta was waiting for him, turning back he gave a confident smile as he took her hand.

"But if you think your words are forgotten, think again. You will find my swords against your own until all thoughts of my woman are beaten from that pig-fucking mind of yours."

Every man on the platform laughed and even Violetta joined, her head resting on his shoulder while they walked down the hall towards her isolated cell.

"He will not touch you." He assured her calmly.

"You mean while you live." She corrected, a familiar worry in her eyes.

"Not while any of the men that stood live. You are safe here Violetta. I gave you my word upon that and, though it is not as safe to believe, so did the lanista."

"Then I will have to offer prayers in hope that he keeps his word to those that I offer for your life's prolongment."

She opened the door to her cell, and he followed close behind. Cassian kept his hands on her shoulder, the tips of his fingers playing with the strings that tied her dress.

"You pray for my life? What else do you offer prayers for, my priestess?" He asked with a tender smile when she turned to face him.

"I offer many prayers, for your life above all but one thing." She replied, reaching out to place her hand above his heart.

"What is that one thing that takes stand above my life?" He asked, leaning closer to press his forehead against hers.

"For just one more chance to spend a night in your arms." She whispered to him, looking up so their eyes met in the waning light.

"Then rejoice, priestess." He kissed her softly. "For tonight those prayers are answered."

CHAPTER 17

Dawn found Cassian woken by the knock of Lucius upon the door.

"It is time to wake you two." He said, opening the door without stepping inside. "I thought I would give your woman the opportunity for the latrine and early bread."

"Trust a Roman to ruin a beautiful moment, waking at your side, with talk of latrine and bread." Cassian said, stretching with a groan before kissing his woman good morning. He was rewarded by the brightness of her smile as she opened her eyes.

"No moment with you could be ruined, even by a Roman waking us with kind thought and horrid timing."

It was with a laugh that they dressed and took advantage of the privacy of the early morning. Cassian was filled with blissful contentment that he had never considered possible. Knowing that Violetta was safe in the infirmary with Arturo, learning medicine and herbology and whatever other lessons the druid was going to teach her, he felt confident that his life was going in the direction that he needed it to, towards success.

Joining the other men on the sands he was eager to begin the training that would see the opportunity to keep his heart nearby permanently. He would tell Tertius at the next opportunity that she needed to be purchased from Census. If the man wanted the best performance from him, wanted him to keep the drive to win, then the games that put her safety in jeopardy had to stop. He would make sure that the lanista knew, without doubt, that this was what he wanted and who he wanted. Everything he had ever wanted was in his sight and he would not lose this vision again.

He and Argus stretched together before beginning the day with the basics of swordplay, the same as they did each morning, but today it felt different. Today the rudimentary practice carried a new weight. His success and that of the man beside him depended on everything going perfectly in Rome. The victories would be enough to have his desire heard by Tertius, and, bloodied by his opponent's death it would be impossible to ignore that he had earned this and earned her safety.

"Get yourself ready for the day Argus. I am going to destroy you if you do not put the best you have into this. There is no room for error, not anymore."

"What changed overnight?" Argus said, taking weapons from Cicero. "The letter Proximus gave to your woman hold some secret that inspired you?"

"The what?" Cassian turned to look at the other German as Arturo and Violetta arrived from the infirmary. "I know of no letter, but I will have answer soon enough."

"Oh fuck." Argus groaned, shaking his head as Cassian stormed towards the opposite group.

"Proximus!" Cassian bellowed from the center of the training sands. "You break words of understanding and brotherhood, yet attempt to use my woman as messenger when you have not the balls to deliver words yourself?"

The men stilled in their early positions to watch the two titans face off.

"The words of such document are not your concern. Nor are my words with Violetta as they do not concern you." Proximus scoffed at the jealousy that Cassian could not hold back, but the man armed himself all the same.

"You will not involve her in any of your schemes. That has been done enough and I will allow no one to make use of her, endanger her, for their own gains. Do you understand me?" The need to protect her blended with the other emotions flooding him and Cassian stood ready to throw weapons aside in order to demonstrate his place as her protector, from any and all that would take advantage of her kind heart, be they slave, Roman or gladiator.

"Cassian, you do not understand." Proximus slowly backed away, his eyes searching the crowd of men watching to the see who would strike first. "Violetta? Tell him this is madness." He called to her, which only sent a fresh bolt of anger through the Celt.

"Do not attempt to have her offer words in your defence. I will not allow you to use her to your advantage." He snarled, swinging one of his wooden blades towards the other man's chest.

"I seek her help to make you see reason." The German replied, blocking the blow with his own sword and gesturing for a shield to be thrown to him.

"I see no reason that you would need to hand your words to her unless it is because you seek her hand in some scheme." He brought his second blade crashing down only to find it blocked by the small training shield. "I will not have her entrapped by you. What was in the letter? Who is so important that you put another life in harms way just to get your message to them?"

"Perhaps I am not the threat you would assume." Proximus replied. "There are others here who hold no respect for the bond between you."

Cassian turned his head to look where the German pointed and saw the accursed Thracian, Tarcarus, leaning above Violetta. He did not seem to understand how her body curling away from him meant that she did not welcome his attention. Arturo was not close enough to see what was happening. Cassian had the choice of continuing the fight with Proximus or dealing with the Thracian. Indecision weighed on his shoulders for a moment, but it was lifted when Argus acted on his behalf.

Blocking a blow from Proximus he watched the younger man storm through the crowd to push himself between Tarcarus and Violetta. He could not hear the words that were being exchanged but it allowed him to continue to back Proximus back towards the far side of the yard.

"Tell me Proximus, who was the letter for and why did you give it to Violetta?" He growled. "I have fought and bled so that she was safe and you...you put her in danger by involving her in your mess."

The man had just opened his mouth to answer, Cassian hoped it was the truth or he would start to injure him instead of sparring, when the voice of their Dominus cut through the air. Every man froze at the sound.

"Cassian. Stay your hand. Argus. Release Tarcarus and attend me." The Roman leaned over the edge of the balcony. "Arturo? Bring your student as well. I would have words."

He narrowed his eyes at the Celt, sending a feeling of dread to the pit of Cassian's stomach.

"What new deviousness is this?" he said, tossing his swords to the ground. With a look at Proximus. "I will kill you if this has anything to do with that letter."

The German walked him off the sands. "The letter is to my own woman, Maya. I asked the girl to put it in the hands of the steward of the house of Titus Claudius. The words are not your business, nor is it known to the lanista or anyone else."

Cassian left the other gladiators and joined the smaller party, taking Violetta by the hand as they walked. "Are you alright? Did the Thracian upset you? Lay a hand upon you?"

She shook her head and he felt some relief before turning his head to Argus. "Gratitude, brother. For all that you did. Tarcarus needs a beating that I shall gladly deliver after this." He grumbled, holding tight to his woman as they ascended the stairs behind the druid. He would find out later why he had let the Thracian get so close without interfering, but for now they needed to be united in the presence of the Romans.

Strolling into the room, confidence like an armor that their words could not pierce Cassian noted the odd presence of Lycithia. She rarely had anything to do with gladiators, even less so in the more recent years.

"We are all here, as you commanded." Arturo said calmly, speaking for the group so that Cassian could maintain his control on his temper.

Suspicious of the look on the lanista's face and the smug smile taunting him in his wife's eyes he reached out to pull Violetta closer. He might not be able to protect her from every threat in this house, but he would do his best to establish the fact that he was not going to take attacks against her lightly. Now that they were under the roof of his own Dominus things would be different and the schemes of the Romans could target someone else.

"It has come to my attention that there have been some rumbles of displeasure about the presence of a woman in the ludus at night. Some of the men hold to a superstition that such a thing brings dreams of defeat and, with the games in Rome approaching as a great weight upon those present, that is something we can ill afford."

"They do not want me among them Dominus?" Violetta ventured to ask, drawing the attention of everyone else in the room.

Cassian did not know if the Romans were prepared for her to be bold enough to speak, but he saw Arturo hide a chuckle behind his hand and struggled to hide his own smirk. She could not have known that slaves seldom spoke to the lanista or his wife unless addressed directly and even then, they only answered the question. This was almost unheard of, but he was proud of her for voicing her question.

"What they want is not the concern Violetta." Lycithia said, gliding towards her with a predatory glare. "A woman does not belong down there, among those animals." Her lip curled as she raked her eyes over both gladiators as if they were covered in blood and stank of shit. "You should never have been placed among them at night and I will see that mistake corrected."

"No!" Cassian stepped between them, rage and insult rushing through him. He was done with the broken word of

Romans. "She stays with me. That was the promise made and it will be kept."

"Cassian." Tertius put his hand on the gladiator's shoulder and Cassian had to stop himself from shrugging the man off like an insect. "There are things I had not accounted for when I said that. Apologies but I cannot risk her safety at night when she means so much to you."

"There is no risk if I sleep at her side Dominus. I will keep her safe from any man foolish enough to make attempt upon her. There is Argus and Arturo as well. Do not do this. I need her with me as she needs me too." Cassian hated to beg any man for anything and to beg the Roman to keep his own word seemed worse somehow, but he was not lying when he said that he needed Violetta with him.

"I am not afraid Dominus. Please?" Violetta added her plea to his own but Lycithia shook her head.

"You are too young, to naïve to know that you should be fearful Violetta. There is no malice or punishment in this. It is simply for your safety and the focus of our champion and Argus who will come to Rome. There is no need to worry. You and Jovian shall share a cell here and be quite content I am certain."

That was the moment that Cassian knew that it was the woman and not the lanista who was behind this. Tertius would never put a woman with his little pet and certainly not one that the boy had shown interest in.

"You take her from my arms, claim it for her safety and then would put her in a room with the biggest whore of the house? Domina that is…"

"Silence, gladiator." Lycithia hissed. "I have given command. Push me further and I will see that her daylight hours are spent scrubbing floors in the villa instead of learning from the druid. Push against this and see how I will bring you to heel. Obey and you may yet have some moments together." She adjusted her hair and snapped her fingers to summon Jovian from the corner where he stood with a barely disguised smile.

"Jovian, show our young medicus to the room you shall both be sharing and help her bring her belongings to it before she returns to the infirmary." Tertius instructed, his annoyance at his wife showing Cassian that at least in a part of this they would be in agreement.

"Of course, Dominus. Come sister and I will show you our room." He purred, sashaying past the gladiators.

The boy barely let his arms drift against Argus' as he passed the German, but he was wise enough to not touch Cassian for he would not have held back making his displeasure known in a painful way.

Violetta's touch against his hand drew his eyes down to hers and he was grateful that she was not afraid, at least not yet. Who knew what the nights in the villa would bring? Between Jovian and the other Syrian snake who slithered the halls this could turn into a nightmare that would last until they left for the capital.

"You are dismissed, with the warning that you are to focus on training and not on playing guardsman to the woman. I would not have either of you distracted from your purpose." Tertius said with that wave of his hand.

Cassian did not stop or linger for the others to catch up with him, stomping down the stairs he looked Lucius in the eyes and growled "Get me wine, plenty of it, and put it in my cell. The damned Roman has gone back on his word and now my woman is to share the room of that little shit, Jovian."

"Cassian, you should not…"

"I will not debate it. If I am going to get through the days knowing that she is there and not with me where she should be then I am going to need wine, and lots of it." He snapped then headed to the sands, not caring who he faced in training because for him they all had the face of the lanista and his pet.

"If they want to see the power of my concentration and control then I will pass their test and rise victorious here and in Rome."

CHAPTER 18

Jovian led Violetta down the hall towards the room he called his own. He refused to call it a cell as the other slaves did. He was not like them, he had the love of their Dominus, why should he act like them.

"You must not worry about being in this room with me. We shall be as brother and sister." He grinned. "Or sister and sister if the mood strikes me to play such games."

She was not returning his smile, in fact, it seemed as though she was displeased at being brought into the villa from the ludus.

"Come, Violetta, be of better cheer. You cannot tell me that you prefer to be down among all that sweat and stench. The villa is beautiful and cool in the heat. There is even a pool, in the hall, where we might cool ourselves at night."

Her eyes were wet and shining. He was beginning to think that she might weep, and it made no sense to him.

"If you are unused to sleeping alone you may always rest with me. There are many nights Dominus summons me to attend to his needs, but I always return to the room."

He put his hand on her shoulder, trying to find a way to comfort her, when she surprised him by turning and wrapping her arms around him.

"Jovian, I do not know what to do. I want to be where he is, where I feel safe. That is what the lanista promised us. I know it must seem awful and dirty to you, but to me, compared to the life in the house if Census it was a new level of freedom."

"You trusted the lanista to keep the promise the same way you thought he meant?" Jovian shook his head. "You're a dreamer Violetta. It is sweet, but naïve. He will always twist his words to his own benefit. You must never trust him completely." He said, trying to be kind as he stepped out of her embrace. He was not comfortable with such displays of emotion and did not know what to do with her.

"I trusted his word only because Cassian seemed pleased with the promise." She sighed, forcing a smile that might fool the Romans but not him, he was too accustomed to the lie on his own face.

"Then let me be the one to tell you that you should not trust anyone inside this villa but myself. In the ludus, I have little experience, but if they have not given you a reason that you should trust them then I would not. Most are savage beasts, your man included." He said with a teasing smile.

She smiled back, a little more genuine than before.

"I will do my best to remember your words. What are we to do now? I should return to Arturo and my training, should I not?" She asked.

There was uncertainty still in her voice while she paced the room and touched the small unused bed that he usually filled with the clothes he was considering wearing for Dominus. Now it would be hers. He wondered if she would become jealous of his things and try to take them? Or would she try to court the favor of Domina to get such lovely gifts for herself?

"I suppose that you should, after we retrieve your things from the cell and bring them here. Cassian will not be in a pleasant mood. You may wish to avoid him for the rest of the day."

"I understand his mood entirely, I share it. That is no reason to avoid his company. I would consider it a reason to seek him and attempt to ease both our hearts in this regard."

She would willingly seek the company of the enraged champion? The woman must indeed be blindly in love to take such a risk. Cassian was surly and difficult at the best of times. Today he would be a barbaric animal of rage, deadly and dangerous. Doctore would not likely allow the newer men to train with him in such a mood, lest his temper cost them their very lives.

"You are braver than I if you would risk his temper." Jovian said, leading her back towards the stairs that would take them to the ludus.

"There is not need to rush the gathering of your things, though. I would tarry and watch the gladiators." He smiled at the thought of Argus, sweating from exertion, and glistening in the sunlight.

"Any gladiator in particular?" Violetta asked as they walked down the stone stairs. "Do you have a favored fighter, besides Cassian?"

"There might be one that has caught my attention, but we shall not speak of him now." Jovian said, helping her down the last of the rough steps.

"I shall wait for you by the door so that you can collect your things in privacy. I will help you take them back upstairs before you resume your training in this place." He wrinkled his nose at the smell that was noticeable from the cells. "I will also return at night to fetch you."

"I will have almost no time alone with Cassian?" She asked, casting a look through the doorway to the sands.

Jovian could hear the pain in her voice, but he had no words of comfort that he could offer her.

"I am sorry, dear sister. I do not know Dominus' mind in this or why they would separate you this way. Perhaps it is that Lycithia, our Domina, is jealous of you?"

"I cannot see what could make her jealous. Unless she wants Cassian?" She shook her head. "That could not be, he would have told me."

"Indeed, he would have and there would never have been the chance for the two of you to be together if Domina desired him." Jovian said with a soft laugh.

They had come to the doorway to the sands and the hallway to the infirmary and her cell.

"Go and gather what you will. I will remain here, as I said."

She nodded and left him to watch the men at their training.

He stood in the doorway, face hidden by the shadows and watched while Argus trained against the giant from Rome. Proximus was daunting, deadly, and completely focused. Even though they were only using wooden swords Jovian was worried that Argus would be injured by the force of the other man's blow.

"I would piss in your bed for that blow." He hissed under his breath, flinching as the German took a blow from the bigger man.

"I do not think that would be advised, my young friend." Arturo said, coming from the infirmary to stand beside him. "Proximus is not the monster that so many would paint him.

He is a good man though his heart is shattered within his chest without the one that he loves at his side."

"He has a lover? Who could love a man of that size?" Jovian scoffed and flicked his hair over his shoulder.

"Every soul has the need and the right to be loved, Jovian." The druid said, shaking his head at him. "One day you might understand that better, though I hope that you do not have to go through the pain that others around you have."

"Arturo, I have the love that I need and more." Jovian smiled. "Perhaps you should find yourself a lover, if it is so troubling to your mind?"

"My mind is not the one that is troubled." Arturo replied

He thought he heard the druid chuckle as he walked away, heading to the sands, but Violetta appeared at his side before he could work up the nerve to chase him down. A quick turn of his head told him that the girl had shed tears that were only barely under control now.

"What happened? What brings tears to your eyes?" He asked, taking her hand.

"On my bed, the one that I shared with Cassian last night, he left these flowers upon it and a small note that I cannot read. I have not the skill. I was never taught." She said, showing him the folded paper and the small cluster of vibrant purple flowers.

Jovian was confused. Violetta was acting as though he had left her silks and gems instead of a scarp of paper and a few common blossoms. It made no sense.

"Do you know how to read Jovian?" She asked, her eyes on her lover swinging his swords on the sands.

"No. Although there are many things that Dominus saw me instructed in that are not the usual things for a body slave to learn that was not one of them. Astrix knows but I would not wish to introduce you to him if it is not needed."

"I will ask Arturo, perhaps he might tell me what it says?" She said, wiping the last trace of the tears from her eyes. "We should go and see these things put away so that I can spend the rest of the day as close to my heart as this work will let me."

Jovian put his hand on her back to guide her down the hall. When he saw the champion pause his practice to watch them, he winked at the Celt before guiding his woman into the darkness of the ludus halls. He knew that the man would be beside himself with rage, not only from the command of the Romans but the fact that the girl was now sharing a bedroom with the only other man in all the villa that might spend the time and energy to seduce his precious woman.

"Hurry now Violetta. You must not be late for the rest of your lessons. Now that you are to stay within the villa itself you may have to answer for all that you do and learn in the day. Trust me when I tell you that it would not be wise to disappoint Dominus. He expects much from you."

He thought the words would be encouraging but, as they entered the confines of his room that they would now share, she shook her head.

"Everyone seems to have an expectation or request of me here, so soon after my arrival. Even Cassian wants to pretend as though the weeks in the villa, or at least the last day that we were there, did not occur. It is much to ask of one that they do not know. Some are putting great amounts of trust into someone they do not know.”

“Who is putting trust in you that should not? Are there secrets in the ludus that you can tell me about?” He asked eagerly. Sitting on his bed while she put away the few things that she had brought Jovian watched her, desperate for the gossip and hoping that it contained some news of Argus that he could treasure.

“I did not say that they should not.” Violetta said calmly, putting away the last few items, small idols for prayer, on the windowsill in the bright light of the sun. “Just that it is strange that a gladiator would. Proximus entreated me for a favor, to take a letter to Rome. He wants for me to try and get a parchment into the hands of his lover, if she still lives.”

“He has a lover in Rome? Who? Why would he think that you might be able to take such a missive to her?” Jovian asked with a delighted smile.

“He has not told me who it is yet but assures me that I should meet her and that it should be easy to get his messages to her. If not then I am to give it to a man he calls his friend.”

“Are you going to do it? Take messages from the former champion of Rome to his lover?” He got to his feet and paced the room. “That would be a huge risk and I am not sure that you are ready for such things. I should be there with you, to help you find her and to see what happens when she gets the letter from a lover she likely thought had forgotten her. It is all so tragic. and you get be there for all of it.”

He sat back down on his bed with a dramatic sigh. “You should help me go to Rome Violetta. You will not be able to do this without me.”

"Well of course I can do it without you Jovian. I have accomplished things of greater complexity without help." She snapped back at him, reminding Jovian that she had not won the heart of Cassian by simply being lovely to look upon. "I would like your company though, upon the road."

"Does that mean you will help me to join the journey?" He asked, hardly daring to hope that she meant it.

"It means that I will do what I can to make it so. You must be as a brother to me until then though, help me in the villa, please?"

"Of course, sister." He said, standing and taking her face in his hands. "We will be a wonderful team, together."

He kissed her cheeks, the headed out the door.

"Come. We must return you to your lessons until nightfall."

CHAPTER 19

Argus had been turning to follow Cassian and Arturo back to the ludus, unsure as to why he had been summoned other than to confirm that he was to go to Rome with the others, when the voice of Lycithia stopped him.

"Argus. A word before you return to your training."

He froze. She had never spoken to him directly in all his years under her husband's roof. He had not even been aware that she knew his name. Shaking himself from his shocked stupor he turned to face her and bowed his head in the expected position.

"Domina."

The word felt foreign, though not as strange as the way she was looking at him. He was not considered to be handsome in the same manner as Cassian, Tarcarus or even Proximus. Some women, in the past, had found his smile to be charming and his green eyes appealing enough that he had been commanded to bed them. He had hated every moment of it, which, unfortunately had seemed to delight them. That had been more than two years ago, but all came flooding back when she put her hand on his arm.

"You are rising quickly within the ranks and now my husband thinks you worthy of the games in Rome. Does that please you?"

"It does, Domina." He replied, trying to keep his voice calm and soft enough that there could be no mistaking his obedience and discomfort. "I am eager to do my part to elevate the house of Tertius."

"I am sure that you will. How far are you willing to go, to sacrifice, to elevate the house of your Dominus?" Lycithia asked, taking his chin in her hand, and forcing him to meet her gaze.

"I do as commanded, Domina." He said, fighting the instinct that told him that he was in more danger than he knew.

"Good. That is what I wanted to hear. You will be called upon to do more than most, more than any other, to elevate this house and you will do so with the same strength and dedication that you bring to the arena."

"Yes Domina. Of course. What is it that Dominus calls upon me to do?" He asked, wishing that it were he that was delivering this speech.

"Dominus will not know about this or this meeting. The task that I require you to perform does not include him having knowledge of these commands."

A feeling of dread sank over him like a net that would drag him to the depths of Hades.

"What do you command, Domina?" Argus asked, squaring his shoulders, and setting his jaw with resignation.

"When the opportunity presents itself, I will summon you." She said with a devious smile. "You will come to me and you will fill me with your seed until it takes hold in my womb. I will have a child in my belly within the year and you will put it there or face the fullness of my anger. I promise you, that is worse than that of my husband. You will speak to no one of this or I will cut off both cock and tongue."

"Domina. I…you must know…I have no taste for women. My affections are towards men and there is one that I hold in special favor. I beg you to choose another for your request." His stomach lurched at the thought of any part of this, especially the worry that Jovian could discover the act, and everything would change between them.

"Then it is good that I do not wish for your affections or devotion. I want your cock and your seed. Nothing more and nothing less. There is no debate, and this is not a request. You will obey me in this and say nothing of it, to anyone." She hissed. The anger at his rejection flashing in her eyes at him. "Now go. Return to the ludus and prepare yourself, for Rome and for the fulfillment of my command. The sooner your seed takes hold the sooner you will no longer be required in my bed."

"You cannot be serious." Argus cried, panic and disgust in his voice.

"You forget yourself, slave." Lycithia snapped.

Her palm struck his cheek in a slap that must have set her hand ringing, but Argus barely felt it. The entire world seemed to spin out of control at the thought of obeying this hideous command.

"You will obey and put a child in my womb, or I shall tell my husband that you once again wish for your cock to service the women of Velletri."

He stared at her with hatred burning through every fiber of his being. His body tense and shaking with the desire to strike down the vicious bitch in front of him.

"As you command, Domina." He said with the slightest bow of his head.

It was useless to fight her will and Argus knew that she would do everything she said and more if he tried to refuse her. As much as the thought of bedding her turned his stomach it could not compare to being offered to any woman with coin once again.

"Much better, my beast." She stroked a hand down his arm. "You will be elevated within the ranks for your efforts. I shall see to it."

She leaned closer, smelling of roses and cloves, and purred in his ear. "It is possible that you might grow to enjoy our times together."

"May I return to training, Domina?" He asked, barely able to hold back to bile rising in his throat at her touch.

"Yes. Go so that no one suspects that I have any special interest in a…beast like you. I will have you in a day or two, when Tiberius goes into the city with those sniveling Syrians and the Druid. You will be ready to fill me with your seed and not disappoint. Understood?" Her voice was hard once more, and he gave only the slightest nod before rushing from the room to try and get away from her touch.

The guards shadowed him to the stairway to the ludus, they were wise enough to not lay a hand upon him. He did not think that he could handle the touch of anyone, even Jovian, after such a meeting.

Argus stumbled down the stairs, his shoulder crashing into the bars before the gate was opened. He could not find the balance to stand upright. The world spun and lurched, hurling him against walls and bars as he ran from the revulsion that was his new reality. His hands reached out to touch the sides of the doorway to the sands, trying to ground himself with the texture of the solid stone.

"Argus? What is it? You look ill." Arturo said to him, turning from the edge of the sands. "Violetta take him to the infirmary. I will join you presently. Get him water and sit him down."

"I will do my best. I think it would be wise if you hurried though."

Argus heard the soft voice and felt the small hands take hold of his arm and guide him away from the sands. She was sweet, gentle, and kind. Why had he been so cruel to her before? She was a harmless little thing and reminded him of someone, who was it? He was lost in his own head. The odious command of Lycithia sending him on a sickening journey through the banks of his memories to try and find some memory of a woman's touch that did not repulse him.

"Come Argus. Sit down and take a drink of water."

He blinked and looked down at the pale face.

"Water is not what I want Violetta. It is not what I need." He started to scan the room, looking for the clay vials that the druid kept his drugs in.

"You can get me something though. Mandrake? Milk of Poppy? What about Henbane? I have heard these names before. What do they do? Can they send a man to a stupor or bring memories back from the dark?"

He got up and started to search the tabletops and pull at drawers and cabinets.

"I know Arturo has many such drugs and I need them, something, anything that can wipe this day and those to come from my mind. I cannot do it. I do not want to, but she will make me."

"Argus you must stop." The girl cried, grabbing at his arm to try and stop his search.

"No! I have to find something to make this sickness stop." He shoved her aside, frantic in his need to find something to cloud his mind enough to deal with what was coming.

He paused only a moment when she cried out, his push having sent her to the ground floor, then ripped open the doors to the last cabinet on the wall before him.

"Thank Jupiter. At last." He grabbed a handful of the small bottles and started to pull the cork tops out of them.

"Argus you must not do this." Violetta cried, climbing to her feet with a horrified look on her face.

"That is where you are wrong, girl. This is exactly what I must do. You could not understand, no one will." He took a handful of the vials and drank the contents. "No one will understand, and no one will know. The agony of the command is not enough but the secret, the secret is what makes it impossible."

"Argus?" Her voice seemed small and far away as the colours started to swirl around. "What command? What secret? I do not understand. You need to sit and drink some water. Arturo will be able to help you."

He let her guide him back to the tabletop and sat on the hard surface, watching her attempt to tidy what he had done to the tools and other clutter.

"You are good to help him, to help me. Kind, you are truly kind." He said, reaching a shaky hand to touch her hair. "You remind me of someone, a long time ago. I cared about her."

"I would help you more. Let me tend your wounds? Your knuckles bleed as does your shoulder. Do you remember how that happened?" Her little voice asked.

"I remember Ilsa, she was kind too. She used to help me when I fell as a boy." He said, smiling at the memory.

"Is that what happened? You fell?" She asked in that voice that sound more like his childhood friend with every word.

"I fell in love with you, Ilsa. When we were children. Did you forget?" He asked, taking her hand in his as a warmth flooded his senses and the light in the room brightened so much that he had to squint.

"I am not Ilsa." She said, turning to look at him.

Her blue eyes turned brown and then back to blue as he blinked. She was Ilsa, or was it something else? He could not remember clearly but he felt comfortable with her, just as when they were children together.

"Of course, little mouse, the Romans gave you one of their names." He slurred, tugging her closer. "When it is you and I though, you do not need to pretend."

The drugs coursing through his blood wiped away every thought but the joy of the reunion with the one woman he had ever cared for, even if she denied being who he knew she had to be.

"Pretend at what?" A harsh voice called from the doorway.

Argus turned to see a pair of men in the doorway. He had to stop running his finger down Ilsa's arm to think of who they were.

"Cassian? Arturo? Come and meet my little mouse, Ilsa. We were children together East of the Rhine and now I find her here, in your infirmary Arturo. Is that not a blessing from the gods themselves?" He was happy, even though Ilsa was trying to pull away from him. She was shy around the other men. How could he have forgotten that.

"Do not worry little mouse. These are friends. Cassian is a gladiator and Arturo is a druid. He will tend any injuries then we can go and talk together."

"You are not taking her anywhere, Argus." Cassian growled at him angrily.

CHAPTER 20

"Argus. I am not who you think I am." Violetta said, struggling in his hold.

He did not look like he was going to hurt her, but that did not help her to feel better about how tight he held her, or how in his state he did not seem to know what was going on. Did he even know that he was a gladiator now? The way he spoke, the name 'Mouse' and the way he smiled, it made her think that the drugs he drank had taken him back to the land of his childhood.

"Hush, Ilsa. They will think you rude." Argus said with an unnatural sounding laugh.

Violetta looked at her lover and her instructor, both standing in the doorway of the infirmary staring in confusion at the scene playing out before them.

"He was crazed. Searching for drugs." She said, gesturing to the table.

"Did he take anything?" Arturo asked, stepping past Cassian and into the room. "Anything at all Violetta?"

"Forget the damned drugs, this is why you should not play with them." Cassia growled.

Violetta looked up to meet his eyes, trying to fight the instinctual panic that was building in the arms of the man that had so recently threatened her with harm who now treated her like a long lost loved one.

"He took a handful. I did try to stop him, but he was fast and determined." She looked at the table and the floor, pointing at the trio of tiny vials laying opened and empty.

"There. I do not think they are broken. What did he take and why is he acting like this?"

"Violetta, come here and let the druid deal with this fool. Since they both seem to enjoy the stupor of his potions." Cassian beckoned her while Arturo crouched to retrieve the vials.

"Fuck yourself, Cassian." Argus growled, suddenly clutching Violetta against his chest. "You cannot have her. Just because you stand champion does not mean that every woman belongs to you. She is mine."

"I belong to no one." She protested, struggling against the firm grip. "Argus let me go."

"It is alright Ilsa. I will keep you safe from him. Arturo, I need to go now. Tell him to get out of my way."

"You all need to calm down." Arturo said, standing with the vials in his hand. "No one needs to get hurt here. Cassian keep that temper calm. No one is going to hurt Violetta. Everyone here is actually trying to keep her safe. Argus, you are not yourself. That is not Ilsa in your arms but Violetta. My student and the lover of your mentor, the man you train with so that you do not die on the sands of Rome like boy fresh from the boats."

Violetta watched the words of her teacher sink into Argus' mind, slowly, but the realization was coming.

"Do you remember the boats? The one that brough you from Germania? Remember that and remember where you are now. Those lives are worlds apart. You cannot go back, even though you want to. Let the girl go, let the past go."

Violetta kept her eyes locked on Cassian's while Argus wrapped his arms around her, hugging her close instead of holding her captive.

"Shh, Argus. It is alright. You can let go now." She said softly. "Just let go."

"No. I cannot let go again. The last time, on the ships, when I let go. They took you away." He said, his voice catching as tears sprung to his eyes. "I still hear your screams. I know what happened, what the Roman bastards did to you. I never saw you again."

Violetta flinched and looked from Cassian to Arturo, the back to the saddened man holding her. Her heart broke for him, for what he had lost.

"Argus, I am not that girl. I am not Ilsa. I cannot be what she was to you. That is impossible, but I can be a friend. You and I, we can be friends."

"We have always been more than friends, Isla. I love you, or I did then, before. Perhaps a part of me loves you still." He stroked her cheek and Violetta looked over towards Cassian.

Arturo was holding him back, her lover's eyes blazed with a rage Violetta had never seen before. He was pulling hard against the druid's grip, which was surprisingly tight. She had not considered that the gentle dark-haired man was strong enough to hold back an angry gladiator like Cassian, but he seemed to be barely straining. If Arturo let go Violetta did not doubt that Cassian would have attacked his friend for daring the intimate contact.

She wanted to bring peace to the German, but how could she without encouraging his illusion and without allowing him to play out more of his memories?

"You love someone else now Argus. Think about who that is, focus on that and come back to the present."

"Be careful, Violetta." Cassian called from where Arturo held him. "He is out of his mind. I swear to Hades if he hurts you, I will bash his brains upon the sands."

"Do not scare the girl, Cassian. You will do nothing to the man. He is not a threat to her."

Violetta struggled to turn her head and look at her instructor. "Arturo? What can I…" She did not get to finish her question. Argus gripped her face in his strong hands and lowered his mouth to hers.

"Hush Ilsa. You are mine again. I will keep you safe." He said before kissing her with a groan.

It was clumsy, awkward and she immediately fought against him.

"No. Stop. Argus I am not Ilsa. I am not the one that you love." She tugged one hand free from his grip and slapped him, hard, across the face. The impact seemed to snap him out of his daze enough that his instincts kicked in. Suddenly Violetta found herself shoved into the table. The impact knocked the breath out of her, and as she fell to the floor something rushed past her.

"Touch her like that again and I will kill you outright." Cassian roared, driving his fist into Argus' face.

Violetta screamed in shock and Arturo reached out a hand to her, pulling her away from the fight.

"Is he going to kill him? I thought that they were friends, training together for the games in Rome." Violetta asked her instructor once they were clear of the skirmish.

"Yes. They admire and respect each other, but how anyone could expect him to hold back after all that the pair of you have been put through at the hands of the men of Census? It is a miracle of the gods that he has not snapped before this."

"We cannot let Argus be killed. It is not his fault, not really." Violetta pleaded, cringing when she turned to see her lover pummel the man who was barely coherent enough to raise his arms to block his face.

"Do not worry yourself Violetta." Arturo said, setting her aside and stepping towards the gladiators. "I will not have a death in my infirmary if I can stop it."

She watched him put a hand to a shoulder of each man and speak with a calm voice filled with unmistakable power.

"You will stop now, Cassian. A chieftain cannot lose control and he cannot beat his own man to death." Arturo said, easing his body between Cassian and the bruised German.

"I am NOT a chieftain Arturo. I am not and never will be in this life. You must stop acting as though I will one day take my father's place. That life, and that boy, are both as dead as the next man that touches her against her will shall be."

"Argus did not hurt her and meant no harm to your woman. He does not see her as yours, not in this state."

"I am not injured, Cassian." Violetta added. Though she was nervous, maybe even afraid, of the big German in this state or sober, when he disliked her, she did not want the man to die for so sad a memory. "Please, let him be. There are greater pains to be born this day than this innocent sadness."

"As you wish then." Cassian said, the anger still burning in his eyes. "I do this for you, not him. If the man lays hand upon you again or speaks words that should be from my lips alone then I shall see if there are brains inside that thick skull of his. Pleading words from friend or lover will not stop me again."

"Cassian…I…" Violetta started to speak but when he stood before her, looking down with those beautiful amber eyes, she could not find words to speak that would calm him and so she simply whispered. "Gratitude."

For a moment she thought he was angry at her, his silence filling the room with his palpable displeasure.

"For punishing him or for stopping?" He asked, taking her chin in his hand, stroking her cheek with a single fingertip.

"For both. I want no one to be hurt on my account." She said, leaning into his touch. "His pain touches my heart, but I am not the one that can mend that hurt."

The Centurion guard, Julius Lucius, appeared at the door. "Cassian, you are commanded back to the sands. You do not want to anger the lanista further today. He leaves for the market. Arturo is to join him. Say your farewells to the woman, you have work to do."

Violetta slid her arms around his waist. The firmness of his muscles, still tense from the conflict with Argus, offered a sweeter comfort that she needed. The scent of him, leather, and sandalwood, calming her nerves and steadying her resolve.

"I will be alright now. Do not vex Dominus further. Though I wish that you could stay we both must do as commanded or see ourselves parted more than we already face."

Arturo was already at the door and Argus was rubbing his face, wincing at the bruises that were already starting to show.

"I will do my best to break words again before you are taken upstairs again." Cassian said, softly, in her ear, as he wrapped his arms around her. "If Jovian makes foolish attempts upon you again I would hear of it. It may convince Dominus to return you to your cell and my arms."

She nodded and rose on the balls of her feet to press a kiss to his lips before he followed his guard back to the sands to train and she was left alone again with Argus. His arms tightened around her shoulders, crushing her chest against his so tightly she could feel the beating of his heart against her skin. Her tongue slid past his lips and caressed his in a subtle invitation that her lover accepted eagerly.

A hand slid up her neck to hold the back of her head, cradling her gently so that he could take a passionate possession of her mouth. Her knees weakened when his tongue swept against hers, and she wanted to hold on to him forever."

"Come, Cupid, before your guardsman must return for you. Lucius hates to repeat himself." Arturo said with a teasing smile, pulling Cassian from Violetta's arms. "She has work to do with sobering Argus and I must attend Tertius and procure herbs much needed if you are to give in to fits of temper such as this."

She smiled when Cassian chuckled, backing away with the pull of the druid's hand, unwilling to break eye contact with her.

"I indeed stand struck by the god's arrow when I am in the presence of my priestess. Will you not let me worship a little longer? I am remiss in my prayers of devotion, old friend."

"Do not linger but hold me in your thoughts as I shall hold you in my heart until I am in your arms again." Violetta called to him as the door swung closed behind their departure.

"Treasure that. The affection between you." Argus said from the table where he sat, holding a cloth to the bleeding nose that Cassian had given him. "Not all of us are so lucky as to be able to display it as openly as you."

She could hear the bitterness in his voice, but the joy in her heart was too pure to hide.

"Someday perhaps you will have it too, Argus. You should not give up hope." Violetta said, offering him some water. "Who is it that you love that you cannot declare your affections for? Does she not feel the same for you?"

"She?" He scoffed in reply. "Though my little Syrian may, at time, dress the part of a girl, he is a man beneath the paint and silk. Though it may be a wish for death to utter the words, he is the one that holds my heart and no other."

"Little Syrian?" Violetta stared at him in shock. He could not possibly mean who she thought he meant. It would be suicide even if it were possible. He could not be so foolish, they would both be put to the cross if either of the Romans made the discovery. "You cannot mean Jovian, can you? Argus? Are you mad?"

"I fear I must be." He hung his head, sadness in his eyes. "Violetta, you can tell no one, even Cassian. I beg you."

"Of course not." She assured him, wondering if he knew the depth of risk he was taking. "I will help you keep this secret, no matter the cost."

Pg 156

CHAPTER 21

Cassian could not help the storm of emotions flowing through his blood. Annoyance at the interruption, along with anger coupled with compassion for Argus. He could not imagine enduring that kind of trauma at such a young age. To survive the works of Census and his spawn as a hardened gladiator was hard enough, but to endure it as a boy, to not ever know what happened to the girl he had loved, was a painful burden that no one should ever have to bear.

"What causes delay Cassian?" Proximus called, tossing a training weapon to each of his hands. "More sweet kisses from the medicus?"

Slapping the flat of a wooden blade to the German's shoulder Cassian grunted. Most days that jest would have brought a smirk if not a laugh and friendly retort, but not today. With the Roman breaking his word by putting Violetta in the same room as the boy who fucked anyone that he could convince to allow it, and Argus kissing her while under the influence of drugs he did not think anything would help his mood outside the realms of sex and violence.

"I offered prayers for your survival to a divine priestess." He growled back.

He was about to square off against the man when he saw Arturo emerge from the cells with his cloak. He had almost forgotten that the druid was to go with Tertius to the city market.

"Hold that blow a moment longer." He said to his opponent before running to his friend.

"I would beg favor of you while you are within the city." He said in a quiet voice.

"You mean besides forgetting to tell the lanista that you lost your temper and took your fists to Argus, who is supposed to be learning from you? What other favor would you ask of me?" Arturo replied with a dry tone.

Cassian knew he was more annoyed than he had hoped, but this was important.

"I will make it up to him." He said in a rushed tone. Tertius was talking to the guards so he did not have much time. "I need things to write to Violetta. If we are to be parted like this, then I will write to her so that she can know my heart."

"That is simple enough. I can and will do that for you, my friend." Arturo replied, his expression softening. "Is there anything else that would help you to stay focused, sane, during this time?"

"I have some coins in my cell to repay this, but there is one other thing that I would ask of you." He whispered.

"Then you should ask it before I go." He said, stepping towards the gate where the escorting guards were gathered and waiting.

"A ring." Cassian hissed quickly. "Something simple, for Violetta to wear. There is no chance of me being able to get one myself. Please?"

"Arturo. What delays you?" Tertius called from the gate. "I would have this accomplished before sunset."

"I make no promise on the ring, but I will do what I can for you. Focus your mind back where it belongs and trust in me as you always can." Arturo said with a brief nod then stepped quickly to join the departing company.

"You have my gratitude Arturo. If they are going to keep us apart then I would do anything that I can to make sure that she knows she is not forgotten. This is not what I promised her."

"The girl is not a simpleton, Cassian." The druid said, putting his hand to the Celt's shoulder. "Have a little faith in her understanding and her fidelity. If you can do that then we shall all sleep a little better in the coming weeks."

"I have zero intention of sleeping or resting at all until I have her back where she belongs." He grumbled, looking back towards the sands. "I do not break promises and I told her, swore, that I would keep her safe."

"Jovian is not going to hurt her, Cassian. The boy is not so Roman as that, not yet anyway." Arturo said with a chuckle. "Go train, I will see what I can procure for your woman. Cassian, you will rest if I must drug you to make sure of it. You are no good to anyone if you are dead on your feet or dead on the sands."

"Get your ass out of here. Unless you are going to join me in schooling these fools. Do what you need to do, old friend." Cassian said with a broad grin.

Knowing that the druid was on his side as well as looking after Violetta's education settled some of his anxiety. She would be safe enough during the hours of the day at least. It was the time that she would spend, at night, in an enclosed space with that two-faced little brat, that worried Cassian. The fidelity of his woman, how she felt about him, was not his concern. He could not stop thinking about how Jovian liked to play his games of intimacy.

The boy had no sense of decency, it was never taught to him. He simply flirted until he got what he wanted. If he wanted to seduce Violetta for his own amusement one night, she would not understand what he was doing until it was too late. The boy would not stop even if she protested and Cassian telling him not to or warning Violetta about his actions would only be a challenge to the boy. His hands were tied just as tightly now as they had been when she was in the house of Census.

Or were they?

What if Argus asked Jovian not to play with Violetta like he did with so many others? The boy seemed to have a developing affection for the German. It might work. It was worth the chance to ask. If that did not work then he would keep such a steady supply of injured men to the infirmary that she would need to be there at all hours taking care of them and Jovian would have no chance to interfere because they would only be in the room together when they were both asleep, if at all.

He was determined to find a way to stop this. Somehow, he would see her safe, back where she belonged, in his arms until it was the gods that parted them and not the will of the Romans.

Arturo followed behind Tertius, playing the part of the obedient slave as was expected but his heart was anything but calm and his will rebelled at every step. He knew that, if he was as wild as his charge, as free with his passionate hatred of these Romans that commanded them, he could have put a swift end to not only the lanista but the centurions and that simpering snake, Astrix. The other man, he refused to think of them as 'fellow slaves', was as spiteful as he was duplicitous which made him even more dangerous that the Romans.

Walking with a forced ease to his step Arturo kept his eyes on the Syrian who was trying to hide his discomfort in his presence. Some of the Romans joined Astrix in their dislike of Arturo's company. Whether it was because he never deferred to what they assumed to be their superiority or because they thought that he was a magical heathen that might use their hair or blood for some spell or offering to his gods. It always made him want to laugh but today it might not be his best plan if he wanted to achieve the requests that Cassian had made of him, as well as accomplish his own tasks within the city. There was no need, today at least, to draw any extra attention to anything he did.

"The herbalist should be my first stop. There are some seeds requested by my new student that she thinks might expand and improve the quality of the care that we give to the gladiators." Arturo said to the lanista.

He hoped that Astrix would avail himself to Tertius' side instead of joining him in the tedious task of selecting sprigs of herbs and inspecting seedling plants. It would make acquiring the writing tools and jewelry much easier if he were alone.

"I can accompany him to ensure that no time is wasted." One of the guards said in a tone that distracted from the eagerness in his eyes.

Arturo was not familiar with this particular man, though that was not hard to accomplish as he avoided all of them as much as he could. He had to wonder why a new guard would be eager to join him on such a tedious task?

"Anything to keep our medicus focused on the task in a timely fashion." Scoffed the lanista. "He is prone to lingering and talking more than he should. If you can keep him on task and be back here before I arrive, I would see you rewarded for achieving what no man in my employ has yet managed."

"Yes, Dominus." He said with a sharp nod and nodded his head towards the alley. "Lead the way medicus."

Acutely aware on the soldier's eyes on him Arturo led the way towards his regular herbalist. The man was consistent in his supply and was also Greek instead of Roman so the pair of them would usually enjoy a few laughs at the expense of those who considered themselves to be the superior nation.

"You are new to the house of Tertius if you think that any reward the lanista will have for you is worth the tediousness of waiting while I select herbs and the few other things that I need." He said, attempting to broach a conversation.

"I did not volunteer for this task because of anything I would get from the lanista." He said as they stepped into the shop. "I was sent from Rome to observe you."

"Observe me?" Arturo took a deep breath, trying to remain calm while he wondered who in Rome would have sent someone to report on him. He had no enemies in this country, not that he was aware of. Though he might have some notoriety in Velletri it was surprising that someone in the capital would be so interested in a druid medicus. "Who would be so interested in my doings? I am nothing but a medic to gladiators."

"You are medic to the Celt Cassian? A friend as well?" The guard said, leaning back against the wall. "My employer has a vested interest in his health and well-being leading up to the match in Rome."

"So why not watch the man himself?" Arturo said, gathering the plants and parchment wrapped seeds that he had selected. "Would that not be a better use of your time?"

"He has Julius Lucius as a personal guard so getting close to him is not required. The girl may become a target as well, but currently you are the one I have been instructed to observe."

They stepped clear of the shop and back into the damp shadows of the alley. Arturo turned to the younger man and met the bright blue eyes with a dark glower. This would be stopped now.

"You may observe me all you like. It will get you nothing as far as secrets or tactics to use against Cassian. Watch him too and Argus, Proximus and the other gladiators at the ludus, but leave the girl alone. She has been through enough at the rough hands of Roman masters. She deserves what peace and joy she can find in this place. The gods know what may happen in Rome. Cassian could fall, though I doubt it. Census could take her back or sell her. There is no way of knowing. I will not, as her teacher and as a decent man, let another force those two any further apart than has been done."

The man blinked in surprise the nodded slowly, understanding that there was more to the quiet slave than he had assumed.

"She is not my charge and I will make note that she is not going to be useful to our purpose."

"Good. Now, there are other things that I require. You may join me or go wait for the lanista, either way, I will be there on time as an act of good faith between us."

"Lead the way. I am not going to interfere with your actions, I shall merely make note of what may be of interest to my employer."

Turning towards the greater area of the marketplace Arturo accepted his shadow, for now.

There were several stalls that sold jewelry, most were elaborate pieces that were meant for the wives of the elite Roman upper class. Though there was no doubt that Cassian could afford them, the man had not spent a coin since the night he met Violetta, but there were few items that the girl could wear without arousing the jealousy of Lycithia or, even worse, Jovian. It needed to be something simple as well as delicate or it would be too noticeable.

The man had asked for a ring, he meant it as a gift of engagement, promise, but that was impossible for a medicus to wear without the risk of the piece being lost. It would have to be a pendant. If he could find something simple enough to be passed off as the property of a slave. It was not until the third stall that he finally found the perfect piece. A smooth, polished light green stone hanging from a delicate golden chain. It would be perfect, and the simplicity made sure that it would be of no interest to the vain occupants of the villa.

He placed the last few items within his satchel. More men than Cassian had sent coin for a few things they desired and would rather deal with him than with Astrix who overcharged for the transaction. The man was as good as his word and said nothing about the purchases. While they made their way back to meet the lanista to return to the ludus Arturo decided to ask one last question.

"Who is it that employs you and takes such great interest in the care of Cassian and my own actions? Is it someone that I might know?"

"There is no harm in that information I suppose." The guard said, shrugging. "Titus Claudius is the man who sent me here. Do you know him?"

"Yes." Arturo almost choked on the word. "I know him well."

CHAPTER 22

Cassian spent the entire day frustrated and distracted. Every noise beyond the gate spun his head to see if it was Arturo returning, but it was not until well past the hottest part of the day that the group returned.

"There are five men missing from the sands, Doctore. Where are they?" The lanista asked, scanning the sands once the gate was closed behind him.

"Our champion is in fine form this day, Dominus. They are being tended by the young Medicus. I doubt any of them shall be withheld from training tomorrow though."

"Good. Keep that fire burning in your soul Cassian. You will need it when we reach Rome. No matter who they throw into the arena against you there is no doubt in my mind that you will reign as victorious in Rome as you do in Velletri."

The cheer from the men around him was encouraging and Cassian lifted his swords in a salute to them, but his mind was full of questions. Some for the Roman and more for his friend who had quietly made his way away from the lanista and towards the infirmary.

"Doctore? Did you send a guard to the infirmary?" Arturo asked, pausing in the doorway, and turning to look at the sands. "To guard the welfare of my young pupil?"

"Apologies Arturo. The thought did not occur to me. You left no instruction for special care. I assumed she could do her job without such a thing."

"Cirandon?" Cassian dropped the swords and rushed to push past the druid to get to the room. He had thought there was a guard. He had been sending men there all day, to keep her busy, not knowing that she was alone. What had he done?

"Violetta? VIOLETTA!" He was practically screaming when he shoved the door open.

He had steeled himself for brutality, for tears and had prayed there would be no blood, that she might have found a way to defend herself. The scene before him was unlike anything that he could have readied himself for. He stood, in mindless shock while his eyes roamed the room.

It was serenity.

Two men were sitting, waiting to be treated, one was tending to the pot of water on the fire while another was grinding an herb. Violetta, his little priestess, was masterfully winding a bandage around the Thracian's bruised ribs and admonishing him for moving too much.

"I would be done by now if you did not squirm like a child. Be still and then your brothers will be able to receive their care." She said to the big man that, only yesterday, had been making jokes about what he would do if he had her alone.

"Yes medicus." Tarcarus grumbled before following her instructions.

Cassian was utterly amazed. Beside him he could hear Arturo start to chuckle and soon he could not stop himself from joining as relief flooded through him. Of all the things he thought he would ever seen in the infirmary it was not his woman ordering gladiators about as though they were new men working in a kitchen.

"Woman, you amaze me. I had though to find you at their mercy or lack of. Never did I suspect to find the reverse."

"You have no idea how right you are, Cassian." Tarcarus said with a grin. "She threatened to turn us out if we made so much as a single joke. How do you manage her, brother?"

"I think you will find that I am not the one doing the managing." He said, wrapping an arm around Violetta's waist. Pulling her close Cassian cupped her face in his hands for a soft kiss.

"You are safe? Tell me if they did, or said, anything to upset you. I will deal with them if needed."

She leaned into his hold and turned her head to press her lips against his wrist.

"I am unharmed. I swear. They did nothing once I made it clear that I would tolerate not a single word out of turn."

Arturo was still chuckling.

"And you were worried? The next thing you know she will be taking up arms and commanding the sands." He said, starting on the next wounded man just as the lanista arrived in the doorway.

"All is well within these walls Violetta?" Tertius asked, stepping inside and gesturing for Cassian to step aside so that she could turn to face him.

"Yes Dominus." She replied, bowing her head.

The smile that he adored so much vanished with the appearance of the Roman, causing Cassian's fist to clench. If they were free men, facing each other in a market square, he knew that he could and would pummel the man for upsetting her. She should always smile. She should always be happy enough to smile without fear of punishment. That was a gift he could only dream of being able to give her.

"Then if there for such a crowd, those not in need of either medicus should resume training while the light lasts." Tertius said, avoiding Cassian's eyes when he added. "One of the guards will come for you at nightfall to take you to the safety of the villa.

"I feel I must remind you that I am capable of keeping her safe, Dominus." Cassian said, dropping a bold but swift kiss to her cheek before he followed the lanista out of the room. "You see how the men already adapt to her presence. Please?"

"Cassian, the decision has been made. Let it be and do not push me to change things further." Tertius said firmly. When he reached out to grip Violetta's chin and raise her eyes. "You will be ready and waiting for your escort upstairs after the evening meal. Do not be late."

"I will be ready, Dominus." She said, all confidence gone from her voice.

Cassian sighed, rubbing his hand down her arm. He wanted to hold her close and comfort her, but there was not time. The Roman's commands saw to that.

"I will see you as soon as I am able. Stay safe in here."

She nodded and leaned up to kiss him, wrapping her arms around his neck to pull him close enough to feel her breasts crushing against his chest. The kiss was filled with longing, but was too short for anything deeper, no matter how much they both wanted it.

"Soon, Violetta. You have my oath. Soon."

Cassian spent the rest of the sunlit hours trying to think of a way to stop this new command from happening without disobeying Tertius or nearly killing someone to keep her in the infirmary overnight. Every solution he could come up with was too dangerous or needed the assistance of another man, neither of which he had.

The evening meal came, and Violetta joined Cassian and the other gladiators who greeted her with a few nods and grunts instead of the crude comments they had been making in days past. It felt so calm and natural, as though this was the way that it had always been. The conversation was light and easy.

Argus and Proximus joined their table. Their presence making it known, demonstrating, that she was to be accepted as one of ludus and not a temporary amusement. It was a glimpse of their life as it could be, as it might be, once he was victorious in Rome and convinced both Census and Tertius that Violetta belonged at his side, that he fought better when she was near him.

"Arturo is not joining us?" Argus asked Violetta, looking back towards the infirmary.

"He said that he needed to sort his herbs and then pray. I was not going to press the issue with him." Violetta replied, leaning back against Cassian's chest.

"When he is in that kind of mood there is nothing that you can do to persuade him otherwise." Cassian said, gently wrapping his arm around her torso and kissing the top of her head. He had not yet had the chance to talk to the druid about the gift he was to have purchased for the woman in his arms.

He had hoped to give it to her tonight, but it would have to wait.

He hated waiting.

"I find his devotion fascinating, though his gods are different from my own. I would like to know more." Violetta said, surprising Cassian with her religious interest.

"I thought medicine was your interest but perhaps my calling you 'little priestess' is more telling than you let on." Cassian replied.

"Why would a woman want to study the gods of any country unless it be the ones to guide her own path?" Argus asked.

"Because, before I was sent to Cassian by Census the gods were, in fact, my path, Argus." She replied, sitting up to emphasise her point.

"What do you mean they were your path?" Cassian said, changing position on the bench and pulling her closer. He rested his chin on her shoulder, drinking in the smell of her before he pressed his lips to her neck.

"I was to be sent to a temple, to intervene on behalf of Felix with the gods. I had not yet taken any vows but if I had not been sent to you when I was, the temple and the gods would have been my life by now."

"Do you wish that were your life? It would have saved you so much pain. The pain brought to you because of me." Cassian said softly, dread at the answer filling his gut.

"Because of us." She corrected him. "Cassian, there is no life I would choose beyond what I have now except to be free, with you beside me."

His heart swelled at her answer, if only he could have taken her to a cell to show her how her words affected him.

"Goodnight, brothers." Cassian said, lifting his woman into his arms and carrying her into the hallway. Lucius or one of the other guards would be there soon to take her from him and he was not going to allow the last few moments to be wasted, not after what she had just said.

"Cassian? Where are we going?" Violetta asked him with a smile and small laugh. "We do not have time to…"

He silenced Violetta's question by setting her on her feet, threading his fingers into her hair and plundering her lips with his mouth. If he could not take her to a bed and bring them both over the edge of blissful release, then he would send her to her bed weak in the knees and filled with thoughts of him.

He lifted her up to sit on one of the rough shelves carved into the wall so that she could wrap her legs around his waist, this way they could get as close to each other as possible. The smell and feel of her wrapped around him was driving him to madness. He wondered how long it would be before they came for her. Did they have time for more? Cassian knew that he could bring her to release in only a matter of minutes and he would follow quickly behind, emptying himself into her, but was there time?

"Violetta…" He rasped against her throat. "Do you want me to…do you want to risk being interrupted?"

"Apologies, champion." Lucius said, coming down the stairs to unlock the gate. "I would have given you more time if I knew what you were up to but the lanista has said she must come now."

"Damn you, Lucius." Cassian said, helping Violetta down from the shelf and straightening her dress. "I never though you would be the man to stop me from being with my woman."

Violetta squeezed Cassian's hand and leaned against him with a barely perceptible sigh.

"Is it truly that time, already?" She asked the Centurion who gave her a smile filled with understanding that Cassian did not know the man possessed.

"It is, medicus. Your room companion is with Tertius, at the moment, so I thought you would like the time to yourself before he arrived." Lucius said, swinging the gate open. "Come along."

"You will be fine." Cassian said, kissing her forehead. "If he does anything, touches you, tell me and I will have it dealt with. If the lanista does more to keep us apart then know that I will write to you. You are on my thoughts, always."

"Cassian…I cannot…if you…" She tried to speak as the guard ushered her through the gate and up the stairs, but he did not catch the end of her words.

Leaning on the locked gate, gripping the bars in frustration, he whispered under his breath.

"If that boy touches you, I swear I will rip his balls off." He muttered.

With a final look at the stairs he walked away towards his cell to try and find sleep. Laying on the hard mat and staring at the ceiling he wondered how it was that, somehow, his bed felt colder, and arms felt emptier than ever before. He stared at the jugs of wine that Lucius had put in the corner at his request and sighed. He was not yet desperate enough to start down that path.

"I will have you back where you belong, with me, where you belong." He said to the dark. "No matter what I have to do to make it happen."

CHAPTER 23

Violetta was trying to understand the words that Cassian had said just before they were parted. He was going to write to her? Did he think she could read? Where had he gotten that kind of idea? That kind of skill? How could she tell him that she could not read more than a few, small words?

"Medicus? Violetta?" Lucius called, putting a hand on her shoulder.

They had arrived at the room she was to share with Jovian, and she did not even remember the journey. Once they had reached the top of the stairs her mind had been solely on the things that Cassian had told her, but now she was faced with the remarkable luxury of her new bedroom and she did not know what to do.

"You can go in. It is your quarters now." The guard said to her with a smile on his face that she could not tell if he was amused or annoyed.

"Yes, gratitude Lucius. I was just lost in thought. Good night."

He nodded before leaving her alone in the bedroom that was as fine as a Romans. Some of the silk on the walls even reminded her of Selenia Census, the daughter of her legal Dominus. Exorbitant taste was everywhere around her. From the draped silks on the walls to the bowls of gawdy bangles and jewelry. She almost expected the detestable woman to enter the room at any moment as some new form of torture concocted by the Romans.

She poured some water into her hand and knelt by the window, sprinkling the drops in prayer and supplication to Mercury as she had been taught and to Hera, Queen of the Gods of her own people.

"Protect your humble servant, I beg thee. For I have been devout and unfailing in my service to you. See me safe from the cruelty of the Roman woman as you guide me on the path chosen for me. Protect me while the man you have chosen to safeguard me has been denied the ability to fulfil that part of his sacred destiny, if that is your will. Please, oh Queen, let me be safe from harm in this house."

"You pray for safety when there is no threat? You are an odd girl, Violetta." Jovian laughed, stepping into the room, and sitting on her bed to stare at her. "What gods do you pray to?"

Closing her eyes to finish her prayer before rising to look at him.

"That is a very personal question Jovian, but I pray to Mercury as I was taught the last four years and to Hera, the Queen of the Gods of Greece, as my mother taught me."

"You pray and make offerings every day? Will it be loud? I like to sleep in the morning, especially after a night of tending to Dominus."

"I pray at least twice a day and, no, it is not loud." She offered him a smile. "I sprinkle the water and say my prayers. If I was alone in a sanctuary, I might say them aloud but here I will be whispering them so that no one is bothered."

"I might watch you. It sounds interesting. Why do you pray so much? I do not know anyone except Arturo that does, except before certain games Dominus will make a sacrifice. We are not really religious in this house."

She watched the younger man stretch out on the bed like a lazy cat in the sun and shook her head.

"That does not surprise me. It does not change anything about how I feel or what I will do. My faith in my gods helped me through many things and I believe that they guided my path to Cassian and that they bend the will and minds of the Romans to help keep us together."

"You think that the gods care about any of us? Our hopes and dreams? Why would they? We are insects to them." He replied, sitting up on the bed.

"I think we amuse them at the very least and that, yes, they care about us. I believe that you do not have to be a gladiator to hold the favor of the gods and that if we find ourselves in their good graces then we should be thankful and honor them for choosing us."

Violetta sat to brush and braid her hair. The skeptical look on her companion's face told her that there was little point in trying to convince him that she was right. He would never be a true believer. The thought took her back to earlier in the evening with Cassian and she wondered if he truly did not believe in the gods, here or in his homeland.

Since her youth as a slave had been spent studying and devoting herself to the gods, as well as avoiding Vitus, they had been her everything. What would she do, how would she feel, if something that mean so much to her meant absolutely nothing to him?

There was a knock on the door that pulled her from her thoughts.

"Who could that be at this hour?" She asked Jovian, slightly nervous

"Oh, I am sure that it is a summons for me. Who in the villa would be looking for you at night unless there was a brawl in the ludus?" He said, opening the door with an expectant smile.

"Domina summons the young medicus." The darker skinned woman on the other side of the door said, looking past Jovian to Violetta.

"Is she ill? I am not yet fully trained. Arturo would still be the best to treat an ailment."

"She did not say. I was simply instructed to bring you immediately. Please come. She is not patient." The woman pleaded.

Jovian nodded "Tilla speaks the truth, Violetta. You should go quickly. Do not be alarmed if I am not here when you return. Dominus often summons me to help him to relax before bed."

Violetta gave him a brief nod before following the other woman through the torch-lit halls of the villa.

"She gave you no indication what it was that she wanted?" Violetta tried to coax anything from the other woman that might let her know what kind of situation she was walking into. After the earlier threat to steal a child from her if she conceived one before the Roman woman did or to find a way to force the birth a child she could claim as her husband's, from a slave, Violetta did not know what she could expect.

She should have told Cassian, but if she had done that he would have been so concerned about the threat that they would never be able to make love with the passionate abandon that they did now. If he did give her a child and the Roman took it from her, from them, he would get himself killed trying to get their child back.

"Only that she waited for Dominus to be gone from the room and in his office for the evening." The woman said. "I am to prepare her bed for the night so the two of you will be alone. Be careful not to make her angry. She will take her wrath out on all of us, not just you."

"I have no intention of making her angry." Violetta said quietly. "Though I do no know if I can do what she wants me to do."

"You will have to find a way, or the entire house will suffer." She said. "Domina? I have brought the medicus as you requested."

Violetta took a deep breath and stepped into the room.

"Domina? I hope the evening finds you well. What can I do for you?" She asked softly, keeping her head down in a gesture of obedience and feigned deference.

"What can you do? You can explain your plan to bring an heir to the house of Tertius." Lycithia said, forcing Violetta to raise her chin and look her in the eyes. "What can you do for me that the druid cannot? What is it that you know that he does not? Selenia told me how you were groomed for the temples, an intimate of the gods. There must be something that you can do that the heretic Arturo cannot. How can a man that does not believe in Juno ever expect to bring her blessings down upon this house?"

Beneath the inane ranting and rage Violetta could see that the woman was hurting with the desire, the need, to have a child. It was hard to tell if her desire was for only for her husband or if she wanted the babe for herself. Was she going to be capable of loving a child the way that it would need or was this simply a way to get attention from her husband for a time and then have someone who she could force to love her when she felt neglected?

"I have prayed upon the matter twice today and await the message from Juno to see what she wishes in homage in exchange for the blessing that you seek. I will continue to pray and make offerings until the solution is made clear." Violetta said, trying her best to sound as knowledgeable as the temple priests so that the dangerous woman would be appeased.

"I know my husband brought you here for the Celt, he refuses any woman but you to his bed now. Even his former favorite whores cannot stir his cock the way that you manage to do. I hope, for your sake, that you are able to stir the same devotion from the gods and see this prayer answered before I am forced to take measures that are more drastic in nature to ensure that this house has it's heir within a year's time. Do you understand? You remember my earlier words of warning well enough that they do not need to be repeated?"

"I remember, Domina." Violetta said, carefully. She did not want to incite the woman's wrath or the sudden violence of her temper. "Shall I go and offer prayers and offering again before sleep? I am eager to return to the infirmary tomorrow and see what herbs Arturo brought back from the city. I had made a request for some that were not in his garden that might help with the keeping of a child in your womb once it takes seed."

"Yes. Should you require anything special for your offerings bring your requests to me and only me. I will see that you are provided with what you need so that my husband does not add this worry to the many that he already carries."

"Of course, Domina. May the gods bring you soothing dreams and visions of the future that they must surely have planned for you." Violetta said, stepping out into the hallway as quickly as she could manage without bumping into anything.

"What do they have planned for me, though, with such madness as my task?" She asked herself in a whisper, walking back to the room.

The relief she felt at finding it empty was palpable. The conflict of her emotions would have been hard to hide from Jovian and harder to explain. She needed the time to understand, to pray for guidance and the miracle it would take to get the older woman pregnant by a husband that seemed more interested in his slaves than his wife.

CHAPTER 24

Jovian would have skipped down the hall to the office of his Dominus if such feminine amusements had not been forbidden by the man. He was thrilled with the little medicus as a partner in his room. There had, of course, been the worry that she would be dull or weeping at the separation from her lover, but she seemed quite adjusted to her reality without excess emotions getting in the way of living. It was possible that they might have a simply wonderful time sharing his room together. It would always be his room. She would never have possessions such as he did and so it would continue to be his domain. He was happy to have her company though, for now.

"I am here Dominus. How may I pleasure you tonight?" Jovian said, practically singing as he sauntered into the room.

"By standing still like a man and not flitting about like some song-bird." Tertius said, his tone harsh and snapping Jovian out of his joyful and flirtatious mood.

"Of course, Dominus. You have always liked me like this, but I am happy to play my part as you like, any way that you like." He said, tilting his head to the side and walking towards the man that had been his commanding intimate, his instructor in the passions of the body.

It was true that he had dreamed of the gladiators, Cassian especially until Argus caught his attention, but he had never been able to achieve his dream of being taught the passionate techniques of the gladiators by one of them. It was his secret obsession, but the look on the lanista's face was so full of rage that he feared it was a secret no longer.

"We do not play your foolish games at intimate touches. Not tonight." Tertius said, holding a hand up to stop Jovian's steps. "Not any night after this. If I want the simpering softness of a woman, I will have one. After this, when you come to me, it will be as a man."

The boy stopped and stared at his master, unable to comprehend what he had just heard. The feminine attire and paints had been the lanista's command from the time Jovian was ten years old. They felt as though they were a part of his identity now.

What would he do without them?

Who was he supposed to be?

"Dominus? Have I brought offence? Is there someone that is going to replace me in your affections?"

"You bring offence in questioning me and still standing here dressed in that foolish attire."

"Apologies, Dominus. I did not know that you wished for anything different. I can go and change now."

He turned to go, and to do as he was commanded but the Roman gripped him by his hair and pulled him backwards.

"You will stay here and do the only thing you are useful for." Tertius snarled, ripping the fabric that had Jovian had carefully draped around his hips.

"Dominus?" Jovian said, struggling slightly.

He did not understand this new game that the Roman was playing. Over the years they had enjoyed everything from tender and gentle to wild and rough, but this was neither of those. Tiberius was angry and when he was shoved Jovian against the table, gripping his hair tight he realized that this was not a game.

The Roman swept his arm across the surface, clearing it of debris and pushing Jovian down on the flat surface.

"Please, Dominus. I will do what you want. There is no need to do this, to be like this. I will be what you want, whatever that is."

His next words were silenced by a piece of silk stuffed into his mouth and oil from the food tray was poured across the cheeks of his ass.

"You are going to do as you are told because you are a slave, my slave." He shoved Jovian back down to the table surface, hard and kicked his legs apart. "You are going to realize that you are not special."

The pain of the penetration was excruciating and so was the pain in his heart. "You are going to realize that you are a whore, my whore and that, no matter who your father is, you will be nothing but a whore, ever."

The wale of pain Jovian let lose had less to do with the pain wracking his body and more to do with the agony of his soul. He did not know what he had thought would happen in the coming years, but it was always something special.

Jovian had thought, perhaps, that he would rise to be his master's right hand. An advisor that was respected and almost equal in consideration to Lycithia had once been his greatest dream. He had assumed that what he had thought was affection from the lanista might even see him freed one day or adopted as a son. He had thought to take over the ludus and have the gladiators under his order, perhaps even in his bed at last.

With every stroke and painful thrust into his body that dream faded further and further away, blurred by the tears in his eyes that dripped onto the table.

"Get yourself from my sight and be ready in the morning to resume your duties. If you wish me to consider bringing you to Rome, then you will have to prove that you can be as useful on your feet as you are on your knees." Tertius said, stomping out of the room and leaving Jovian to see himself out.

He felt physically broken and emotionally disillusioned. All Jovian could think of was getting back to his room and tearing down all the beautiful finery and decorations that he had there. It was all reminders of the lie his life had been until that moment and he could not bear to look at any of it, not anymore.

"If he wants me to change then change is what I shall do." He screamed, storming into the bedroom and reaching for the first piece of fabric he could find and ripping it to the floor. "No more soft and sweet night. Just a slave. To fuck and be fucked."

"Jovian?" Violetta sat up, staring at him while she clutched the blanket to her chest. "What is this? You were so pleased to be summoned. What happened that has upset you this greatly?"

"He has fucked me for years, but this was the first time I felt like a slave, like I was nothing but a whore." Jovian said. "I do not know what happened or why, but everything I am is to change. I am no longer allowed to dress as I like. I must come to him as any other slave, as a man and not his special boy."

He wanted to throw himself on the bed and weep for all the hurts that he was suffering. There was no time for that though. He had to change everything in the space of one night and be able to appear at the lanista's bedside in the morning looking as though everything was as it should be. He could not look as though his entire world had changed in the space of a few minutes.

"That is a strange command." Violetta said, getting up to help him with the silk. "Why did he say that? Why did he hurt you?"

"Because I am a slave, no matter who my father is. That is what he said. What does that even mean?" Jovian said, sitting on the floor surrounded by the bright silks he used to treasure as decorations. "What does my parentage have to do with anything at all?"

"I could not say. Who are your parents?" Violetta asked, sitting on the floor next to him and taking his hand.

She truly was sweet, sisterly in many ways, but pretty as well. Jovian was beginning to see why Cassian was so taken with her, even if she were not as lovely as he could be when he wanted. In the past, not anymore. He could never be pretty again, by the lanista's command.

"I do not know. I have never known." He said with a sigh, laying across the silks on the floor, and putting his head into the girl's lap. "I have always been here in the villa. No one has ever mentioned my parents to me before, other than to say I was unwanted. I have always assumed that one, or both, were slaves."

"What if your father were a gladiator of note? Or a Roman?" Violetta suggested, stroking his hair. "Then Tertius would surely know of it."

"It does not matter to him. He said so." Jovian said, turning to his side to face her. "Why would he say that unless he already knew though had no intention of telling me?"

"He must know." Violetta said. "It must be someone of note to keep it from you. He is keeping it from you as we prepare to go to Rome. Perhaps it is someone there, but he does not want you to look like yourself so that they will see you. He wants you to blend in to make sure that your father does not find you."

"Why would he care if my father found me? I am a slave. I cannot choose to leave him."

"He fears to lose you." Violetta suggested, stroking his hair soothingly. "That does not excuse the hurts he has caused you but all folk lash out when they are afraid."

"Is that why Vitus hurts you so terribly? He fears to lose you?" Jovian asked. What remained of his innocent heart wanted her words to be true, but some people were only monsters, her Dominus, and his children among them.

"No. He never had me to lose. His lust combined with hatred makes him deadly. If I am returned to that house it will be a death sentence."

He sat up to look at her, expecting tears in her eyes but there was nothing more than quiet resignation reflected at him. She believed her words, that the return to that place would mean her death. Did Cassian know this? Of course, he must. That was why he was training so hard, fighting as hard as he could. He was trying to save her life by keeping her here.

"Then you cannot go back. We must all work together to keep you here." Jovian touched her cheek. "I do not want you to die, especially at the hands of those Romans."

She smiled so sweetly that he wondered if he had finally said the right thing to her, was she finally able to understand him as he was?

"You know, if I am to start behaving as a man, like a gladiator or a Roman, you could help me with that. If you want to." He said with a teasing smile, twirling a long strand of her hair around his finger.

"I would be happy to help you in any way that I can Jovian." She smiled, shy but with her eyes on him. "Do you want me to help take down the silk and pack it away?"

"There is something else I would like your help with first." He leaned a little close, as though he might whisper in her ear. She smelled so sweet and was offering to help him. Surely it would be not too much to ask that she help him feel like a man for the first time in a long time.

"What is it you would have of me Jovian?"

There was the hint of a tremble in her voice, but he could wipe it away with the few soft touches that he knew to use on those that faked innocence. They could have some fun together if she would let him.

"Help me practice the passion of a man. I would not hurt you or risk bringing a child into your womb, but if I am to be as a man now then I need to practice. Lay back and let me, please?"

CHAPTER 25

Violetta had barely slept all night. She was worried that Jovian would make another attempt to kiss her. It had been hard to stop him the night before and she did not think she had the energy to do it again. Whatever had happened with the lanista had made him forget that she was devoted to Cassian alone.

It had taken a hard slap to his cheek coupled with tears on her own to stop his advances, but she was able to convince him that he needed a good night sleep more than anything. He seemed to have slept well but every sound had startled her so much that rest was impossible.

As soon as the first traces of light from the dawn had appeared in the window Violetta had risen to offer prayers to her gods. In the not so distant past when she would sacrifice her own blood to Mercury, trying to earn or buy enough of his favor that she would be safe from the hands of Felix and Vitus, but it was only water that her god required her to sacrifice now.

Once her prayers and offerings were finished, with Jovian still asleep, she found Julius Lucius who was so often at Cassian's side, to take her down to the ludus. She hoped for a few moments of peace in the infirmary to rest before the day's work began

"Medicus?" The voice of the cook called to her as she stepped out onto the platform. "You arise earlier than usual. Would you like to break your fast now?"

She smiled warmly at him.

"Gratitude. That would be much appreciated."

When he brought the fresh, hot, bread, they broke it together and watched the sun rise over the hills.

"It is beautiful here, is it not? Before the fighting begins? When it is still?" She gestured towards the sand and the view from the cliff.

"It is. The fighting has a beauty of its own though. If you take the time to see it. The motion of the gladiator has a grace to it that is remarkable in its grace. Like a dance between the Titans and the Gods that is as deadly as it is beautiful."

Violetta considered his words and tried to consider the horrifying violence as she remembered it when she had been on the pulvinus with the Romans to watch Cassian fight in the arena. Even though it had been terrifying she could see some of what the cook said in how the men moved.

"You know much about their life for the man that simply cooks the meals." She looked down at the scarring on his leg she had never taken the time to notice. "You were a gladiator once? Some years ago?"

"Some long years ago it seems though, I suppose, it is not as distant as it feels. I was wounded in the arena but lived and was granted this position. Though I will never raise arms upon the sands again I do my part by providing as nutritious food as I am able for the men that I once would have called brother. They do not see the man that I was then, only the broken man that I am now."

"There is more to any man than his ability to lift a weapon to take a life. Not all men are destined for glory in the arena, that is not the only way that a man can rise, not the only way that he can honor his ancestors and the gods." Violetta said softly.

"You truly believe that?" The cook said, rising to his feet with a strain on his face that spoke of the pain that wracked his body still. "You may not want to try to convince your man of that. It is not the way of gladiators. Death and blood are our, their, path. The only path to the glory that they seek. They will not be dissuaded from that by any means. Though I am sure the means that you possess are more tempting than anything they have been offered before, especially our champion."

Violetta blushed and looked back towards the cells.

"I do not know much of his past, but I hope that his future and mine continue to be upon the same path. I believe that the gods have united us, and that my prayers keep them happy."

"Then I hope you are right, and you get to stay at his side. Cassian is more driven and more bearable since you have entered his life. The lives of the rest of us are easier for your efforts too." He said, heading back to the ludus kitchen to finish the rest of the bread for the men.

With a smile on her face Violetta walked towards the infirmary, still hopeful that she might have a few moments to rest before the rush of the day or at least before the arrival of her instructor.

The room was still, a peaceful tranquility that was instantly soothing when Violetta shut the door after stepping inside. Almost everything was where she had left it the night before and those items that had been moved had been done so by Arturo.

The connection she was building with the druid was different from the one with Meridius, but soothing. He held no affection for her, fatherly or otherwise, but they might come to share a respect. Perhaps they would even become friends. He had so much to teach her and she felt as though she could teach him about the plants she knew, and he didn't. She touched the seed pouches with a smile.

It would be good to plant them in the garden area on the south side of the villa. How Arturo had gotten permission from the Roman's to use the small square area behind the olive trees and oregano bushes she did not dare to ask. Neither Tertius or his wife seemed to be the kind of masters that would understand that even slaves needed something for themselves. They all needed something of home or a moment in the day where they could believe that the world was not as bad as it often seemed. That garden might easily become her favorite place, besides Cassian's arms.

Preparing the fire for the day, she wondered how he was. What was he thinking of? Was it her or was his head already in the mindset of the warrior in training for the match in Rome? Closing her eyes, she tried to focus on the possibilities should he be victorious, the idea of his loss was not one that she could bear. What if he won his freedom at last?

"Violetta?"

She heard her name through the cloud of sleep.

"Violetta, wake up."

Opening her eyes, she found Arturo's deep brown eyes staring into hers with a twinkle of amusement.

"It would be unwise for a gladiator, or a Roman, to find you in such a state. Are you unwell that you need extra rest?"

He asked, handing her a cup of heated water with the juice of lemons stirred into it.

"Arturo, good morning." She said, sipping slowly. "I am well, simply tired. The first night in the villa was not one of ease or comfort."

"The woman of the house give you grief over your youth, disguised as a lecture regarding your conduct when inside the villa or in the company of her 'proper Roman women' that she likes to parade the gladiators in front of?" He asked, tinkering in the medicine cabinet that was still not completely restocked from Argus' attack on its contents.

"No, she did not, yet." Violetta said. "There were words with her that did cause sleep to become elusive, but it was the words that the lanista had with Jovian that proved to be the greater trouble."

"Jovian? Gods, what did that child do now?" Arturo asked with a chuckle.

Violetta was not sure that he would take her words as truthful. Jovian was so well liked by the druid and others that she doubted they would believe that he had tried to convince her to go to bed with him. Cassian would believe her, that he had tried, but would he have faith that she had resisted the persistent boy? He was known for getting exactly what he wanted from anyone he wished. Why would anyone believe that he did not get it from her, if they even believed that he made the attempt?

"He disrupted my prayers with his flirtations. He made it difficult to find rest enough to sleep. I am fully capable of following instructions though. I have done harder work on less sleep." She said, rising to her feet.

"I imagine that you have." He said, putting the seeds and plant cuttings from the market into a basket with a few tools.

"Would you like to plant the seeds from yesterday's journey to the market? Or would you rather that I do so?" She asked, smiling back at the druid when he offered her a kind expression.

"I will take you to the garden and let you have some peaceful time there. You can join me beside the sands when it is done." He patted her hand and picked up the basket he had prepared. "If you carry the seeds and smaller plants then I would like for you tell me about your gods and how you worship them. Your lover tells that you were trained as an acolyte, is this true?"

"It is true that until Felix made the decision to gift me to Cassian, I spent years training to serve the gods at the temple. I had looked forwards to it. The years I would have spent without worrying if Vitus or his father would be abusing me would have been peaceful but without Cassian it would have been empty." She said with a smile, walking beside him to the garden.

"Would you have recognized the emptiness for what it was? If you had never known the love and passion that you share with Cassian, would you have seen that your life was empty, or would it have been fulfilled by the grace of the gods?" Arturo asked, opening the gate to the garden.

"I think, if I had never known love, that I would have been able to convince myself that the life of an acolyte was enough. With the knowledge that I have now that would be impossible. I have no desire to live without him."

Violetta could feel Arturo watching her.

"What will you do if your Dominus takes you back to his villa after the match in Rome?"

"I am going to die if I go back there. It will not take long for it to happen with the temper of Vitus pushed to the edge of his limited control by my being here and out of his reach."

The druid stopped and, with his hand on her arm, turned her to face him.

"You think that he is that dangerous? His father would not stop him?

"Yes, he could and would do it. He would be punished for it and I believe that Meridius would find a way to kill him for it. If I return to the house of Census, I will die the next time Vitus lays his hands upon me."

"Then we have to do whatever we can to make sure that does not happen." Arturo said with a smile.

She thought he meant for the smile to be calming, and it was to some extent, but it made her wonder if he had begun to plan something.

He was as crafty as the Roman's claimed, the difference being that he plotted ways to work around their devious cruelties. It would not surprise her if he tried to find a way to have her kept safe no matter what happened in Rome.

"All we need, all I need, is for Cassian to live, to be victorious in Rome." Violetta said, stepping into the grove where they were going to plant the seeds from yesterday's market trip. "If he dies, when I die, we will find each other in the afterlife. I am not afraid of death, though waiting for it to come will be excruciating, terrifying." She knelt in the ground and began digging in the sun-warmed earth. "I am afraid that if he is victorious, when he is victorious, that the Romans will still part us and that I will never speak with him again. I might only see him in the arena, and that is only if I am taken to the games by Felix."

"You think that after the games in Rome, Tertius and Census will cease their bargain and part you both? They know Cassian loves you and that he fights better, more passionately, since you have been put into his life." Arturo said gently. "They would be fools, cruel ones, to part you."

Violetta looked up him and shook her head.

"Arturo? Have you ever known them to anything else?"

CHAPTER 26

Cassian was walking the line between frustrated and worried. He had not seen Violetta all day. He had not seen her since Julius had taken her upstairs, where she had spent the night in the same room as Jovian. What had happened in that room? Had the boy painted her up like a Roman whore again? Was that why she did not come to the sands with Arturo?

He had to find out, and it had to be now, before the distraction saw him injured.

"Arturo? A brief word with you?" He said, nodding his friend towards the water barrel.

"You do not seem yourself this morning Cassian." Arturo said with that infuriatingly calm smile he was known for. "Is something troubling your mind?"

"I think you and I both know what troubles me. Where is your student and what is her condition?" He set down the pair of blades that he practiced with and watched the druid over the edge of his water cup. "I would also see the gift that you found for her at my request."

"I do not know what it is that you are asking Cassian." He said, digging into his pocket and placing a small bag into his palm. "Look at that later."

"Did that little brat do anything to her that I need to see corrected? Did he force himself on my woman? Is that why she hides from my sight today? I would not hold it against her but against him, she should know that." Cassian said, tucking the precious pouch into his subligaria.

"How would she? If that were what happened then the girl would be right to be afraid. How would she know any different? Think of that house and what her life lessons were. Who taught her about men?"

Arturo was trying to comfort him, but he did not know about Meridius. If Violetta had mentioned the blue-eyed Spaniard to her teacher Cassian was certain that she would have left out the man's attempt to kiss her. If she had, the druid would not have been talking about the lessons of that house for they were all based upon pain and lechery.

"I have been teaching her about love." Cassian said, shaking his head. "I would hope that she would know that she can come to me with anything and see her words met with understanding."

"As you met the boy's attempt to decorate her with his paints?" Arturo said pointedly.

"It was his attempt to kiss her that sent me to a rage. She does not need that kind of paint; she is not like that hag of a Roman upstairs." Cassian said with a chuckle into his cup. "Where is she Arturo? I need to know that she is unharmed and not afraid. I bled to keep her safe."

"I know you did, Prince." Arturo said softly, putting a hand on his arm.

"Do not call me that, not here." He growled. "I am not that boy anymore."

"Or you are more that man than you like to remember and so you try to forget."

Cassian set down his cup.

"You avoid the answer to my question, more than once. Where is Violetta and why is she not at your side, learning, as she was brought here to do?"

"She is in the garden, planting the seeds that I brought yesterday. I do not know why she has not yet broken words with you, nor is it my business to ask. She is safe, unmolested, though tired. That is all I can tell you save for one more thing."

"What is that? Did she send you with a message for me?" Cassian asked eagerly. He hoped that she had sent some message with the druid so that he could focus on his training that was to be used to secure her to the house of Tertius and free her of the terror of Census forever.

"It is a message that she did not express for your ears but one that I think is most important. Live or die in Rome, she fears that her return to the house of Census will see her dead at the hands of his son, Vitus. Something must be done, must be secured, to keep her under this roof or there is nothing that you can do to save her. Everything you fought for, everything that you feel, will be for nothing. This is the test of the gods."

"The gods test my love for her? That is easier to prove than anything I have ever been challenged with." Cassian shook his head with a smirk, thinking of the ways that he could prove his love for her.

Passion had always been his gift and when combined with the love that he felt for Violetta there was nothing that was impossible or unattainable, except the marriage denied to him by the words of the Romans.

"The gods test your resolve, your skill and, perhaps, your love for her. If you fail this test, fail to convince Tertius that she is worth the price the merchant may demand, then you will lose her as well as your title. Stand victorious, in word and deed, and everything that you ever wished will be at your fingertips. Pass their test and secure her safety. That is your challenge now."

"Have I ever backed down from a challenge? Especially one with such dire consequences, such personal consequences?" Cassia said, with a grin that was filled with the anger and deadly rage he felt.

"Only once. When you were four years old and could not yet swim. You were smart enough not to try either." Arturo said, chuckling at the memory.

"Then you should have no concern about my ability to meet this test head on and destroy any and every man or woman that makes the attempt to get between her and I."

"Then keep that focus and do not worry about her safety. She is well looked after by me during the day and the lanista's wife thinks that the girl can help her conceive a child. You know that means that she will be as safe as possible inside the villa. Focus on your training and the time will pass swiftly enough to be endured. You will have the right to ask for her the night before you go to Rome and the ride to the capital to enjoy each other again."

Cassian laughed and returned to the sands to train. He tried to imagine the great Circus Maximus, the greatest arena in the Republic, but knew that nothing he had ever seen could possibly be the size and grandeur of the great Roman spectacle.

"How fitting that the monument to Rome will be the scene of my greatest victory." He muttered to himself, getting ready to face off against Proximus. "You fought there, the great Circus?"

"More than once." He said, engaging with his own swords. "Is that where you are to fight in the city? I can give advice if you would take it."

"If it will help me to stand victorious or to ease my woman's time in the cells of the medicus, then I will hear it."

As they sparred with each other Proximus went over the details of the halls and cells, the infirmary and the altars that were all within the confines of the great arena.

"There is a temple for Mercury there? Violetta will be pleased with such knowledge. He is a god that she offers prayers and offerings to."

"Your woman prays to him? That city will be filled with things and places that will interest her." He paused. "Do you think the lanista will parade you about the city like he does here? It will give her the chance to see so much."

"Proximus, we are going to fight not to tour the city for temples and shrines. I would like for her to have the chance to see the temple at the circus. It would mean something to her, but there is little chance that I could arrange that."

"Your guard will be there with you and so will Arturo. I am sure that someone can take her to see it, while you are in the waiting cells." The bigger man suggested with a shrug.

Refocusing his attack Cassian rained his swords down on the shield that Proximus raised at the last moment.

"I want to be there, to see her face when she steps into that space." He shook his head. "Your own woman, the one in Rome, must have something or somewhere special.

Something that has nothing to do with Rome or her affections for you. If you could, if it were possible, would it not be important to you to see the realization of her joy for yourself? To be a part of that moment? That is what I want, for Violetta and myself."

"You want a moment with her in complete joy. I understand now." Proximus nodded, a sadness that Cassian knew all too well in his eyes.

"Something that the Romans cannot touch or take from either of us." Cassian said, following his opponent off the sand when it was time for the newer men to attempt to mimic the fight that the senior men had demonstrated. "They have taken enough already."

"All they do is take. I have never met one that gave back." Proximus said, smirking. "A few pretend, for a time, that they care or that they are different than the rest. They promise to help you achieve your heart's desire, so that you agree with what they want and then, when it is too late, they tell you the price."

The men looked at each other, the sound of the sword practice filling the silence of understanding between them. Both men had suffered at the soft hands of Roman women and they knew that the fairer sex could be, by far, the more vicious. It was part of why Cassian felt such concern for Violetta to be in the villa where Lycithia could do incomparable damage.

He leaned back against the wall and tried not to think of what the woman could do to Violetta, could command her to do, and she would have no one to advocate for her. As much as he despised the Spaniard, Meridius, the man did his best to keep Violetta safe. Jovian would not do the same, no matter what was happening to the delicate girl. He would not risk the wrath of the Romans to help anyone. His silks were more valuable to him than any person would ever be, even if he considered the person a friend.

That thought sent a feeling like a rock straight to his stomach.

"There is something that I must do." He said to Proximus and left the yard.

He rushed through the halls to his cell so that he could grab the parchment and ink Arturo had brought him. He had to finish the letter for her, she had to know what to watch for in that house. What he was planning to do and how he was determined to see her safely kept from the house of Census. If he did not tell her what he intended to then who could tell what madness and foolishness thc Romans might fill her beautiful head with, or what Jovian would say, carelessly, that could wound her heart or give her doubt about him.

How else could he keep from going mad with worry instead of focussing on the training that was playing out before him?

He opened the small pouch and let the gift fall out onto his palm. It was not the ring that he had hoped for, but the green stone was beautiful and would look lovely on the delicate chain around Violetta's neck.

He would purchase something else for the day when he would be allowed to wed her.

Cassian knew that he needed to assure Violetta that his desire for marriage did not fade with the first refusal of the lanista and her own master. He would try again. Cassian would do whatever it took to keep her with him and, someday, he would find a way to make them man and wife so that the laws of the Romans could be used against the masters instead of the slaves for a change.

His pen flew across the paper, spilling words of devotion and romance that he might never be able to say out loud but, somehow, filled every possible inch of the paper before him as he poured out his heart to the woman he loved more than his own life.

CHAPTER 27

Violetta stared at the paper in her hands with utter confusion. Julius Lucius, Cassian's shadowlike guard, said that her lover had written it for her but gave her no other indication of what might be contained in the strong decisive strokes.

Was he angry? Happy? Or trying to send her a warning of some sort that she needed to give an answer to? It was impossible to tell. She could not read a single letter beyond that of 'C' which was the same as the brand she bore from the house of Census.

"Do you wish for me to tell him anything in response?" The tall, dark-haired Centurion asked, looking at her expectantly. "Do his loving words of devotion please you?"

She closed her eyes, grateful that he had, unknowingly, given her what that she needed.

"You may, apologies, I mean, would you please tell him that his words bring a smile to my lips and a warmth to my heart." Violetta said, pressing the paper to her chest. "I shall treasure it."

The Centurion chuckled and turned to depart back to the cells below. He would make sure that the champion of the house was safe and secure in his cell before he returned to his own quarters near the back of the villa with the other paid guardsmen and the man who worked the steel in the forge. He paused and turned back to face her, making Violetta a nervous that there was some darker message or threat to be delivered from the protective Roman.

"I am sure that response will please enough, but I have a question of my own. The answer of which may bring peace of mind to both lover and teacher."

Relief brought another smile to her lips. This was a man that was kinder than any other Roman she had ever met, despite his surly demeanor.

"I would be happy to answer anything that might bring the peace of a good night sleep to both men that I hold in such high regard."

He leaned close so that he could whisper in her ear, low enough that no one could overhear the conversation.

"Are you safe here? Unmolested by Romans or the boy you share a room with? The Celt could barely hold his focus on training today, his concern was so great."

"You may tell them both that though threats have been made and a singular, forgivable, attempt as well, I stand safer still than had I been returned to the Villa of Census. They may rest as easy at night as they do in the day. I am unharmed."

"Lucius, what has you standing in corners whispering with slave girls?" The voice of Tertius disrupted their conversation when the man appeared with Jovian at his side. "Does Violetta hold your cock in hand as well as my champion's?"

"I can assure you that she does no such thing. The woman who holds my heart in her hands is far beyond this city and bears no more than a passing resemblance to Cassian's woman. Your boy, when dressed in his silks, looks far more similar to my Tanaquil than Violetta, in coloring at least though my memory of her soft curves beneath my palms would put them both to shame were her glory standing before us now."

Violetta could not be sure, but it looked as though Jovian had jealousy in his eyes at the mention of the guard's lover. Did he lust for Julius as well as Argus?

"I did not know you had a woman, Lucius. I invite you to join me for a drink and tell me of this secret beauty of yours. You are excused Violetta. Your work tomorrow will suffer if you do not sleep, or so I am told."

"Thank you, Dominus. Pleasant sleep to you and you as well Lucius." She said with a quick bow of her head before leaving the two Romans and Jovian to their talk of the other woman.

She was grateful that she did not have to stay and listen to the crude dialogue that many men turned to in the absence of their wives. Hopefully, the nature of that talk and the alcohol the Romans consumed would keep them occupied for most of the night so that she could sleep without worry of Jovian's flirtatious attention.

Now that she knew Cassian and Arturo were worried about her, she would make a point each day of telling them that she was safe. It was an unexpected kindness from her instructor and a sweet gesture from her lover.

Her thoughts returning to Cassian and the letter that Julius Lucius had brought, Violetta looked down at the paper she could not comprehend. She could feel the smile on her face, it did not match the one in her soul.

He made her happier than she had ever thought she would live to be. Even if she could not understand the words he had scrawled across the fine, luxurious parchment, she was grateful to have a physical manifestation of his love that she could hold in her hands, slide beneath her pillow and keep as a treasure for the rest of her life.

Perhaps, she thought as she lay down to sleep, after offering her prayers, there might come a day when Cassian would be able to teach her to read the letters he had written. If he could not then she would beg Arturo, who certainly could read and write, to teach her the skills as well.

She would have to tell him that it was to improve her skills as a medicus. She doubted that he would do so in order for her to be able to read and reply to love letters written by a man who should have been focused on his training instead of the flowery words of a love letter.

Touching the paper where she had hidden it Violetta wondered if he had written to her with poetry or if he was a man of practical prose? Had he told her of the plans he would have for their life together if they were free together in his homeland or here in the Republic?

The joy of these thoughts guided her to sleep and blessed her dreams until the light of the dawn woke her to a new day and her swift return to the presence of the man she loved. It was bound to be a wonderful and beautiful day.

Her routine of mornings in the ludus were becoming a thing of ease. She had even begun to enjoy a teasing relationship with the cook and a few of the other gladiators. It was a feeling that was new to her, belonging. This is what it felt like to belong. Meridius was the only one who had ever made her feel as though she was a part of something.

The thought of the blue-eyed Spaniard that still served at the feet of Felix Census brought her a moment of sadness. He was the sole part of her past that she missed. His fatherly guidance and their shared moments of prayer to their own gods in the morning had been so peaceful. His strange attempts at seduction after Cassian had taken her maidenhead were something she still did not understand. She had not told her lover all the details, he would rage and hate the man she held to heart as family. It would not matter now. They would never be in a place where they would have to know each other

"Good morning, little priestess. What brings such serious thoughts to your face as the sun rises?" Cassian said, appearing as though summoned by her thoughts to stand behind her.

"Does the sun rise? I find it faded and dull in comparison to the god before me." Violetta said, turning her head to look up at him from her seat.

"What a clever woman I have to say such things. I wonder if it is because she has an unspoken desire she wishes to see fulfilled? Or simply to be spared the base company of mere gladiators?"

"You jest, Cassian. The only desires I have are to be with you, alone." She said, looking around the gathering company. "Though there have been offers, you alone are who I choose."

"Offers? Who in Hades has propositioned my woman?" He sputtered, looking around in curious rage.

Violetta laughed softly, putting her hand on his arm.

"Cassian. There is no one, but your jealousy is as endearing as it is without need." She said, rising to her feet. "I shall return to watch you train later."

He watched her walk towards the infirmary, his eyes fixed on her buttocks and the way that her hips swayed while she walked away. His cock was hard simply thinking about thrusting into her. The next time that they lay together he would take her from behind so that he could keep his hands gripping the swell of her hips. The thought was so immersive, so overwhelming to his senses, that he did not notice the arrival of Argus until the younger man clapped a hand to his knee.

"Where is your mind Cassian? Planning your next dance upon the sands? Or does the champion dream of Rome on such a fine morning?" The younger man said with a laugh.

"What thoughts press upon my mind are not your business." He said with a smirk, rising to his feet to begin the day. "Your own should be bent upon training or when we depart for Rome you will be making your final farewells."

Argus laughed and joined him on his feet.

"There are precious few here that would deserve such words from me." He said with a glance towards the balcony that was so swift Cassian nearly missed it. "At least you can rest assured that your woman will ride with us on the way there."

"When I win it will be to ensure that she is there on the way back as well. I have yet to think of the way that I will convince Tertius that this is what needs to happen, but I will find it and keep her here."

Agrus nodded and took his opening stance.

"If there is anything that I can do to aid you, all you need do is say the word."

"Much appreciated. Now, begin." He said, moving into the attack position.

They faced off, waiting for the command to start from Cirandon. When the word came, Cassian forgot about brotherhood or comradery and gave in to the base, primal viciousness that coursed through his blood.

He attacked Argus with a growl, swinging one sword and then the other. His frustration equalled his pride when they were both deflected with a skill that bordered on excellence. It was possible that the German would return from Rome after all. They began to circle each other slowly. Cassian had a broad grin on his face as he watched the progress that his pupil had made in a short period of time. Argus had a look of deep concentration, but his guard was still down on his left. A hard lesson would have to be taught if he were to survive an honest attack against him.

Cassian was ready to rain down a series of blows that might have bruised the boy's ribs when the opening of the gate caught his attention and the voice he hated most in the world called across the sands to Violetta where she sat studying with Arturo.

"There sits my father's great whore, the prize of the champion of Velletri basking in the sun like a cat. Is this how you inspire victories? Or is that work done upon your knees as the men wait their turn upon the sand?" The Roman cried with a laugh, waving to Tertius on the balcony. "I could not waist the chance to see the men train by coming in the front door, Tiberius, I hope you will forgive my eagerness. If not then the words from my father may help to lessen your dismay."

Cassian did his best to finish the match, but it was certainly not up to his standard. When he turned to look at Violetta, hoping to encourage her with a smile, he found that she had buried her face in her arms and pressed herself against the wall, as if the stone could encircle her within itself and hide her from the Roman monster.

"Roman cunt." He snarled to himself. "Has to make an appearance and ruin her day and mine."

"My apologies Cassian but it looks like he is not quite done yet." Cirandon said, joining him on the sands and pointing to where Lucius was drawing Violetta to her feet while Arturo argued with him.

"What in Hades is this?" The Celt snarled, trying to leave the sands but finding the way blocked by his Doctore.

"Do not cause a scene. If you do that will only make things worse for her. Be patient and pray for her safety. Arturo goes with her, so be appeased in that at least."

There was nothing that was going to appease him while his woman, his heart, was in the presence of the monster parading as a man. There was wisdom in the words of his friend though, and so Cassian waited until he could no longer see Violetta or Arturo before he returned to his work.

"Give me something that I can hit, Doctore." He said, choking on wrath until Proximus joined him for a match. "Get ready to fight as though your life depended on it, for I wish to take a life this day."

CHAPTER 28

Violetta stood, numb, listening to Arturo argue with Lucius. This could not be happening. Vitus could not be here; in the place she was supposed to be safe. It had to be a nightmare. It could not be real. Arturo cursing in Greek brought her back to the present.

"Arturo I cannot help what the lanista demands. You may come with us, but the girl is coming upstairs at the command of her master. All your blustering and curses do not change what I have to do."

"I am not going to have that fool of a Roman disrupt my day and I certainly will not allow my student to be accosted." Arturo said with guttural growl that sounded remarkably like Cassian's.

As comforting as the sound was and as reassuring his presence would be, there was nothing that could make an audience with Vitus anything other that terrifying. She wanted to run and hide, as she had done in the first few years living in the house of his father. There were so many places in the ludus that she could hide, and Vitus would not be allowed to walk the halls to look for her.

The firm line of Julius Lucius' mouth told Violetta that she would not be allowed the childish indulgence she craved, even if she begged him. The monster would simply have to be faced. Since it was not possible to have Cassian at her side she would simply have to have faith that the two men that he trusted would keep her as safe as they were able in the presence of evil.

"Medicus this is unavoidable. Do not make a fuss and make this harder on everyone involved." The centurion said, as kindly as he was able when he was obviously frustrated.

She nodded and sighed to herself.

"Yes, of course. Vitus will not grow more patient and I do not think that the lanista will appreciate extending the time spent in his company either." She said, following his lead with a glance back to where Cassian stood upon the sands, watching her go with wild eyes.

"He can survive being without your attendance for the short time that we will be upstairs, Violetta." Arturo said in a low voice, for her ears only. "I will do my best to ensure that Vitus is kept in check. It may not be possible, for Tertius will do nearly anything to kiss the ass of men who he thinks can elevate him or this house, but I will try."

Violetta could not help smiling at his accurate description of the Roman while she followed her teacher and the centurion. The dread she felt was a weight on her shoulders, growing along with the volume of Vitus' voice. The sound was more obnoxious than she remembered, which was impressive, especially considering that she had spent her days in the company of men that would be considered the rudest and crudest in the republic.

Arturo turned to look her in the eye before they reached the door to the balcony.

"Remember, you are not a scared little waif any longer, Violetta." He said to her with a calmness she wanted to latch on to and hold tight to her heart. "You are a student of medicine. You do the will of the gods by saving lives, and you will have their knowledge in using herbs to take lives as well. You do not need to fear a little man with no future.”

He was right. The realization of what that could mean for her, in this house or that of Census should she ever return, washed over her as she followed Arturo and Julius Lucius onto the balcony to join the pair of Roman men. Lycithia had not yet joined them and Violetta wondered if the lanista’s wife, like so many women, had found a reasonable excuse to avoid Vitus’ company.

“Ah here is Lucius with the young medicus, and her instructor as well, of course.” Tertius said, but Violetta wondered if Arturo joining her threw his confidence or if there was some other plan that the presence of her instructor would affect?

“I recognize the guard of the gladiator but who is this one? I have never noticed him before.” Vitus said, rising to his feet to circle Arturo.

That kind of inspection, with the predatory look in Vitus’ eyes, had always been terrifying for Violetta. It was when he would pinch, probe and grope through the thin material of her dress. Usually these encounters would leave her in tears, but Arturo was standing calmly, as if nothing were happening. If she did not know better she would have guessed that her teacher was bored, he was so casual and detached, or so it seemed.

She knew better though.

He was taking in every aspect of Vitus’ persona. There were things that the druid could and would learn about the despicable Roman simply by how he walked, how he moved his head or how he second guessed himself before reaching out to touch Arturo. Every weakness and flaw that was possible to find would be discovered and ways would be found to use the information when it was most needed.

Violetta found herself curious as to what he would discern and, if like his reminder of her new skills, how it would change how she felt in his presence. Though she felt less fear now than she had, there was still something about the son of the man that owned her which set her every nerve on edge and made her want to hide safely away from his vicinity.

"That is my senior medicus, Arturo, a druid from Britannia that was captured with my champion, Cassian, years ago. He is of little interest to you I would think, Vitus." The lanista said, handing Vitus a cup of wine. "He was captured and sent into my house with a pair of instructions from his captor and proper master."

"And what might those be? That he not fight? Like the other barbarian? Or is it that he not be fucked? I am sure that command, or both, must leave you aching, either in coin purse or loins. He's an amazing specimen and they say the druidic barbarians possess magics. Do you?"

He directed the final question to Arturo who barely blinked his disregard for the question.

"What skills I have could hardly be called 'magic' except by the most foolish or children who do not know better." Arturo said at last with a calm, cool smile that was sure to agitate the Romans, and distract them from any plans of harassing her.

"I think your medicus just called me a fool Tiberius." Vitus said, sipping his wine with an arched brow.

He was glaring at Arturo, which would have sent shivers down Violetta's spine, but there was no doubt that her teacher held no fear of Vitus.

"I would say that he does not know better Vitus, but I will not lie to a man of your intelligence." Tertius stated, trying to get between the two men.

"You mean a man with his lack of intelligence. He could not possibly understand half of what I could say."

Vitus struck out at Arturo and Violetta cried a warning that could be heard around the villa and the yard, but it was unneeded. Arturo's raised his arm to block the blow from landing, and he took a step back to put himself out of reach of a second attempt.

"My captor in Rome takes a strong dislike to my being harmed. You should think hard before making such an attempt again."

Violetta had never heard him mention a captor in the city, certainly never in the capacity of being owned by the man. He never mentioned being a slave if he could help it, perhaps to deny that part of his reality. Even now he stood with all the confidence of a free warrior, a brilliant intellect among his inferiors.

"Celtic dog." Vitus snarled then joined Tertius closer to the rail. "Why not have the beast destroyed like the rabid animal he clearly is, or at least send him to the sands so that the gods can have their will done upon him?"

"I have been asking my husband that question for several years now, Vitus, and have yet to receive a satisfactory answer." Lycithia said, breezing into the room with Jovian in her wake.

Violetta noticed that her friend had been struck hard enough to leave marks on his face and arms. She could see that he had been crying and that his nose and lips had traces of blood around them. She tried to get his attention so see if he needed medical attention, but his eyes were cast to the ground until he made his way to the rail of the balcony where his face lit up in an adoring smile.

She knew just who he had seen to make him forget any pain he was feeling.

Argus.

Violetta knew her friend's joy because it mirrored her own each time that she saw Cassian or heard his voice when he called instructions to the newer men training with him on the sands.

"Lycithia you are a vision in the morning light." Vitus said with a smirk, stepping away from the slaves to greet the woman.

"Well, I thought that there ought to be some decoration, some proper decoration, when there is such an esteemed guest in out house." The woman said with a sniff of disdain in Violetta's direction.

While the Romans began to talk of the upcoming journey to Rome, who they would see and what they hoped to accomplish, Violetta joined Jovian at the edge of the balcony to watch their men training against each other while Proximus and Cirandon each coached one of the competitors.

"Are you alright? Are you badly hurt?" She whispered, letting her finger touch his hand. "Do you require my attentions? I have a few supplies in our room if you do."

"Gratitude.

"I am well enough. I will explain things later, Violetta." He whispered back. "I want to watch them, since I do not know if I will get to see it much longer. What if he does not come back from Rome? What if he is killed in the great Circus and I have not had the chance to be with him, to cheer for him with the other voices of a crowd? What will I do then, with my broken heart?"

Her heart ached for him and her mind raced with ideas of how she might be able to help him achieve the greatest desire of his heart. Though Argus was improving each day there was no way to know if he would be good enough to best his opponent on the sands when the day finally came. Violetta thought about how she would feel if it were her, if she were to be left behind while Cassian went on to fight without the chance of a final farewell between them. She had to do something to help him and Argus have a chance to be together at least one time.

"What if I can find a way to help you into the wagon so that you can come with us? It would not be the most private or comfortable, but it would put you within an arm's reach of the one you love. Would you take the chance?"

He turned his head to give her a soft, but hopeful, smile.

"You would help me to join the journey to Rome? Violetta? That could place you in danger as well. Dominus' wrath would be horrible, Domina her would be a monster of rage. She does not want me there. I think she is worried that my parents would see me, would want me back."

"Why would she care about the desires of slaves? If she hates you so much I would think that she would want you to be gone from this house." Violetta replied with a quick glance over her shoulder to make sure that they were not being watched by the Romans. "She should want you to go so that they ask their Dominus to buy you."

Jovian shook his head and leaned close to whisper very softly.

"My parents, at least one of them, is a Roman Violetta, and one that she knew well enough to take me from while she was in her elevated social circle in Rome. My mother, I think, was someone of great importance and Domina does want her to see how I have been treated."

Violetta was not sure if he was telling the complete truth or if he, like many children with missing parents, was simply creating a fantasy to ease the pain of his rejection. It was obvious that he believed what he was saying, so she smiled and kissed his cheek.

"I will do whatever I can to help you find the chance you desire with Argus and the opportunity to find your parents in Rome."

CHAPTER 29

The moment of peaceful companionship was shattered when Vitus place one hand on her shoulder and the other on Jovian's.

"What are you two doves whispering about over here?" Vitus said, rubbing his thumb up and down Violetta's arm with possessive suggestion. "Concocting ideas of sweet pleasures? Or simply sharing memories of the same?"

Violetta had thought that she would be braver but his salacious suggestion and lecherous touch here where she had been safe from such things was as unsettling as it was disgusting. She wanted to speak, to say something that would make him walk away and leave them in peace, but she could not find her voice.

"We have no such memories to share, Dominus." Jovian said, turning the face the Roman with the smile and voice he used in his flirtations. "A plain looking thing such as her would never be put to such use in a house where form and beauty are prized above all. Look at how she cowers, her bones sticking out of sundried flesh."

He turned the man back to Lycithia and the lanista.

"When there is a gem of the city, such as my Domina, among us how could any man lust after such a skinny bird, unless he favors a touch with slightly more strength though just as soft and pleasing?"

Violetta could hardly believe that he would make such an offer the man he knew to be a monster simply to save her from his debauchery. He must truly desire the trip to Rome above all things.

"And what sort of things do you do in this house, pretty boy?" Vitus asked, letting Jovian lead him away from Violetta who was still too in shock to move.

She did not hear what her friend replied but turned to look down at the sand. Searching for Cassian's face, hoping to find strength and comfort in his eyes, Violetta found that his face was a storm of worry and wrath. He must have heard her cry out and thought that the Roman hurt her or had tried to. His face looked as though he was ready to kill the next man that he came against.

She wanted to sooth him, wipe the rage away with a stroke of her hand. He was fire and death, only soothed by the taking of a life or the touch of her hand. Watching him take his frustration out on the men around him, frustration that he could not help her the way he wanted, have her the way he needed, tugged at her heart. Violetta wanted, more than anything, to ease his life, ease the pain that he felt. How could that happen when Vitus was determined to destroy the bond between them, or simply destroy them utterly?

Finally, he looked up. His golden-brown eyes met hers for a moment and she flashed him a hopeful smile. There was no other way to tell him that she was safe, despite the presence of Vitus.

A nod and soft wave of her fingers was all that she had time for before the Centurion drew her away from the edge.

"Come, medicus. I dislike this task but, you are to give a display for the son of the merchant so that he can report of your training and treatment to his father."

"No. Lucius please. I cannot let him touch me again. Is there nothing to be done to stop it? He hurts me and he likes it." She pleaded in a whisper.

Understand of what she meant washed over his face and Violetta was surprised to see that the idea of her being so roughly abused upset the Roman guard.

"He will not have that chance, medicus." He replied carefully, through gritted teeth. "It is your training with the druid, which makes you more valuable and unique, that the pissant wishes to see."

There was some peace to be found in that explanation, though the lack of injury made it difficult to think of how she was to give an accurate demonstration.

"Dominus." She addressed the trio of Romans with a bowed head. She was sure that Lycithia would be either glaring at her angrily for drawing attention away from her or have that look of utter disdain that was meant to remind her of their difference in station and how worthless the other woman considered Violetta to be. "How can I offer my services to your pleasure?"

"Vitus would like a demonstration of the results of your lessons here, my dear." Tertius said with a smile.

The endearment from the lanista's lips made Violetta want to cringe. Like slime between her toes, his words and false sentiment disgusted her.

"What can I do to offer such demonstration Dominus?" She asked, hoping her unease could not be heard in her voice.

"I think it will suffice to see you tend a mortal wound." Vitus said with a laugh.

"Apologies. No one here has such an injury." Violetta said, shaking her head.

The Roman monster grinned, took up the knife from the table where Tertius had been breaking his night's fast and slashed it across Arturo's stomach.

"There is now." Vitus said, setting down the knife and taking a drink of wine.

"Save his life. Save him with your newly learned skills and impress me." He said, sitting down with a casual amusement. "Well? Proceed, medicus."

Violetta could not breathe. Could not think. The blood was starting to seep through Arturo's fingers and all she could do was stare at the wound. Vitus had injured Arturo, and no one was going to do anything to him?

How could this be allowed?

"Violetta?" Arturo gasped, pulling her attention back to the present. "Do not overthink it. You know what to do. Forget that it is me and fulfill your task, quickly, please."

He sank to his knees, pale and clutching his wound. When he blinked up at her, trying to speak through his pain, Violetta moved to act.

"Lucius, pressure on the wound, please. Jovian, go and get my kit from our room. Hurry please." Violetta said, stepping into the role that she had been training for.

She eased her teacher onto his back and took over from Lucius, praying that Jovian arrived soon. There was more blood than she had expected, and everything was faster, more urgent than she had anticipated. She had to stop thinking about the potential loss of a friend, and about the Roman audience in this twisted game that they were playing with lives. The only thing that she needed to focus on was saving the life of her patient.

"Violetta." The druid whispered, clutching her hand. "You can do this. Remember what I taught you, forget the patient and focus on the medicine. You are capable."

"Here are your things, Violetta." Jovian said, returning to the balcony and putting the small satchel down beside her before Tertius pulled him to his side. "Save him."

"On your own, girl." The lanista said with a wicked smile on his face.

They had planned this, to harm Arturo, and they had all walked right into it blindly.

There was no time to think about that or to think of what she could say to the men in the ludus below to explain it, she had to save him first.

The wound was clean and precise which made the medicine simple. Violetta tuned out the chatter of the Romans, the whispered prayers of the Centurion and began to work. Every piece of advice that Arturo had given her ran through her mind. As did the lessons, the hours of practice and the quiet observations that he had made to her while they had both watched the men training upon the sands was running through her mind and out through her fingers.

Stitches and bandages were soon in place and though her dress was stained red with blood that had pooled on the ground, there was no more seeping from Arturo's body. All that she needed now was for him to open his eyes and speak, confirm her victory over the wound and the vicious act of Vitus.

The silence was deafening, even the men below had stopped their combat making Violetta wonder if they had been told what had happened. She looked at Julius and then Jovian who gave a slight nod.

He had said something to someone so that the gladiators knew. They were all waiting for Arturo to wake, to survive.

She wished that she could tell them all that the wound was not deep, there was no reason she could think of that he would not wake up unless she had miscalculated the amount of blood loss.

"Arturo? Can you hear me? Wake up and come back to us, please?" She whispered, checking his pulse, and squeezing his hand. "Wake up. I know that you can."

"Have you failed so deeply that you have killed your instructor?" Vitus laughed, weighing the knife in his hand. "You have no business in this place unless it be upon your back. I should take the waif back with me now. She is utterly useless."

"You will do no such thing, Vitus." Lycithia hissed over Violetta's head. "The agreement was made with your father, not you. As long as Felix lives you do not have the authority to break the agreement, besides, you have injured our medicus. Despite her training not being completed, the girl is all we have tending to our stock. She certainly will not be leaving until the druid is well or replaced."

"My wife is correct. Lucius, return the druid and his student to the infirmary. Jovian, go with them and return to me the moment he awakens." Tertius said, with what looked like a slight nervousness in his eyes.

"Yes, Dominus. I will have a stretcher brought to carry him." Lucius replied, then quickly left the balcony.

Violetta wondered if the lanista were worried that if somehow Vitus was able to convince his father that Tertius had offered a great insult to their house the invitation to Rome would be retracted. How would he react if she told him that Felix would take the word of most of his house slaves more seriously than he took the word of the son he despised?

If it were Selenia before them it would be a very real fear that she could change the old man's mind if she wanted to, Vitus was almost nothing.

"I will make sure that Jovian brings you word of his waking the very moment that his eyes are open, Dominus." Violetta said with a bow of her head as the guard returned with the stretcher and men to carry it.

"Yes. I wish to know immediately." Tertius said with a frown.

"Load him carefully, please." She said, doing her best to ignore the fuming Vitus while her instructor was loaded to safety on the canvas stretcher. "Your words, my will, Dominus."

They made their way carefully to the infirmary. The stairs from the villa to the ludus were more difficult than Violetta expected but the guards were as careful with Arturo as they might have been with one of their own. Their care made her wonder how many times Arturo had taken care of their illnesses as well as the gladiators that he was charged with? They had always seemed to fear him, so she had never thought that they might be his patients as well.

"Please, put him down on that table." Violetta pointed to the lower of the wooden slabs. "Jovian, you may sit where you like. Julius Lucius? Will you tell Doctore that I cannot return to the sands until Arturo is awake."

"Yes, Medicus. He will want to know how the druid fares as soon as possible, as will I."

She looked up at him, there was something different in his tone. His long, angular face was a mix of frustration and concern. Violetta wondered if he was one of those rare Romans that disliked the enslavement of others.

"Julius?" She said his given name softly after his fellow guards had left the room. "Do you have slaves of your own at home? Did you grow up with them?"

She noticed that Jovian lifted his head from where he was looking at Arturo's surgical tools, curiosity on his pretty face to hear the answer from the handsome man that he seemed to admire.

"My father did not believe in such things." Julius said calmly. "Nor do I. I have felt the sting of a master's whip in my life Violetta. Never would I lift my hand in such a way against another or seek to call another man, or woman, my possession. Those who do are lacking something in their soul."

"You guard them though, help the oppressors to keep their slaves." Violetta said feeling confused. "How can you act in such a way that is opposite your belief?"

A dark cloud passed across his face and she worried that she had offended him.

"Because there has to be someone who sees it. Who bears witness to it all. I try to do anything that I can to make things easier, when I find the chance."

He reached out and caressed the top of her head as though she were a child.

"We are not all monsters, Violetta. I know it may be hard for you to believe, but some of us are good men. Vitus, though, will never stand among us, we know what he is. The coward will be cast out by his peers one day."

"I hope that I live to see that day, Julius." Violetta said with a sad smile.

"As do I, young Medicus. As do I." He nodded and left her and Jovian alone with their thoughts.

CHAPTER 30

Cassian was doing everything that he could to maintain his control. Why must the Romans test his restrain at every breath? What could Arturo have done to Vitus to have deserved the wound from that demon in a man's skin?

He should have killed the Roman piece of shit when he'd had the chance in Census' villa. Then none of this would have happened…including Violetta's presence in the infirmary.

Damn the man. He had to influence everything in Cassian's life now that she was at the heart of everything he wanted.

Would there ever be a day when the name Census was not a thought for either of them? When those bastards were nothing more than a fading memory, easily forgotten with the touch of a hand or a kiss?

There were very few things in this life that he wanted as much as he wanted to be free of the curse of that name. He would not sacrifice Violetta or the depth of their bond, but anything else that he could do to separate them, not him, but them, from that place, he would give if it would make it so.

He wanted to go to the infirmary and sit by Arturo, wait for the man to wake and comfort Violetta at the same time. He was grateful that Cirandon had told him what he knew about the events that brought the druid to the infirmary, but he wanted to be told by those that were present what had happened.

He wanted to know how it came to be that a man who had never raised his voice let alone his hand was injured in the company of the lanista who owned the men the druid spent years saving from the depths of Hades. He wanted to wring the lanista's neck until the words fell from his gasping lips or beat it from Julius Lucius who was supposed to guard Arturo with the same care he took with Cassian's well-being.

Instead he was training.

He was always training.

Training for battles in a war that he would never win.

Testing his skill against men that he knew he could best. Before he ever met them he knew that he could defeat them, because he knew one simple thing that they did not.

Cassian knew, without a breath of doubt, that he would not die as a slave in the arena of this small town so far from his home.

He glanced at the balcony and the silk clad monsters that stood gazing down at them all as though they were animals, as if they were mindless cattle, and a spark of rebellion lit in his heart. They deserved to die, each of them, for this and countless other acts. He was capable, maybe even expected, to lead such a rebellion and regain his freedom. He knew it and so did every being withing these walls. The only question was, would the risk of such a thing be worth the chance?

Could he risk all their lives for the chance to live?

Yes.

Once he had secured Violetta to the house of Tertius then he would begin his plan to find freedom for all of them. Gladiators, even the new recruits that were half trained, were more deadly than the soldiers in the ludus. It would not be hard to overpower the lot of them and escape into the hills.

They would simply take the clothing of the Romans and set fire to the ludus as well as the villa.

No one would be looking for slaves that should have died, locked in their cells while their master's property burned to ash. They would be able to return to their homes, with coin in pocket and the sweet taste of freedom on their lips. Take ships, travel the roads, with no one hunting them. They would move through the empire like insects and find their way home.

He would take Violetta to his homeland and, before his family and the people of his tribe, he would wed her according the customs of his people and make her his wife, his Queen. They would live their lives free of the commands of other and build a family, with children that would never know the sting of the lash.

He grinned to himself and spun the weapons in his hands. His thoughts were focused on the way that he would feel when he made this dream a reality. When he stood over the corpse of Tiberius Tertius and his bitch of a wife it would be a good day, but if the day came when he could laugh down at the dead face of Vitus Census it would be one of the best days of his life.

That day would never come while he was a gladiator in the house of a lowly lanista in Velletri, so he had to pass these foolish tests of skill and patience, for now. He would bide his time and watch for the opportunity he needed. He swore to his gods and those of the Romans that before he left the Republic he would find a way to look down on the dying face of Vitus and smile.

"Tertius." Vitus called from the balcony. "Since I am here on my father's behalf I should have better news to report than that the girl can do stitches. Have the big man, no, the trainer, fight against my father's choice for Rome."

"Vitus? The Doctore does not face the men and steel is only used upon the sands. I do not ever have it used upon the training sands. It is too dangerous."

"I want to see that the man has risen higher than those that taught him. If he is going to fight upon the same sands as the champions of the Rome, against the best men in the Republic, then I want to see for myself what he is capable of. Now."

"Now I must fight against my brother, my teacher, to amuse that piece of shit? Just to pass their test. A test that will send me to Rome to fight another man, to take another life." Cassian growled.

"Still tongue, Cassian." Cirandon said firmly.

Cassian looked at him. They had not lifted blades against each other since the day before Nala died. It was with the claim of consoling the injured pride of a young man that Nala had come to his cell that night while her husband was being celebrated in the villa by the lanista and his supporters. She had brought a more potent wine than he had ever had before, proper Roman wine, and reminded him of how close he had come to victory.

That reminder, which was meant to comfort, had also carried an unseen threat he had not realized until years later. She had seen him not as a friend, but as a threat to Cirandon's station as Champion of the house. Her plan had slipped past Cassian, who was besotted with the older woman and wracked with guilt over lusting after the wife of his friend, his teacher. He had never thought that she could mean him harm and struggled now with the memory that she had meant to kill him.

He had not crossed steel with Cirandon since that match because he worried that his guilt might allow an injury to take place that would only deepen the guilt of one of them.

"Dominus? To do such a thing would be foolish. If I were to injure Cirandon then who would train the men and if he were to injure me, which stands more likely, then what of the match in Rome? Who would fight for the house of Census and for…other causes?"

"Does his whining on behalf of that little bitch never cease? It seems as though that is all I hear talk of. It would almost be better if my father would sell the girl and see her removed from the city and the thoughts of all those within its circle."

Cassian could feel the blood drain from his face and his hands tightened around the swords in his hands. He wanted to scream. This could not happen. They had been through so much because of that piece of shit. Too much.

He had to do something to secure Violetta as a permanent part of this house before they left for Rome. If the lanista would not agree then Cassian would not fight, would not go to Rome. It did not matter that he had dreamed of fighting in the great Circus Maximus since he had taken the title of Champion of the house of Tertius. He would give up that dream if it were what it took to convince the lanista to buy Violetta.

She had to be here, under this roof, when he made his fight for freedom. If she were anywhere else then there would be a chance that he might not be able to find her, to save her.

This had to go his way, which meant that the Romans needed to think that it was going their way.

"Cirandon?" He rarely used the man's given name and never in front of the lower ranking men, but this was a different situation. "Join me in putting on a show, Doctore?"

"Because it is you who asks, if our Dominus allows it, I will gladly cross true blades with you again."

Cassian knew the lanista well enough to know that he was weighing the risks against the advantage. He could practically see the thoughts running through his mind. He was worried that his champion would be injured and unable to perform in Rome in less than a fortnight or that his Doctore, the man who shaped the skill of every man that fought upon the sands in his name, would be permanently injured and unable to carry on that unique task.

Some men could fight in the arena, only half of them could win, less than a quarter of them would ever come close to the title of champion, but less than that number were the men that were able to achieve all of that and teach others to do the same. If one man in a hundred had what it took to become a champion, then one man in a hundred champions could become a Doctore.

"Dominus. If the son of Felix Census wants to see a match between the two most well-known gladiators of your house then who are we to deny him such a sight, even if he is unable to comprehend the skill involved."

Cassian ignored the warning glare from Cirandon and continued, his eyes locking with Vitus.

"If the lowest man in Velletri can bear witness to the greatest fights in the Republic for mere coins then why not let the son of a mere merchant enjoy the show? Since stabbing your senior medicus was not thrilling enough, why not allow the greater entertainment?"

"See Tertius? Even your wild dog understands the value in entertaining the wishes of your ally." Vitus laughed, which made Cassian want to stuff his fist down his throat and rip out his heart.

"Dominus." Cirandon spoke at last. "It will not take long to remind Cassian why I am the Doctore and he is only a gladiator, a champion, but still a gladiator."

"Then see it done." The lanista said, sipping his wine and still looking nervous.

It was moments later that there was the weight of real steel in his hands and Cassian was stepping onto the sand to face his instructor. He could remember a time when this had been his greatest desire; to face the once great Cirandon and prove himself the best in the city. Now he knew that there was no honor in such a thing, and it had been pride, and pride alone that had craved it.

"I give you my word that I will do my best not to bring you any injury, old friend." Cassian said quietly, taking his beginning stance.

"If you hold back the lanista will know and he will think that we have mocked his command." Cirandon countered, rotating the weapon he had once wielded with complete supremacy. "Do your best, I hold no concern. We will promise each other that there is to be no loss of life or of limb.”

“Agreed.” Cassian nodded and waited for the word to strike.

“Begin.”

There was no chance to hold back, no moment to consider his opponent. Cirandon began the match with a brutal assault that gave Cassian no choice except to fight back at full strength. The Romans watching were forgotten, as were the other men of the ludus. This match was between the two great warriors with the spectre of death waiting on the sidelines on the chance that one of them would lose control.

The steel sang out and the men moved to its rhythm. There was no falseness or pretence to the match. They may as well have been on the sands of the arena with the roar of the crowd echoing around them.

Cassian had never fought against someone who anticipated his every move. If he wanted to win, to have to victory needed to impress his audience then he needed to do something that Cirandon had not taught him, even if it was dangerous. A quick spin with his weapons backwards, meant to disarm and distract, was something that he had learned from his father.

Cassian thought that Cirandon would block the pair of blades but be distracted enough that he could be tripped, land on his back and thus end the contest. He never thought that the blows would land, embedding the steel tips deep into the muscle of Cirandon’s thigh.

What had he just done?

CHAPTER 31

"Kill him. Claim the victory!" Vitus yelled from the balcony.

Cassian looked up to see Vitus and the lanista, as well as his wife, staring down at the sands. Their faces were full of surprise but not one of them had concern for the life of the man bleeding on the sands.

"I will do no such thing. This was not a proper contest but a match only for the amusement of the merchant's son." Cassian called up to Tertius. "Dominus, there is no need for death here. The injury itself was an accident and he needs the medicus or there will be nothing further to debate."

"Come Tertius, he is only a slave, besides is that not what you have trained the girl you spirited away from my father's house." Vitus said with a laugh.

"Tiberius? You have the man from Rome that could easily take his place if needed. Proximus is just as well reputed as Cirandon. If it is better business to let the man go." Lycithia added.

Cassian could not believe what he was hearing, instead he gestured to a few of the gladiators to pick up their teacher and head towards the infirmary. Damn the man for allowing this to happen. If Cirandon were to die then the weight of it would be on Cassian's shoulders for the rest of his life. Just as the weight of Nala's death, though it was not at his hand, still weighed on him.

"Violetta?!" He bellowed, shouldering the door open. "Cirandon's leg, two steel gladii'. Help him? Please?"

He could not remember asking a woman for help with such desperation, but there had never been a woman since his mother that he had trusted so completely.

"Cassian?" Violetta looked up from the herbs she was tending in the window. "Steel? How did this happen? Why was there steel used?"

She rushed to the table where the gladiators laid their teacher on his back. The concern on her face did not ease the worry in Cassian's gut.

"Any man that does not need to be here should leave. I need space and he will need peace to recover." Violetta said in a voice so firm and confident that Cassian could not help a half smile.

"Get out, all of you." Cassian growled, standing next to Cirandon's head. He looked at Jovian, who was staring at the blood soaking the bandages that Violetta was quickly pressing to the wound. "If you aren't going to help her then get out. There is no need for an audience here."

"Cassian I would help if I could." The boy stammered awkwardly. "I do not have the training for this."

"Then get out."

"It is alright Jovian. You can come back to check on Arturo for the report required from Dominus." Violetta added to his command.

Cassian was staring at the wound and the swift work that Violetta was doing to mend it. Once the door closed he waited a few moments before speaking.

"You can save him? Arturo has taught you how to do this?" He asked her, looking up to meet her eyes. "Tell me that you can do this, Violetta."

"Come hold this bandage tight so that it slows the blood flow." She replied, turning to put a blade into the fire. "The would is deep and his lack of consciousness is worrisome, but I can do this. With your help I can do this."

Cassian gripped the fabric that was working as a tourniquet and watched Violetta burn and stitch Cirandon's wound closed. It was like a magic to see her at work. Her fingers moved quickly, confidently, to form stitches so fine that he could barely see them. Even Arturo was not as skilled with the needle as she was.

"You are quite skilled at this, Violetta. I stand impressed." He said, flashing her a smile.

"Gratitude, but stand a little to your left so that the light is better, please?" She teasingly replied with a wink. "The skill with the needle comes from years of with silks, but the skill mending flesh was the lessons of Arturo."

"Never did I think that you would be using those lessons upon my flesh, Violetta, but I am glad you are as devout a student as you are an acolyte." Arturo said from the table, with a groan.

"Arturo?" Cassian said with a grin at the sound of his friend's voice. "It is about time you woke up. There is no time for napping while the son of Census is in the villa."

"I am glad to see you too, both of you." The druid said, reaching to touch Violetta. "What is the injury and course of treatment?"

"Shallow stab wound with the tip of both Cassian's gladius. It would not have been dangerous had it not been so close to the artery. I have almost finished the stitches." She said, without looking up from Cirandon's leg.

Cassian was impressed with the intensity of her focus. It was a whole new side to her that amazed and intrigued him. She was capable of so much more than anyone in her life had ever considered, perhaps even himself.

"She worked fast to seal the wound. You would be proud."

"I certainly stand such or lay as the case may be." Arturo said with a chuckle that ended with a wince. "I had actually been inquiring after my own health. What happened on that balcony?"

Cassian was grateful that the druid had asked the very question that was weighing on his own mind. All he knew was that Vitus had wielded the blade that caused the injury and that the lanista had not so much as raised his voice in protest.

Once she finished the final touches to Cirandon's leg both Arturo and Cassian listened while she told the tale of what had happened. The gladiator's hatred for the man was growing with every word from her beautiful mouth.

"Why in Hades do they want you dead? If the lanista does not want you here why does he not send you to Rome and whoever this mysterious man he claims is the one who owns you." Cassian snarled, pacing the small room.

"The man in Rome does not want me in his house, that is why I am here. We have an understanding." Arturo said, laying his head back on the table.

"Who is it?" Violetta asked, moving from Cirandon to check Arturo's wound. "Why would you have an understanding with a Roman?"

"So that I could be where Cassian is, since he is the reason that I was in the battle that saw us both captured. I made a deal with him so that our fates were bound together, so that we would be together now matter what happened."

"That is a noble thing." Violetta said, adjusting the bandage and looking up at Cassian.

"You never told me that." Cassian said, stepping over to the table and look down at his friend. "You could have been in Rome all this time? With soldiers? With intellectuals? And you stayed in this pisshole with me?"

"You are worth every miserable moment, my prince." The druid said, making Cassian smile while cringing internally.

"I have asked you not to call me that, Priest." He replied, clasping his hand. "Now I will have to explain that title to a certain young medicus who is staring at us both as though we have the three heads of the Hydra."

"It is not a title one hears often in the Republic." She said with a small smile and the lightest blush on her cheeks.

"Well…Now that your instructor is awake I might take you to your cell for a conversation that requires some privacy."

"Do not let Cirandon and I stop you." Arturo said with a save of his hand and a shared glance with Cassian.

"I appreciate the assistance, as always, old friend."

Taking Violetta's hand, he tugged her out of the infirmary despite her protests that there was still work to be done and that her patients needed to be watched over.

"Woman." He said closing the door of the room that was her cell behind him and pulling her tight to his chest. "The men in that room have seen more blood and injuries than you can imagine. They are fine and we are within the call of a voice if you are needed…there."

He could feel the soft cushion of her breasts through the thin linen of her dress and wanted to simply rip the laces, push the fabric away then shed his subligaria before seducing her body right there against the wall.

There was something so arousing about watching the woman he loved mend the bloodied flesh with her newly grown confidence. He had fallen in love with the frightened girl but when he saw the woman she was growing into he fell all over again. The damn Romans were the only thing in the way of him showing her that, every single night.

He wanted to bare his soul to her, tell her every dark secret he had ever had and hear hers as well. Cassian wanted to know who she had been before the bastards of the house of Census had tried to break her spirit. To hold her and listen to the stories of her youth. He would learn all there was to know about her while he planned the future that they would have together once they were free of the will of the Roman bastards that played games with their lives.

"Cassian? You said you would tell me why Arturo calls you his prince." Violetta said, placing a hand on his cheek that he could not help leaning into.

"He calls me that because, at home, in Britannia, that is who I am, or who I was." He said, turning his head to kiss her wrist and her palm. "My father is a Chieftain, sometimes called a king. The druid served our people and so he calls me that, particularly when he wishes to remind me of how he thinks that I should think of myself or how I should behave."

"I can see you as a warrior prince." She said with that smile that struck his heart like a dart. "What does it mean: how he thinks you should think of yourself?"

Cassian pressed a kiss to her cheeks and smiled against her skin when she gasped.

"It means when he thinks I am being a savage and he wants me to be rational or tactical at the least." He chuckled, wrapping his arms around her waist and pulled her closer. "He forgets that the violence that keeps me alive and the savagery makes me the best."

She looked up at him, leaned her small frame against him in a way that suggested her desire was as strong as his own and placed her hand on his chest.

"What else does your savagery help you with? Prince?" She whispered, pressing her lips to the base of his throat.

"Careful woman. Release the beast and you could find yourself utterly ravaged." He said, sliding a hand beneath the fabric of her dress to rest on her backside.

He wanted her so badly he could taste her. The nights they had been kept apart seemed like an eternity. It was worse, in some ways, than when they had been in different houses. To have her so close and not be allowed to touch her was a new torture he was not prepared for.

"Perhaps that is my wish?" She replied, pressing a trail of kisses across his chest. "I have missed your touch Cassian. Why did they bring us here simply to keep us apart again?"

"I wish that I had that answer for you, Violetta." Cassian replied, slowly sinking to the ground to sit against the door and pull her into his lap. "The only answer that I have is that they seek to test my control and my obedience by setting you, once again, as my prize."

"Is that how you see me? Champion?" She asked him, turning her body to straddle his hips, and slowly shed her dress from her shoulders to reveal her breasts. "Am I a prize?"

She amazed him. The sexuality that had teased below the surface of her demure timidity was blossoming along with her confidence in her training. She was so sensual, so innocently erotic that he had to hold back his need for her, despite her bold words.

"You, my priestess, are so much more than a prize."

He slid his hand from her backside to rest on her hip and allow his thumb to rub the sweet spot of nerves and bring her to the height of arousal. When she rolled her hips against his touch Cassian captured her mouth in a kiss filled with all the passion that he had been forced to hold back on the nights without her, the longing and desire that was for no other woman but her.

"You, my love, are so much more than a gladiator."

When she pressed her lips to his in a fevered kiss, Cassian pushed the rough material of his subligaria aside and gripped her hips with both hands. With only the slightest shift of both their bodies his cock slid home between her thighs.

Violetta gasped and when her head rolled back Cassian felt her hair dance across the backs of his hands where he held her body tight against his own. The feeling was as luxurious as it was erotic. Never would he allow for her hair to be cut and he would beg for her to never bind it tightly in braids so that he could touch it any time she would let him, just as he wanted to touch all of her every chance that he was given.

Her beautiful body was moving with him, her slender hips rolling to meet his thrusts deep into her core. Cassian was about to move so that he could lay her on her back and pound his passions frustration into her welcoming heat when she put her hands upon his shoulders and leaned into his chest to whisper in his ear.

"Lay back. Hold my hand and let me show you."

He eased himself back on the floor, took her hand and put the other on her hip as his sweet little priestess began to ride his cock with a wild and passionate frenzy. Her body moved, rolled, rose, and fell with a tempo that left the gladiator mindlessly floating in a sea of ecstasy.

His shaft throbbed with the need for release and he could feel Violetta's core tightening around him. Her body was trembling within the throws of her frenzy, so he tightened his grip on her hip and whispered to her.

"Let go, Violetta. I will guide us both."

Her answer was a wordless moan that thrilled him as she firmly planted her hands on his chest. Both of his hands on her hips, thundering his cock into her core, Cassian inhaled the scent of her hair as it fell around them like a curtain.

"Cassian, I…oh gods." Violetta cried, suddenly arching her back and clasping her hands over his as she shattered in release.

It was a few moments later that he allowed his own body to give in to the most primal need. Pulling her down as he drove up in one final thrust, Cassian called her name as he poured himself into his woman.

"Violetta, no matter how long they keep us parted, I love you." He whispered, kissing the top of her head, and wrapping his arms around her as she nestled against his chest. "For all time."

CHAPTER 32

Jovian left the infirmary and closed the door behind him. What was he to do? He could not return to Dominus without the information that he wanted, but he did not have it to give.

Most of the men had returned to training while they waited for Cirandon to reappear, but, as he snuck a peek around the doorway, he saw that Argus was not among those on the sands.

Where was he?

The boy began, slowly, to search the halls and cells for Argus. He wanted to see him, even if it was just for a few minutes. The German's eyes had been haunting his dreams since they last spoke. He had to see the sparkling green shining at him the way it did when he laughed.

Jovian wanted to be the one that made him laugh, that made him blush and stammer. He wanted to be the source of joy in Argus's life and the subject of his fantasies, as the gladiator was for him already.

"Argus? Are you here?" He said, stepping into one of the darker corridors. "It is Jovian. I was told to leave the infirmary and I could not go out onto the sands alone. I came to find you."

"And find me you did." The familiar voice said from the shadows. Argus stepped into the dim light with a raised eyebrow. "Why did you come looking for me? Does Dominus grow bored and send you to the ludus or will there be guards coming to tear you away again?"

"No one is coming. I am to wait until Arturo wakes and report his condition to Dominus. Until he wakes there is nowhere I am required to be." He said with a teasing smile, leaning against the doorframe.

"And why, exactly, are you not still in the infirmary? Should you not be in the company of the young medicus? You share a room now, surely you share each other's time as well?"

He was jealous of Violetta? If Argus' face were not so serious Jovian would have laughed. It was inconceivable that the girl could mean more to him than the man that haunted his dreams.

It was foolish to even suggest it.

How could he think this?

"No Argus. I have no wish to spend all hours of the day with Violetta. Being forced to spend my nights in her company is enough for me. Cassian told me to leave the room and not come back until Julius Lucius came to find me, so of course I came to find you."

His heart raced when the gladiator reached to touch his cheek.

"You have no special attachment to the girl? You do not share a bed?"

Jovian shook his head. He did not want to mention the one attempt that he had made. It would upset his gladiator and bring the wrath of Cassian down on his head. Violetta would never tell anyone so the lie would be a secret kept between them.

"There is only one, in all the ludus, that I wish to share my bed with, and he stands before me this very minute." He said, staring adoringly up into the face that appeared in his dreams every night.

"That is a forward thing to say, Jovian." Argus said with a smile. "And I had thought you to possess all the manners of a proper Roman."

"Such things are in my possession, though they have little need in the ludus. I have thoughts towards more base impulses when I am here."

It might be forward and almost dangerous to flirt so boldly, but the chances to do so were so few and far between that he felt he had to make the most of this opportunity.

"What base impulses are you inspired to pursue down here in the depths of darkness and depravity?" Argus asked, rubbing the pad of his thumb across Jovian's lips. "I might be able to assist you in achieving your goal."

"You are my goal Argus. To be the kind of man that you might desire is what I want, almost as strongly as I wish to be a gladiator, like my father before me."

"You are the son of a gladiator?"

"That is what Dominus has always told me. My mother is the wife of a wealthy and powerful Roman, but my father was the gladiator Saif. He died in the arena shortly after I was born." He said proudly. He had treasured that story ever since he was a small child. Jovian was not sure that he had the courage to become a gladiator like his father, he was, however, sure that he would always be proud of who he was and who his father was.

"I have heard of Saif." Argus said, sounding impressed with Jovian's lineage. "I did not know that he had fathered any children. You should tell the gladiators. They would not be so quick to mock you if they knew."

"I think that I am the only one. He fought in Rome so perhaps while we are there I will be able find out. Find someone that knew him." Jovian said with a dreamy smile, reaching out to touch Argus' arm. "I will also get to see you fight and cheer you on to victory."

"You are coming with us to Rome?" Argus gripped Jovian by the shoulders. "This is joyous news. Do you travel with Dominus or in the wagon?"

"Violetta has agreed to help me hide in the wagon. I shall be with you upon the road." His voice was full of excitement. He had not dared to hope that Argus would be this pleased. It meant so much and yet there was now the danger that the guards might hear him speak of it and report to Dominus, which would see the plan ruined. "In truth, Dominus does not know, and I do not intend that he should until it is too late to turn back and return me to the villa."

"That is dangerous Jovian. He will be furious with you when he finds out that you have lied to him. How will you explain yourself?"

Argus sounded genuinely concerned for his safety. Jovian had not thought about the lanista's reaction to his presence being anything other than one of great joy. Since it was his wife that had declared that the favored slave would not be allowed to join the journey the boy had thought that his master would be pleased to see that he had found a way around the angry woman.

"I will simply say that I did not wish to be parted from his company for so many days." Jovian said, shrugging his shoulders and taking Argus' hand. "He need not know that it is your company that I do not wish to be parted from."

"As much as I feel the same, Jovian, I would not want you to risk the wrath of those upstairs. Domina will be dangerously wrathful."

They both knew, as did the entire house, that Lycithia had some special hatred for him that was a mystery to all. Jovian wondered if there was some offence he had committed as a child that had caused her to hate him so vehemently.

"You are worth the risk Argus. I ask that you keep this secret and let me worry about the Romans."

The look of worry on Argus's face made Jovian want to kiss away each concern. He wanted to see his eyes lit up with joy instead of shadowed with dark thoughts.

"I will worry, regardless." Argus said.

"Then let me give you something to distract you." Jovian said, reaching up to draw Argus down to him.

The gladiator did not resist and there was a flash of excitement in his eyes that Jovian did not miss before their lips connected. Perhaps he had waited for this moment for as long as Jovian had.

When their lips touched there was a sudden jolt that scorched through Jovian's entire body, unlike anything he had ever felt before. How was it that this man, this rough and rugged, violent man, was the one to spark this feeling deep inside him?

Was this what love felt like? Was he in love or falling in love with the gladiator he had been lusting for? Could that be possible?

He slid his hands around the firmness of Argus's torso while the German cupped his face, his thumbs stroking Jovian's cheeks while their lips connected carefully, with tentative passion. Jovian held on tight, pressing his body tight against Argus'. He wanted to commit the feeling of the defined, muscular chest to memory. The gods alone knew when there would be another chance if things went badly in the days before they left for Rome.

Would they be able to kiss, to touch, in the wagon on the way to Rome? Or would Tiberius command that he join the Romans in their cart? It would only be two nights travel, but how torturous would it be once the lanista discovered the truth of Jovian's desire? There was little chance that he would be understanding and a great chance that he might even use the time in Rome to broker a sale of one of them if Argus survived his match against the other gladiator.

With well practiced nudge Jovian slipped his tongue between Argus' lips, holding back a smile when the gladiator groaned. He could feel the eager response to his touch. Argus wanted this as much as Jovian did.

Had he been waiting too? Was this a moment of his dreams coming to a reality as well?

"Argus?" Jovian whispered, moving his lips to the cords of Argus' neck. "Tell me that you want this too? This is not in my head?"

"I want you, Jovian. I want you more than I know how to say." Argus whispered hotly in Jovian's ear, burying his fingers in his hair.

"I want you too. I have dreamed of this moment so many nights that I have lost count. Even now I wonder if it is real. Are we really here or lost in a dream together?" Jovian said, kissing across the broad chest before him.

"If this is a dream then I never wish to wake from it." Argus said, breathless and smiling.

Jovian was about to say something more when Argus tugged him further into his cell and firmly against his body.

The younger man ran his hands over every inch of the defined and muscular chest. His fingers teased at the top of Argus' subligaria. Would the bigger man be brave enough to go farther this soon? He could feel the size of his arousal through the fabric and his own body swelled in response to the thought of what could happen next. What bcautiful passion they could make together, would make together, when the time was right.

"Jovian, I…" Argus started to speak, pausing to kiss Jovian's lips again, but whatever he was going to say was cut short by the voice of Barrius in the hall.

"Argus? Dominus wishes for you spar against Proximus. Have you seen his pet Syrian? Or the young medicus? Arturo is awake, as is Cirandon, the Romans will be wanting their condition reported."

Jovian was trying not to giggle when Argus put a hand over his mouth to silence him.

"I have seen neither of them Barrius. Tell the giant that I am ready to send his ass to the sand, if that is the wish of our Dominus."

"I would like to see that." Barrius chuckled, heading back down the stone hall. "Hurry before the wagers get beyond what that Syrian snake Astrix can calculate."

Jovian waited a few moments before rising on his toes to press a kiss to Argus' cheek. "You should go first so that there is no suspicion that we were together. I shall go to the infirmary and then pause to see your match before I rejoin Dominus on the balcony."

Argus gave a brief nod and headed to the sands, leaving Jovian more than slightly crushed that he had not given any affectionate farewell. Was it simply that he was in the mindset of a gladiator, ready to fight, with no room for tenderness in his mind? Or was he embarrassed that they had almost been caught by one of his brothers?

Had he ever been with a man before? Jovian could not think of a time when he had even seen Argus even flirt with another man.

This was all that he could think of when he reached the end of the hall and saw he man he had just been kissing practicing against the dual blades of Proximus with a spear and shield. Primal grunting filled the air in accompaniment of the sound of wood against wood. Both men wore expressions of such savagery that Jovian was shocked. There was no trace of sensuality or passion on his face, furthering the confusion that was flooding Jovian's heart.

He had no idea what he was going to do next.

A sound and motion at the gate stole his attention away from the fighting. The iron bars swung open and Meridius stepped into the yard of the ludus.

With all the grace of a panther and eyes the colour of the skies, the Spaniard strolled into the ludus as though it was his home instead of the fighting ground of men he had never known. Jovian was in awe, absolutely mesmerized by the grace and power the man exuded.

He was about to go and greet him when Violetta rushed past him to throw her arms around the man's broad shoulders, with a joyful cry.

"Padre."

The Syrian boy looked back to see Cassian in the doorway, crossing his arms with a look of tolerant amusement.

Was there about to be fight between the two powerful men? Over Violetta's affections?

CHAPTER 33

Cassian watched Violetta joyfully embrace Meridius. As happy as he was for her reunion with the other man that she cared so deeply for, he was mildly annoyed at the smugness with which the man received it. The arrogant smirk that the Spaniard wore while he wrapped his arms around Violetta's shoulders was infuriatingly possessive and while she was present there was nothing that Cassian could say or do about it.

He would love the chance to cross knuckles or swords with the man, if he had the skill to wield them, which he doubted. The arrogant nature of the man irritated something in Cassian's mind almost as strongly as the remembrance that he had attempted to push himself on Violetta.

For that alone he wanted to kill the man.

He would have found a way to do it if the loss of the man would not have hurt the woman he loved. That they both loved. It was the only thing about the man that Violetta had said that Cassian could agree with. Meridius loved Violetta dearly. It was not the shared, passionate love that was between Violetta and Cassian, but it was love all the same.

Once the Spaniard released Violetta from his embrace he followed Hector as well as Auctus past the gladiator and towards the stairs that would take him upstairs to the presence of the Romans. Cassian was pleased that Violetta did not follow them past the doorway where he stood but leaned herself against him instead.

"I never thought that I would see him again." Violetta said, slipping her fingers through his. Her smile when he kissed her fingertips was as sad as it was beautiful.

"You miss him?" Cassian asked, draping his arm across her shoulders, and turning them both back to the sands, noticing Jovian watch Argus and Proximus battle on the sands.

The boy looked as though he was ready to eat the younger German alive. Had those two been foolish enough to become involved? It was dangerous and deadly. If Argus were not smart enough to see this then he would have words with Jovian and remind him of the risk he was taking, not only with his heart but with both their lives.

"I do. He was the only part of that house that was not a horror." Violetta said softly. "That is why I am so glad to be here where, so far, the greatest horror is what happened today on that balcony."

He placed a kiss on her cheek.

"I hope that is the worst that you will face here. I will do my best, all that I can, to make it so that you stay here, with me, from now until we greet the gods."

"No matter how hard the Roman's test you, test us, we will rise above their challenges and survive." She said with a smile that spoke of her determination.

"My priestess, we will do more than survive." Cassian said with a grin. "We will thrive. I want, more than almost anything, too see the day that we arrive in Britannia as free as the wind."

"How could that ever happen?" She asked, staring up at him with hope in those beautiful blue eyes that inspired him everyday. "Do you think you might earn your freedom in the arena? I do not know of how I might earn my own."

He wanted to tell her of his idea of leading a rebellion against the Romans then running from their hunters until they were safe in Britannia, but the fewer people that knew the more likely it would be that he might succeed in the moment.

"There is a possibility, after Rome perhaps. When I win there then I will convince Tertius to let me begin to put my winnings towards purchasing your freedom."

"Mine?" Violetta asked. "What about your own?"

Cassian smiled and brushed his fingers down her cheek.

"I will win mine upon the sands all the sooner knowing that you are free and safe from the assault of Romans."

The hope on her face was inspiring and he prayed that it was never proven to be misplaced. The day that he was able to tell her that freedom was near would be one of the happiest of his life, only less than the day he knew that she loved him and the day that he was allowed, at long last, to marry her. That day, when they became man and wife, would be more glorious for all the simplicity that their ceremony would be.

As slaves there would be no special gown or feast. The lanista might feel generous and give them wine as well as some food from their table. So, unlike the beauty and revelry of his homeland. As the son of a chieftain there would be celebrating for days. Either version of the day would make him just as happy. All he wanted was to have her as his wife.

Cassian nestled Violetta against his chest, his arms wrapped around her while he dreamed of what things should be like when he married her. The handfast would happen over a holy stone. Arturo would protest, only because it was not the formal ceremony that he would want. They would speak their intentions over the stone and toss it in the river so that the water would carry it to the gods. After the ceremony he would give her the same gold medallion that his father had given his mother to show his commitment to the prosperity of their future and then they would get their marriage tattoos. He wanted them over the brands that marked their slavery, then all of this would be in the past and there would be nothing left to remind them of the hell they had been in when they had met.

That was what he wanted most for Violetta and himself; to be able to put this house, this city, this Republic behind them forever. Somehow he would find the way to make his dream a reality. He had to, for both their sakes.

"I should go and see to it that Arturo and Cirandon are ready to leave the infirmary and give Jovian the report for Dominus." Violetta said, pulling him back to the present moment.

"Yes, it would not do to enrage the man after the day we have already have. He is likely to command some new form of foolishness that would see another man to your care in the infirmary." Cassian said, dropping a kiss to her cheek.

"Perhaps it would be you and I battling with sticks." Jovian laughed, joining Violetta on her walk back towards the infirmary.

"You had better hope not, boy." Barrius said, joining the joke. "I should think the woman of the city champion would know a thing or two about the use of a sword."

The entire gathered company joined the laugh and Cassian considered the practicality of the older man had said. Why not teach Violetta how to use a sword? Even if it were just a few basic strikes so that she could defend herself if needed or convince an attacker that she had the skill to do damage. If he could teach any number of fools over the years then he could certainly teach his woman who was more intelligent than any three of the men he had taught over the years.

He would write about it in the letter that he would pen to her that night. Somehow it was easier to put his thoughts on paper than it was to say them out loud. It was certainly easier than trying to find moments where he could whisper in her ear, or, even rarer have a conversation that was not going to be interrupted by Arturo, another gladiator or one of the Romans. The knowledge that she alone would read his words of romantic affection, see the softer side of him, brought him a smile of comfort while he watched his brothers train for a battle they did not even know was coming.

Meridius loathed the son of his master as an incompetent, savage, monster, and the fact that he, as a slave, could not give voice to his thoughts was likely the only thing that had kept him alive. Listening to Vitus while he laughed about injuring the man that was teaching Violetta the skills that she needed to be useful in this place infuriated the Spaniard. He wished, not for the first time, that he could lay the beating on the man that was more than a score of years in the making.

He had grown up a few years older than Vitus, having been bought to serve Felix when he was twelve and Vitus was eight. The younger boy had been cruel, even as a child. He teased as Meridius learned the language, called him 'the Spanish stolide', which translated to 'the stupid Spaniard', and there was no one who would stop him other than his mother, and occasionally his father. When the Domina of the house died due to a fever Felix stopped caring what his son did, and, instead, focused all his attentions on his business, his daughter, his occasional lovers and, eventually, Violetta.

When she arrived, fifteen years after Meridius had, all three men, Felix, Meridius and Vitus, were all mesmerized by the innocent beauty. When Felix discovered that she was the daughter of a Greek Priestess he made sure that no one made an attempt on her virginity, which meant paying attention to nineteen-year-old Vitus. He also brought priests and priestesses to the villa to train the girl for the temple. The merchant had been determined that the girl would petition Mercury on his behalf.

That had been the plan until Felix had decided to sacrifice her to the gladiator instead of the gods.

It was the only time that Meridius had ever agreed with Vitus about anything. There was no reason good enough to let that savage brute touch her, ever.

Meridius had, for several years, been hoping that when the time came Violetta would have seen the affection in their relationship and trust him with her transition into womanhood. He had never had any woman in his life that he had cared for in a way like this. There had been a man once, a long time ago, but Felix had commanded his death and the most severe punishment for his beloved blue eyed boy that he could bear when he had found out that Meridius cared for the other man. After that Meridius had never let himself get too close or care too much about anyone, except for Violetta. He had never considered that she would not want him, and he still held some doubt that she truly felt nothing more than familial affection for him.

What could Cassian have that he did not have himself?

From what Meridius could see and what he had heard, the man was rough, crude, undeniably violent and had bedded most of the women in the elite circle, or to be more accurate, had been bedded by them.

It was the sole thing that they had in common.

Meridius knew that he was treated better than most slaves, even the body slaves who were often favored to the point of being considered spoiled by their less popular counterparts. He had robes made for him, instead of wearing cast offs of his master or his children or a linen subligaria. Felix was his only concern and duty so there were many times that he had no responsibility but his own amusement.

When he was able to speak it had been a time of devious conversations, and whispered flirtations that led to passionate liaisons with anyone that he desired. Felix had a deep love of beautiful things so, with a few exceptions like the cook, Irissa, that he never saw, most of the slaves in his house were beautiful men and women. This made them a wonderful group of sensual playmates for Meridius. There were few in the house that had not shared his bed at some point.

Even Violetta had come to him, not for sex but for comfort and consoling. He had never attempted to make more of their time than it was, with the singular exception of the kiss after she had been with the gladiator. He had not wanted to scare her away.

Meridius wondered if Cassian knew about that part of their relationship?

Had Violetta ever told her lover that Felix had summoned them both to his bed before and after he had given her to the gladiator? The old man got a thrill from forcing the girl to watch the two men together in the throws, abusing her innocence long before he had had the girl's body. Meridius would have dared to argue against it, had he been able. He hated to be a part of anything that stole the innocence of anyone, the way his had been stolen from him years ago.

"Meridius?" Vitus' voice broke his thoughts. "What, exactly, is it that my father sent you here for? It has been years since I needed an escort from one house to another."

Barely acknowledging the agitating viper Meridius offered the scroll in his hand to the lanista. He had no thoughts to what it contained. The merchant wrote it in private that morning while Meridius had been attending to his morning prayers.

His reaction was as genuine as the Romans around him when the lanista closed the scroll and announced with a surprised smile.

"Felix has offered me the sale of Violetta, for the price of half of Cassian's winnings over the next year."

CHAPTER 34

Violetta changed the dressing on Cirandon's wound with a smile still on her face. After making quick and passionate love with Cassian she had not thought that her day could have improved any further, but she was wrong. When Meridius had appeared at the gate with that familiar smile she thought her heart would burst with joy.

For the briefest moment she thought that, perhaps, Felix had sent her friend here to be trained by Cassian. That would have been the most wonderful news she could have received, other than Felix selling her to Tertius. That would never happen though. He treasured her possession like kings treasured gold. She meant almost nothing to him, he simply enjoyed owning her as though she was a thing and not a person.

Her farewell to Meridius, when he descended from the villa with the others, had been brief due to Vitus' rage and impatience, had been strangely emotionally. If she did not know better she would have thought this was the last time that she was going to see him. He held her tighter, longer, than he usually did, and she thought that she saw moisture in his eyes.

Had something happened on the balcony to upset him?

She tried to ask him, but he made a few obscure gestures that made as much sense as the sadness in his eyes. The only one that she could clearly discern, before he left with Vitus, was Rome. She worried that he was trying to tell her that, though she might arrive in Rome with the lanista, she would be leaving with the merchant instead.

How would she tell Cassian? Would he believe her? He seemed upset by the other man's presence and their shared affection. He had not said a word about it, but she could see it on his face, in his eyes. Her champion would never admit to feeling threatened by the other man, but there were few men in the world that would not be.

Her padre was one of the most beautiful men that had ever walked the earth. He knew it, she knew it, anyone who saw him knew it. She knew that he thought that he was immeasurable, incomparable to any man, but he did not know the quality of the man she loved. Perhaps even Cassian did not know the truth of his own quality. Violetta knew his quality though. She knew both men in ways that they did not know themselves. Neither man was the Adonis that he pretended to be. Not perfect, nor invulnerable. They were, however, the two most caring men that Violetta had ever known, and she loved them both.

"Your hands are doing their work well, considering that your mind is not here." Arturo said when she moved from Cirandon to check his dressing.

"Apologies. Meridius was here. He went up to the balcony to speak to the Romans."

"I thought you said that the man does not speak but uses hand gestures." Cirandon interrupted from where he was laying.

"Yes. Of course. I meant that he came bearing the words of Felix to be delivered to Tertius." She said, backtracking with a smile. "He did not tell me what was in the scroll. I tried to get the information from him, he was too upset and rushed to tell me. Something is wrong though. I can feel it."

"Wrong? By the smile on your face I thought you to be daydreaming about a certain man well cared for by all in this room." Arturo teased, his dark eyes sparkling.

"Oh, well, yes. I cannot deny those thoughts any more than I can deny the blush upon my cheek. I did not think that either of you would want to hear them given voice and so I brought forth a more interesting topic." She said, her blush deepening at the teasing of her instructor who was showing the more charming side of his personality.

He was quite an attractive man, which often made her wonder why he was not involved with any of the women in the house. More than one of them had commented on how fortunate she was to be working with the handsome druid.

"You never need to hide the truth of your thoughts inside these walls, Violetta." Arturo said, trying to inspect his own bandages. "This is your sanctuary as well as your place of work."

"You are correct, and I am the one who is working. Not you, Arturo." She said, smiling and covering the bandage with her hands. "Trust my lessons were well learned and leave that bandage be."

Cirandon chuckled, sitting up carefully.

"It seems your student has, in fact, learned lessons better than you thought, Arturo. The girl sounds just like you."

"Well, I suppose, yes she does." The druid sputtered in surprise and the trio shared a laugh until there was a knock on the door and the guard Hector stepped inside.

"Domina sends word for the girl to attend her, immediately." He spat, making Violetta think that he was another of the Romans that was uncomfortable in the presence of her teacher.

"Are you both feeling well? Do you need me to stay or any further attention?" Violetta asked both her lover's instructor and her own. "I can ask one of the men to stand watch in case you need me."

"Would you fall to command." Hector barked from the door. "Your Domina awaits you with little patience for your delay due to these two. Move your feet, girl."

"We will be well enough. Go upstairs Violetta and do what you can for her." Arturo said, carefully standing and putting the water pot over the fire.

"Send word if you need me and stay off that leg Doctore, for at least a day." Violetta said, following Hector up into the villa. She was careful not to get within arms reach of the surly guard. She did not forget biting him the first night she came to the villa and the look on his face told her that he had not forgotten it either.

It was strange to feel relief when they arrived at Lycithia's chambers but the anger that was smouldering in Hector's eyes told her that she was not wrong. He was dangerous and she needed to be careful whenever she was near him. She also could not tell Cassian. He would want to act on her fear and that was something that could not happen. If he assaulted a guard then the lanista would not forgive him easily and the whole journey to Rome would be put in jeopardy.

"You certainly took your time answering that command." Lycithia said in a bored voice. "One would think that you did not take the summons as seriously as changing a few bandages on men who are as capable of the task as you are. Is that true Violetta?" She asked pointedly.

"Of course not, Domina." Violetta answered quickly. Being used to the temper of those of the house of Census she knew just how to placate the Roman. "I simply wished to ensure that there would be no need for us to be disturbed. Thoroughness is a great partner to efficiency."

"Let us hope that you are that efficient at the task that I have assigned you. Tell me what you have discovered that will see me with child before the month is out."

"I have no clear answer, Domina." Violetta said, carefully. She removed a few candles from a scarf she had grabbed as she exited the infirmary and began to arrange an altar on the nearest table. "I wanted to start by praying to the gods of my mother's land in the manner that she taught me. If the gods of Rome are not listening then perhaps those of Greece will."

She offered the Roman woman a warm smile and lit the candles before inviting her to sit at her side.

"I do not see how it can hurt to ask for the help of the gods by any name." Lycithia said, sitting down beside Violetta.

"Then let us pray together Domina, for blessings and guidance." Violetta said, lighting the incense and bowing her head.

She did not add that she was also praying that she did not come to bear a child herself, at least not before the Roman woman who would be sure to snatch the babe from her breast to claim it as her own. That would be more than any woman could or should be made to bear and exactly what Lycithia was capable of without a second thought to the pain and agony it would cause.

This was likely the reason that the gods had denied her a child, even so, Violetta would petition them with every prayer to grant the request. It might be for selfish reasons, to protect her right to a child of her own blood from being taken from her arms, but she would do anything that she could to ensure that the older woman had a child of her own. The heavens knew what might happen to them all should the request not be granted.

For hours Violetta prayed, lit candles and incense, made offerings and hung charms about the room. She hoped that it would bring the attention of the divine and grant the requests for a child and for safety. There was nothing else that she could do, at least for now. Perhaps the trip to Rome would reveal some new method or prayer that she could use, otherwise this might be a lost cause.

Finally, the lanista arrived, dismissing Violetta with a kind smile. If she thought he was capable of the feeling she would have thought that he was grateful for her efforts with his wife. She had not thought to ask the man if he wanted a child as much as his wife did. What if this was against his wishes?

She was too tired to try and understand the dynamics of the relationship between the Romans. How could she hope to understand the minds of people who chose to treat men and women as possessions instead of living, breathing, people?

Arriving back at the room she shared with Jovian Violetta was grateful to see that Jovian was fast asleep. She would not have to answer the dozens of questions that he would have about what she had been doing since her return to the villa. There was no way that she could have deflected every question without letting something slip that would get her in trouble with Lycithia.

She shuddered to think about how the woman's rage would manifest. If she saw nothing wrong in how her husband behaved then how could she be any less vicious when in a fit of temper, such as the one that the betrayal of what she was trying to accomplish would bring?

Pouring water into a basin Violetta began to wash the dust and grime of the day from her skin, offering prayers to the gods for safety and guidance within the madness that was her position now.

How could she maneuver herself within this new circle and thrive?

The only way would be with the gods on her side.

Carefully, she made her offering to Mercury, hoping that he would hear her prayers.

Leaving the water to sit in the glistening light of the moon Violetta turned to her bed, prepared to sleep deeply after such an intensely trying day.

Setting her dress over the stool beside the bed she slid her hand beneath the coverlet and to smooth the material. The luxurious texture was still a marvel to her, and she savored the touch of it every night, but tonight there was something besides linen under the blanket. Curious to the unexpected texture Violetta withdrew a folded piece of parchment from beneath her pillow.

How had such a thing been placed there? By whom?

Jovian was asleep and she was fairly sure that he did not write. If he did then he would not have put something under her pillow but would have left it where she could see it immediately. He would have been waiting to see what her response was.

That meant that this was from someone else, but who?

Stepping back to the window Violetta scanned the dark scribbled markings to see if there was anything that might reveal the author to her. Again, her name was at the top of the page and there was another word, alone, at the bottom. The 'C' told her that it must be from Cassian, but what did it say?

She sat on the sill of the window and traced her finger over each swirling letter and wept in frustration. For all the knowledge that she had gained in this place this was one that she continued to lack. It seemed that each day revealed yet another way that she was lacking in the simplest of skills owned by those around her.

How could she reveal to anyone that she could not read? Would they think her a simpleton or see that it was the decision of Felix to make sure that her education never included such a simple thing?

She hoped that Cassian would not think her less for this and, just as important, she hoped that Arturo would still let her practice medicine.

CHAPTER 35

Cassian could not understand why Violetta had not answered his letters. She had not even answered his question when they were dining together. It made no sense.

When he had written to her that he wanted to marry her in the manner of his people, no matter what the Romans said, he had thought that she would answer right away, but she had not even mentioned the question.

Was she afraid of the wrath of the Romans? Or had the Spaniard said something to her, in the rush of gestures that he had made at the gate, to dissuade her from accepting his offer?

He wanted to ask Violetta herself, but, even if his pride would have allowed him to, she rarely appeared at the side of the sands this week. Arturo said that she was busy with the preparations for the arena of Rome. As an aid to the attending medicus she would be expected to be ready for any emergency and as it would not be safe to run to a market in the gigantic city they had to take as many supplies as possible.

She was busy at the work he had brought her here for and he had to fight his jealousy that it took so much of her time. It would have been a little easier had she not also been spending more time than he had anticipated in the villa. Nearly every day it seemed as though a guard came to fetch her. Many of those days she did not return to the infirmary until late if she returned to it at all.

What was going on and why did he not know about it?

Cassian hated secrets. This one was too close to home and heart to be born. What other option did he have though? It was not as though the lanista would grant him an audience tell him all that he had planned and whatever it was that the damned Spaniard had brought from Census.

He was still stewing over possible ways to find the answers to his questions when Argus joined him at the table to eat.

"Only days until we leave for Rome." The German said, his excitement obvious and his energy contagious.

Even Cassian could not help but smile at the younger man's enthusiasm. He would learn soon enough what the true energy of the arena was, and they would learn what the great city was like, what the crowd was like, together.

Hopefully, they would both live to tell the tale of that discovery.

"Argus, the trip to Rome will be a day, perhaps two, locked inside a cart that rattles down the road hard enough to jar your stomach into your skull." Cassian said, getting up from the table and gesturing for him to follow to the sands.

"Is that supposed to worry me?" Argus laughed. "That kick of yours does the same, so the feeling is not one I am unfamiliar with."

Cassian let his head fall back as he laughed, letting the worry slip from his shoulders while he took his position in the one place that never changed. No matter his confusion about love, life, or Romans, he knew that the sands and the God of Death would always welcome him to test the fates again. The day would come when he would lose, succumbing at last to the divine call and the ultimate challenge for any gladiator: death.

"Come at me then, boy, and I will increase your knowledge of it."

Argus spun the shaft of the spear and brought it down in an attack that surprised Cassian with its ferocity. Each thrust was well aimed and harder to deflect than it had been even a few weeks ago. Something had happened to inspire a greatness in the man that had not been there before.

Perhaps he had found a cause to fight for at last?

They sparred, again and again, each time Cassian became more impressed with the power and passion behind Argus' attack. He had prepared himself for the death of the German in the Roman arena. Now there was a good chance that he would survive his debut upon the sands of the greatest arena in the Republic. They both would.

"I stand impressed Argus." Cassian said, tossing his arm across Argus's shoulder. "Something has changed. I may not be saying a funeral prayer for you after all."

"You thought you would?" Argus sputtered with a grin. "Gratitude for your faith in my skill. Does Cirandon know that you hold such little faith in his teaching?"

"What is Cassian holding of mine now?" Cirandon said, joining them with a slow limp.

"Besides your cock?" Barrius called, sending every man among them into a fit of laughter.

"Your great student thinks that your teachings only worked for him and that I might fall in Rome due my lack of education." Argus said when the laughter slowed. "The man is surprised that I came near to besting him, more than once."

"I am not surprised because you were not near to besting me." Cassian chuckled, sharing a glance with his old friend. "I am merely shocked that anything that Doctore said made it through your thick German skull."

"At least it was not a sword through his thigh." Tarcarus said, directing his jibe at Cassian.

Wearing a smirk on his face the Thracian stepped from the platform onto the sands. He was deliberately antagonizing Cassian, trying to pick a fight so that he could show the lanista standing on the balcony that he should be on the wagon to Rome as well as those who would already be jammed within it's confines.

"More than most here you should know that accidents happen upon the sands." Cassian said, stalking towards him and leaving Argus and Cirandon behind. "How many men have you sent to the infirmary trying to display skills you have yet to master? If you think to attempt to shame me for the accident that led to Cirandon's injury then say it with a sword."

"Cassian, there is no need for that. I know you did not intend for the injury." Cirandon said, stepping up to both men and placing a hand to each shoulder. "I would not have further blood shed for such a thing."

"You forgive the man too easily Doctore." Tarcarus said, staring Cassian in the eye. "He brings offence, injury, and insult to you, to all of us. I would challenge him for title of champion of the house if you would give me your backing."

"Have you lost what sense the gods ever gave you?" Cassian barked at him. "I could put you in the ground here and now, but I do not wish to have to cover the cost of your worthless life from my winnings which have a greater cause than ever before."

"At least my mind is not lost between a pair of thighs." Tarcarus said, scoffing.

Cassian did not pause to hear the next word but smashed his fist across the Thracian's mouth. The spray of blood carried a certain level of satisfaction, but not the same level as the indignation and rage on his face. A face that Cassian was about to permanently change.

"Speak such filth again. Do it and see what your face is like come the dawn." He snarled. "I promise you that she will not put back together what I am going to break. You will be lucky if you are able to lap up gruel like the dog you are."

"You are the one barking like a neglected dog, Cassian." Tarcarus laughed. "Your little bitch will do as commanded and tend to my wounds. Perhaps I will have her 'tender ministrations' for the pain in my cock as well. We shall see how she enjoys a spear of Thrace compared to your Celtic cock."

Wrath consumed Cassian and he lunged at the other man. The tackle caught him off guard and knocked him to the ground. The champion straddled his torso and started to rain blows down. He did not care that the man was supposed to stand as a brother or that what he had suggested was all but impossible with Arturo in the infirmary.

He was tired of every man thinking that Violetta was available to them simply due to her work within their reach.

They were better men than that, or he thought that they were until things like this happened, repeatedly. He could feel the breaking of bones beneath his fists, but he did not care. Not today.

He could feel the hands of his brothers grabbing him trying to stop his murderous assault. They would not stop him from teaching the Thracian a lesson. Faintly he could hear Violetta calling his name, Argus had likely fetched her from her work, but she did not know why he was fighting. He would explain it to her later while she wrapped his knuckles and shook her head at his need to defend her.

Just as he raised his fist for another hard blow the tip of Cirandon's whip wrapped around his wrist and held it steady while a trio of gladiators lifted him to his feet.

"To his cell. Take him to his cell." The voice of the lanista bellowed from the balcony. "I will attend him at my leisure. Get the other man to the infirmary, see him tended and that girl removed to the villa."

Cassian had intended to go quietly, certain that he would be able to explain his actions to the lanista's satisfaction. When Tarcarus laughed as he sat up, curled his finger to summon Violetta and called across to her.

"Come on then, lanidica. There are aches all over my body that need your tenderest touch."

All thoughts of calm compliance flew from his mind at the crude slur and Cassian spun on the ball of his foot to deliver a savage kick to the side of Tarcarus' head. The man dropped to the sand, unconscious and therefore no danger to Violetta.

"Cassian!" Julius said, gripping the back of the Celt's neck. "That is enough. She is safe enough for now. You have other things to hold your concern now. The lanista is furious."

"Not as furious as I am." He grumbled, letting the guard lead him away.

He gave a look of apology to Violetta as they passed but the Centurion gave him no time for anything else. He hoped that she could understand what he did and why he did it. He prayed that she would find a way to come and see him before she was taken upstairs. He would have to explain to her why he lost his temper, but he would get the answer that he needed about his letters.

"Bring her to me if you can Julius." He asked, hoping for understanding from the only Roman he could trust.

"You know that he is going to tell me that she is to be brought to him immediately." Julius said while they made their way through the dark halls. "I will do what I can. If there is a chance."

"That is all I ask."

"And all I ask is that my champion gladiator not attempt to kill every man…"

"Every man that threatens to rape the woman I want to marry? What would any man do in the moment, Dominus?" He wanted to choke on the word, but humility was the only chance he had to get what he wanted.

"Is that what happened?" The lanista paused, looking from Cassian then back towards the sands. "You would raise arms against your brothers for her sake?"

"I would do anything to keep her safe. I want to marry her. It does not matter to me that Felix denied my request. My heart is set upon it."

"Then you would make sacrifices to see her purchased? For her to become a part of this house permanently?"

Cassian felt a spark of hope in his heart and raised his head to look Tertius in the face. Did the man mean it? What would be the price of such a thing?

It would be worth paying no matter what it was.

"Yes. Dominus, as I said I would do anything to keep her with me. She should be safe, at my side, as my wife."

"One feat at a time Cassian." Tertius held up his hand with a smile. "First I must secure her sale from Felix. The man is unlikely to be inclined to sell her. You are prepared for the cost? Anything beyond the price of a common body slave would need to be covered from your own earning."

"I understand Dominus." He said, trying to contain his excitement, his joy that she might finally be safe from the monsters of that house. "I would give all that I have to see her free of that place."

"You do understand that this does not free her, Cassian. She would be a slave of my house, training with Arturo as a medicus to treat all the men. You would not own her, nor would you have the power to stop her should she choose another lover."

Cassian had not thought of such a possibility, but he knew that Violetta loved him as he loved her and there was no man within these walls that could break their bond.

"I understand Dominus. Would you give me you word that, once the debt of her purchase is settled that I will be allowed to make her my wife with all the rights and ceremonies? That she would be protected as my wife? No man, slave or free, will be able to force her to their bed once she stands as the wife of the greatest champion of the Republic. Can you promise me this?"

"You must also stop trying to kill every man that looks at her or there will be no gladiators left in the ludus and that is bad for business."

"I will find other ways to educate them, Dominus, besides sending them to the afterlife."

The lanista extended his arm. "Then I will see her price arranged and you shall pay it. I give you my word."

CHAPTER 36

Argus' head was still spinning from the kiss with Jovian. Even though it had been a few days the surprise and its residual effects were still fresh. His heart was racing and his cock throbbing each time he let his thoughts wander to the soft lips and smooth touch of Jovian. That the boy had been daring enough to find him in the dark halls of the ludus cells was impressive enough but that he was daring enough to act so passionately had astounded Argus and left him with must as many questions as it did answers.

How could the boy be so reckless? So foolish? So gloriously passionate?

The grin on his face as impossible to hide. He had to tell the others that it was his excitement and his enthusiasm for the coming match in Rome. The risk that Dominus would find out the truth through one of the other men was too great for him to share the true cause of his joy.

If they were caught or if anyone suspected that there was affection between him and the Syrian boy the wrath and violence that would rain down from the villa would be as deadly as it was sudden.

That was how it had been with his brother, Darius.

Older than Argus by two years Darius had been wild hearted and hot tempered. Despite that he had been well liked by all. Even Cassian had enjoyed his company and the man was not known for being friendly. He had been a skilled fighter, making his way through the ranks towards the better fights in the arena. Darius had seemed as content with his life as a gladiator could be.

That was why the fire he had set had come as such a surprise to everyone, everyone but Argus.

What no one else had known, except perhaps Arturo since the druid seemed to know everything that happened in this place, was that Darius was miserable. He hated having to kill for sport and even more than that he hated the attention that it brought him from the elite of the city. Nothing was worse than having to bow and scrape and pretend to care what their captors thought. Unless it was having to bed them.

Darius hated the Roman habit of sleeping with the slaves that interested them, and he was a man that had always caught someone's interest.

He was tall with hazel eyes that sparked like the sun through the forest of their homeland when he laughed. He had fought as a Murmillo, with sword and a small shield, and had so often spent extra hours training with Argus. When he was not commanded to the rooms designated for the pleasing of Romans that is.

It was something that happened to many of the men, and it was usually wealthy women with old husbands who could not give them children. Other times it was men with a wife at home that they were tired of or that they had given children to but were not truly attracted to. It was the combination of the two that had sent Darius into the spiral of emotions that had led him to set fire to his cell.

It was etched into Argus's memory as clearly as the memories of his homeland, the night that Darius had descended from the villa in a wild state. He was angry, frantic, and muttering about the impossibility of what had just happened.

When asked what had happened, Darius looked Argus in the eyes and said.

"I cannot be a father. It cannot be mine."

"What? Who? A father?" Argus asked, confused.

He had not understood what he meant. He did not know then the things that Romans would use slaves for, the perversions and the pleasures. Argus had been an awkward and gangly young man then, at the beginning of his training and did not have the attention then that he had come to receive in recent years.

"She claims that the child is mine." Darius said. "They want me to be sold and sent far from the city so that no one will ever see a resemblance."

"They cannot send you away for something that is not your choice. They did this to you and now they wish to punish you for it?" Argus had asked.

He reached out to touch his shoulder, trying to calm his older brother. It did not work though. Darius began to pace frantically, raking his hands through his short dark hair.

"I never thought such a thing would happen to me though I have heard of other men who have been used to give these women the children denied them by their gods." Darius shook his head. "I do not want to go. I cannot leave you here alone."

"Me? You are to be sent…somewhere, and you are worried about me?" Argus shook his head. "I would think that you would be more concerned that it would be the mines or a cross? I can survive, here with our brothers in arms. You would be alone though. We can ask Dominus not to let this happen."

"Argus do not be the fool they think you are." Darius snapped. "With enough coin put to his palm that man would sell any man among us, except his champion and that pretty little Syrian child."

"I am not the fool that you seem to think that I am." Argus snapped back. "It could succeed. What if we offered to fight a match together, as a team, against another house? The draw of the crowd would more than match whatever they have offered to him. Who is it? Who says that you fathered a child?"

"What does it matter?" Darius cried, slamming both his fists against the wall. "If it is mine then I will never know or know the child. If it is not mine then it will be the same except that I will be far from all the family that I have for the rest of my days."

"It matters." Argus said with a teasing tone. "I would hate to one day be face to face with my brother's son and be cursing him as fool Roman without knowing his true identity."

"You are such a child he would probably be more of a man at eight than you will ever be." Darius said rolling his eyes. "Go. Practice your sword work. You will need it soon enough."

"I will need it to school your tired ass come morning." Argus said with a laugh, heading down the hall towards the sands. "Try to rest."

"Try to live." Darius called after him.

Those were the last words he heard his brother say.

A few hours later smoke filled every hallway and lifted to the villa, waking every slave and Roman with coughing fits.

Everything was frantic, yelling and swearing, while everyone tried to escape the flames and smoke. Once the gladiators and slaves from the house were under guard upon the ludus sands a few of the guards began to search for the source of the fire. That is when Argus had realized that Darius was not among them.

He had begun to call his name, alerting Doctore to the fact that he was missing and asking the others if they had seen him. No one had.

Argus started to struggle with the guards to try and get into the ludus to try and find him. Darius had been so upset and it was possible that he was unconscious, drunk, somewhere in the tunnels. He fought harder against the hold of the guards than he had ever fought in the arena. Kicking, and throwing punches whenever he got a hand free of their grasp, he was desperate and fighting like it.

"Argus! What in Hades is wrong with you?" Tertius bellowed.

"My brother is in there." Argus cried, pointing to the smoking halls.

"Darius? No. He is not in the ludus. I sold him an hour ago, I was paid to sell him and made money on his sale. He has not been in this house since sunset."

Argus had collapsed to the sands. Darius had been taken away. Gone. Sold.

"Dominus? Why?" His mind spun at the realization that he would never see his brother again. "Where is he gone?"

"He is gone because he offended those I embrace as friends of this house. Offended me by that offence and so he is gone forever. He was deemed unworthy of this house, so it does not matter where he is gone."

Argus was crushed, angry, confused. He wanted to fight but he could not think of who he would fight. The guards? The Romans? Another gladiator?

Perhaps if he attacked one of the guards then Dominus would sell him to whoever he sold Darius to? He had only taken a few steps towards the captain of the guard, intent on striking him, when he felt a fist connect to his temple and knew no more until the morning.

Cassian had taken it on himself to stop Argus from making a mistake that would likely have seen him to the cross not the auction block. Though he had been angry at the time he could see now that it had been done to save his life and he was grateful. The man had been through more at the hands of their masters than most ever would.

It would be the wiser thing to take his advice whenever it was offered, even if it would break his heart. He could not pursue Jovian. He recalled that Proximus had given the same words of counsel against the union. Surely two champions would not lie to him. They wanted him to rise within the ranks, to join them in honoring the house of Tertius in the glory of the arena.

It was time to choose between his life's goal and a chance at love.

Neither was promised no matter what he chose, and death was almost guaranteed.

What was he to do? What was the right choice?

The choice that would save a life, even if it were not his own.

Tertius would kill Jovian the same day that he would have Argus executed. How could he choose something that would see the one that he cared about to the same risk of death that he was facing? It was not fair to the boy who did not know what the risk would be. Argus had to be responsible for him too. Jovian might not understand the reason that Argus was doing this, but it had to be done. Argus would make the sacrifice so that Jovian would never have to.

He looked up to the balcony and met the gaze of his would-be lover. Those dark eyes were full of hope and affection, and though soon they would be filled with hurt and anger. Pain that he would cause by doing the right thing. Why did saving a life have to break the hearts of those with everything to gain and just as much to lose.

He turned away without offering the beautiful boy a smile. He could not bare to see the confusion that would cause, so he focused instead on the weapons in his hands. It was possible that he would die in Rome and save them both the agony of living each day and never knowing what they could have had. Then this would be for nothing. All of it, but it still had to be done.

"Argus."

Doctore called his name and drew him back to the present.

"Yes, Doctore."

"Spar with Proximus if you are done daydreaming of Rome. I would have you survive, at least long enough to return and inspire those lesser men not chosen for this honor."

"Yes Doctore. I will show all who would doubt why I was chosen and why I will return victorious." Argus said, stepping onto the sand with all the confidence of the Celt he wanted to emulate so badly. "Proximus, prepare yourself to meet the sands."

"Come one then you little shit. Show me what you can do."

Argus charged at the bigger man with a laugh. His countryman met him with all the embrace of a brick wall. The impact of their swords meeting was enough to knock Argus off his feet. He had to roll quickly out of the way to avoid the stomp of Proximus' foot. It fell like an anvil, burying him up to the ankle.

The momentary pause in Proximus' attack let Argus rise from the sand and drive the pommel of his sword into the hollow of his knees. Moving fast, he slapped the flat of the wooden blade into the crevice of the other knee, knocking the big man to both knees. One more quick blow to the back sent the giant of a man facedown in a cloud of dust.

"How is that for the work of a 'little shit', you blustering boulder?" Argus said with a laugh before offering his hand to help Proximus rise.

"Better than expected. Let us see if you have what it takes to do it again. Take position, Argus."

With a quick glance to the balcony that was more reflex than intention Argus squared his shoulders and nodded. If only it was a sword that he would be using in Rome.

"I can do this until the sun sets and old men, like you, fall asleep. Begin!"

CHAPTER 37

It had been two days since Cassian's burst of temper that had seen Tertius to his cell and an accord struck to see Violetta purchased from that monster of a silk merchant, but nothing had changed. Not a damned thing was different than it was.

Violetta was not back to her cell in the ludus at night, and due to the strange, secretive, summons to the villa she was rarely beside the sands in the heat of the afternoon when Cassian spent more of his time watching the younger men training. He had not had the chance to talk to her about the letters and the fact that she had said nothing in answer to his question.

It was burning in his heart. He had to know if she still wanted to be his wife. It was haunting him that she might say no, or that the lanista had been unable to secure her sale. He needed to settle his soul if he were to reign victorious over the Republic in a week's time. He needed to talk to his woman and not be interrupted by the timeline of the Romans or one of the other gladiators. If they were to leave for Rome in the morning then he would demand that he be allowed to have Violetta to himself for the night.

The lanista might still be enraged that Tarcarus was still recovering from the beating he had laid on him, but there had to be some benefit of being the champion of his house. If he refused then Cassian was prepared to argue for his right to the woman he loved. He was not going to be kept from her any longer. She was his love, his life, the only heart that spoke to his soul. He needed her more each day and the longer they were kept apart the more agitated, the more savage, he felt.

Perhaps that was the damned Roman's idea. Driving Cassian to his wits end by denying him the only thing that soothed him was something that Tertius was absolutely capable of. Despite his soothing words and promises to see Violetta purchased and secured to the company of the ludus, the man was a liar.

He was beginning to wonder if anything that Tertius had said that day was the truth. How was he going to buy Violetta from a man had been so adamant about keeping her as his own? Felix would know that once she was permanently part of this household Cassian would marry her as soon as possible. If he knew that meant that Vitus would know as well. The son would do anything that he could to make sure that Violetta did not find the happiness that she truly deserved.

That poisonous son of a hairless bitch was bound to spend his lifetime making hers a misery. His plans would not include letting her go from his father's house without a fight and as many attempts to give her misery as he could.

Was that why he had come to the ludus? Had he hoped that the lanista would give him the chance at assaulting her once again and when that did not work he had injured Arturo in frustration?

It was making him insane to have no answers and even more so to be denied the company of the one who could tell him everything that he needed to know.

"Lucius." He turned to speak to the Centurion in his shadow. "I would seek an audience with Tertius. There are words that must be broken before we are set to depart for Rome, and they can wait no longer."

"Cassian? Are you sure that is wise?" Lucius asked. "You know how he gets when he as to face the elite. He is not going to be in a giving mood."

"I do not care what kind of mood that fucking shit is in. I want my woman and I want her now. Whatever in Hades is going on in that villa that takes her there daily, for hours, when she should be attending the sands. When she should be learning her skills. When she should…"

"When she should be watching you adoringly? Instead of making herself invaluable to the woman who truly runs this house?" Lucius said with an infuriating logic.

"Can you blame me for wanting her eyes upon me at all times? Those eyes are like the blue of the Tenerife Sea and I could swim in them forever."

"You are a hopeless romantic Cassian." Julius said, shaking his head. "To try and keep your woman at your side is an admirable cause, but is the lanista going to listen to you? Is he going to be able to give you anything that is going to sooth you?"

"He can give me my woman and leave me alone with her until dawn comes." Cassian said, following his guard up the stairs to the main part of the house. "You must convince him to see me. I cannot wait until the return from Rome to hold her."

"You are so certain that you will return and that she will be here if you do?" Julius asked, leading him towards the lanista's office. "Rome is not Velletri and the gladiators there are not the piss-ants that you are used to fighting."

"You, of all people, doubt me?" Cassian laughed with an arch of his eyebrow.

"Not for a second. I only ask how sure you are so that I know how to place my bets in the city." He joked before nodding to Jovian to announce the gladiator's presence to the lanista.

"Take the best you can get and know that your coin will be well invested. I intend to give Rome a show unlike anything they have ever seen before. They will be screaming my name and begging for my return by the time that I am done with their champion. All the Republic will know my name, Lucius, and I will take every advantage of that."

"Your confidence is encouraging Cassian." Tertius said, looking up from his desk. "What brings you to my presence, absent command, on the eve of our departure to Rome? If you were any other man I would as if you were suddenly afraid of what you are to face. That is not your affliction, is it"

The lanista knew better than to ask such a foolish question. There had never been a time that Cassian had been afraid of a fight. Even when he had been taken captive as a foolish youth, not much younger than Jovian was now, he had been fearless to the point of recklessness.

"I believe you know that the answer to that question has never been in doubt, Dominus." Cassian said with a slight bow of his head. "I also believe that you know why I have petitioned Lucius to bring me before you tonight."

"There is something that you desire? Wine perhaps?" The lanista said, his voice infuriatingly distracted while he sorted through the parchments on his desk.

"Something more inspiring, something warmer." Cassian said, holding back a growl that threatened to pour from his throat. He was in no mood to be teased or have his mind played with.

"What would you have Cassian?" Tiberius asked, looking up from his table of work.

"I would have my woman in my arms." He said tensely.

"She will be with you in the wagon. You will have each other's undivided attention for nearly two days." Tertius returned his attention to the papers. "Why would I disrupt my household for a night when you will have what you want in a few more hours?"

"I would not dishonor her with intimacy in the company of Argus and Proximus." Cassian exclaimed. "Was it not you who said to me that I should take care of her, protect her?"

"So, you were listening? I had thought your mind too occupied with the drama of the night to understand me." Tertius said with a smile that Cassian found discomforting.

"I heard and understood. That is why I know that you will keep your word regarding bringing her, permanently, into this house. Why you will aid me in keeping her safe from the monstrous behavior of Vitus and Felix both."

"You are so sure of me and my word are you?" The lanista said, once again giving Cassian cause to doubt his sincerity. If the Roman was surprised at his trust it was possible that he should not have it at all.

"I am sure that you mean what you say, Dominus." Was his careful reply. "That is why I would like to have a night alone with the woman who inspires me to fight before we leave for the greatest games of my life."

He waited while the lanista appeared to debate with himself, tenting his fingers while he watched Cassian who was trying hard not to let his frustration show. Was he going to deny the request of his champion? Every man in the room knew that Cassian was well within his rights as her protector, her lover and the champion of the house and city to want Violetta in his bed, even Jovian who was lingering in the doorway knew this. The only question was if the Roman would honor to tradition or not.

"I suppose, when my wife has no further need of Violetta tonight, and she is fully prepared for the morning departure that Lucius may escort her to your cell."

"Gratitude Dominus." Cassian said with the smallest dip of his head that he could manage.

He hated to even pretend to respect this small-minded little man, but it was worth it, for now, to achieve his goals. He hoped and prayed that when the time came it would be his blade that found the lanista's throat. For every lie the man told, for every manipulation that cost a man his pride, his dignity, or his life this man needed to bleed. As much as the lanista needed to bleed Cassian needed to be the one to make him bleed.

He had to avenge so many fallen men, brothers lost to the amusement of the Romans. Because of what he had been before he had come here, who he had become among these men and who he was going to be when he returned home, he had to exact vengeance for them all. Every last one of them.

"You may go and make whatever preparations you need. The girl…"

"Violetta." Cassian interjected.

"Violetta will be brought to you at the end of her day and left in your cell until we leave an hour after the sun rises tomorrow." Tertius said, with the false benevolence that made Cassian want to smash him across the face with his fist.

"I will be waiting for her with eager gratitude, and a bottle of wine." Cassian said, stepping out of the office with his guard.

He gave Jovian a slight glare, just to remind the boy of who was the man in Violetta's heart and mind. If the boy had any thoughts of interfering with her coming to him that night then the reminder of the temper he would be agitating would do well to change the boy's plans.

Nothing and no one would stop him from having the woman he loved in his arms that night. Nothing.

Once they were down the stairs and back within the torchlit stone halls of the ludus Cassian looked and Lucius with a grin.

"I stand in your debt for that assistance and would like to add to the balance by requesting your aid in acquiring a bottle of wine that I might share with her tonight. Do you think you can manager it?"

"I do not see how it would be a problem, as long as you have the coin to cover it?" The Centurion teased.

They both knew that he was well paid for the games he competed in and that he had not been drinking as much wine since Violetta came into his life. There was simply less need for the oblivion provided by copious amounts of cheap drink.

"You know that I do. Ass." Cassian chuckled. "Make it something worth drinking if you can. I would have this be a special night for her."

"I will do what I can." The guard said with a nod before he departed.

Cassian set himself to turning the dank, dark, cell into something that could be soft, inviting, romantic, the kind of thing that women liked. It would be easier to ask why she had not answered his letters when she was thrilled at the effort that he put into the air of seduction for the night. As much as his pride was hurt he knew that he had to be careful to make sure that she did not think that he was angry with her over it.

He simply wanted answers. Answers and the tenderness of her touch on this night and all others that followed.

CHAPTER 38

Violetta was buzzing with excitement when Jovian told her that Tertius was going to allow her to spend their last night in Velletri with Cassian. She had been missing him terribly and it seemed as though it was part of Lycithia's agenda to make it impossible for them to see each other, let alone give them a chance to break words or share a kiss in a stolen moment. She knew that she had to help the woman, and a part of her wanted to, ordered to the task or not. It was heartbreaking to see a woman who wanted to be a mother so badly denied the chance. Still, she did not want to neglect Cassian simply to help Lycithia, even if she felt bad for the woman.

"It feels like an age since I have been alone with him, Jovian." She said to her roommate while running a comb through her hair. "I cannot wait to have his arms around me, to feel his kiss."

She paused when she noticed that her friend was pouting while he combed oil through his own hair.

"Am I upsetting you Jovian? Apologies if my joy reminds you of your desire to spend the same time with Argus."

"No need for apologies." He said with a sigh. "I am sure that the memory of his kiss will sustain me for one more night. Tomorrow we shall all be in the wagon together. Surely there will be a moment where a kiss or some other embrace might be stolen."

"You honestly think so? Even with so many of us in the small space?" Violetta asked applying a subtle touch of the scent that Jovian had offered in a moment of generosity.

"The small space is what ensures that I will be closer to him, for longer, than ever before." Jovian teased with a waggle of his eyebrows.

They were both laughing when Lucius knocked to announce his appearance.

"Violetta? It is time to go, young medicus. Be sure to bring all that you have prepared to take to Rome. There will be no returning to this room until we return from the city itself."

"I think that I am as ready as I can be." Violetta said with a smile, shouldering her bag. "The other is in the infirmary."

"That can be easily grabbed in the morning, but do not forget it. I would not want to think of what would happen if you were to forget your instruments." Lucius said with the smile that she was coming to learn was his kindest. The one he kept for friends.

"I should think it would be a catastrophe that needs to be avoided, at all costs." Violetta said with the seriousness that the situation required. She needed him to know that, despite her joyful exuberance, she took her work as the medicus as seriously as he took his work as the champion's bodyguard.

"Then let me get you to your man. His patience is as thin as the lanista's hair."

All three of them shared a laugh before Lucius pointed at Jovian.

"Do not speak a word of that to him."

Jovian held his hands up with a broad grin.

"Dominus will hear nothing from me. I will not be in his cart on the journey to Rome, remember?"

He was speaking to Julius, but his eyes were looking at Violetta. There was no doubt that he was doing his best to remind her that she had promised to help him get into the wagon. She still did not know how she was going to achieve it, she had to try though. He would never forgive her if she did not do everything she could to get him inside with the rest of them.

"Ready to go Violetta?" Julius asked, pulling her attention back go the moment. "He's waiting for you."

"Take me to him, please." Violetta said, joining him in the hallway and leaving the expectant Jovian behind in the room they had been sharing. "How did he manage to convince Dominus that we should have this time together?"

"He asked." Julius said, leading the way through the darkened hallway. "He also reminded the lanista that it is his right as a champion to ask for his woman. I am sure that you will get a good rest tonight."

Violetta was grateful for the darkness. It hid her blush at the Centurion's tease.

"I am sure that we will be well rested for the journey. Cassian is in peak condition and ready to fight."

"He is ready to do more than fight Violetta." The guard laughed and opened the gate. Gesturing to the man stepping free of the shadows. "I shall see the two of you in the morning. Have a good night, Cassian. Get that rest, medicus."

"Rest?" Cassian said, sliding his arm around Violetta's shoulder. "I cannot promise any such thing tonight. I will hold you in my arms while you sleep in the wagon tomorrow though, if that would meet the Centurion's approval?"

"Goodnight Violetta. See you both in the morning." Lucius said, locking the gate and heading back up the stairs to the villa.

"How stands my beautiful priestess this night?" Cassian said, pulling Violetta into his arms.

With a sigh of delight Violetta settled into his embrace. He was warm and strong, with comfort in his touch that spoke to every unsettled nerve in her body. It was magical how he had the ability to calm her with such simple affection. There was nowhere else in all the world that she wanted to be other than in Cassian's arms.

"I am as happy as a woman can be in the arms of the man she loves." She said, resting her head on his shoulder. "Perfectly satisfied."

"If you are satisfied now I wonder how you will feel in an hour?" He said, tilting her chin up so that he could press a kiss to her lips.

It was soft, tender, without demand or possessiveness and she reveled in it, in him.

"I imagine that, when I close my eyes to sleep at last, I shall be the happiest woman in all the Republic and more satisfied than the gods themselves as I rest in the arms of my beloved," Violetta said, wrapping her arms around Cassian's neck and stroking her fingers through his hair.

"As I told Lucius, I doubt there will be much rest for either of us this evening. I doubt there will be any regret either."

He looked down at her with that teasing smile she adored and brushed a strand of hair from her cheek.

"How does that appeal to my priestess? A night at prayer?"

"You must not say such things, Cassian." She chided with a shake of her head. "You are so irreverent. The gods may one day take offence to your teasing. I pray it is not this night though, or this fight."

"The gods love me, almost as much as you do. They will not smite their favoured son for so small an offence."

"You assume much of the gods, and me." She teased him, standing in the doorway of his cell, and looking inside. "It looks as though you have been preparing for me."

She stepped inside, leaving him to watch her as she turned slowly, taking in all the subtle changes to the cell that he had made, for her comfort alone. There were soft candles around the room, on shelves and in deep crevices of the walls. There were even a few in clusters on the floor where they would not be knocked over. His cot looked as though there were not only extra, thicker, blankets on it, but that by some miracle he had found or borrowed some cushions as well to increase the comfort and comparative luxury for their night together.

"Cassian, it is amazing."

"You like the candles then?" he asked with an uncertainty she was not used to hearing from him.

"I think it is completely beautiful. Gratitude for this." She placed a kiss on his cheek and smiled up into his eyes. "You are a thoughtful man, Cassian. With facets that most would not believe."

"No one else needs to believe. You are the one that matters." He said moving her hair from her shoulder and pressing a line of kisses down her neck. "In this life, and the next, you are only one that matters."

"As you are for me." She whispered, flicking her tongue against the pulse at the base of his throat. "Always."

He paused and looked into her eyes for a moment, almost as if he wanted to ask her a question, then scooped her into his arms and carried her the few steps to the bed. There was no need for words between them after that.

Slowly, with a touch so soft Violetta could hardly believe he swung swords with deadly force each day, he unfastened the shoulder laces of her dress and lowered it down her body. His tenderness made her shiver. It was just the slightest of trembles, but it brought her lover's hands to a halt and his eyes back to hers.

"Do you want me to stop?"

Opening her eyes, she pressed her lips together and shook her head.

"Please, do not." She stroked the side of his face. "I have missed your touch, your company. Oh, Cassian, I have missed you these past days. There are so many things I wish to tell you."

He chuckled and kissed her navel, the vibration of his laugh bringing a smile to her lips.

"Tell me in your letters, I want tonight to be for passion. There may be time for words and whispers of secrets in the days to come, but not tonight."

She was going to protest, to try to tell him that she was too uneducated to write a letter back to him, but his mouth pressed against the aching heat in her core and all other thoughts flew from her mind. The first wave of pleasure brought by his tongue crashed over her only seconds later, making all the worries of the journey seem far away. Cassian's finger slowly joined the work of his tongue, pressing into her, sliding deep inside, aided by the slickness brought by her pleasure.

The feeling of him filling her, even with just his hand, was exquisite bliss. Her hands threaded into his hair, freeing it from the braids at his temples so that she could bury her fingers in its softness.

Was there nothing that this man was not a god at?

Each sweep of his tongue was matched by the press and stroke of his fingers, testing, and teasing her nerves until she felt outside her mind. The tightness coiling within her was beginning to make her knees weak. Just when she thought that she might fall to the floor Cassian's free hand slid up the back of her thigh to cup the cheek of her ass. He held her tight against his mouth while the strength of his arm kept her from collapsing to the floor when the first touch of release flashed through her body.

"Cassian, I cannot stay upon my feet." Violetta pleaded, feeling as though the breath had been stolen from her body. "Please?"

When he looked up at her the light of the candles was flickering in his eyes. He looked positively devilish, like a delighted demon risen from the underworld.

"Pleading, my priestess?" He teased.

Rising slowly to his feet, his hands didn't leave her body. The rough calloused fingers danced over every inch of her flesh, setting her entire body on fire once again.

"Pleading for you, Champion." She replied, her body flushing as she pressed against his chest, revelling in the feel of his granite cut chest against her softness.

She watched the wildness she had come to know and love creep back into his eyes. She had come to recognize it as a sign of his passion and the depth of love he had for her. It thrilled her every time she saw that look in his eyes, even though it scared her just a little.

"Then you shall have me, my love."

He scooped her up into his arms and carried her to the bed, just as he had the night they had met.

Laying on the thick woven blanket it was Violetta's turn to caress her lover. His physique was a collection of contrasts that thrilled her. From the softness of his hair to the rough, short beard he wore, the soft curls of his chest hair and the smooth, hard, shaft that she now had in her hand, he was a blend of mortal man and divine god.

A god that was at her mercy.

Her hand worked up and down his cock while Cassian lay on his back, soaking up her attention, her affection and basking in her power to arouse him. His body was so tense and rigid, with every muscle defined, like carved marble, that she thought he would be cold to the touch when she pressed a kiss to his shoulder. She was surprised to find him so hot that he was almost feverish, with sweat glistening like dew at dawn.

"Cassian? Champion? I need you, now."

He grinned up at her, gripped her by the waist and flipped her beneath him.

"Then you shall have me, priestess."

CHAPTER 39

Cassian was utterly captivated by the woman laying beneath him. She was glowing divinely in the candlelight and the warmth of her body was inviting, but it was the confidence in her eyes that stirred something stronger than lust in the champion's soul. She was growing stronger, more sure of herself and her skills every day that she was beneath this roof. That was why she had to stay, why he had to do whatever it took to make that happen. That was why he had to treasure every breath between now and the moment the lanista told him that his wish had been granted.

Moments like right now.

She was arched against his body, needing the same thing from him that he was needing from her: the immediate consummation of their desire, followed by all the hours of the night in each other's arms.

The damp heat from between his woman's thighs greeted the head of his cock and he slid like silk between them. A brief pause at her entrance to help her to wrap her legs around him was over in a breath and then he was deep inside her core and Violetta was gasping at the sudden intrusion while she gripped his shoulders tight.

Her head was thrown back, taking away his view of her impassioned face, but giving him a glorious view, and access, to her bared breasts. Slowly thrusting into her Cassian lowered his head to lathe his tongue in a teasing circle around her nipple, sucking it into his mouth as she gasped. Releasing one delectable bud he moved to the other. Dragging the edge of his teeth across the flesh above it, Cassian smiled when he felt her tighten against his tongue.

The way her body responded to him was a gift from the gods. It was an arrow from cupid's arrow that went through his body from head to toe. Instead of being deadly the bolt was inspiring.

Lifting his head from the bliss of her bosom Cassian slid his arms beneath Violetta's slender shoulders and gathered her tight against his chest while he rose to his knees and settled his lover firmly upon his cock. Keeping one hand her back and the other upon her hip he drove up into her body with a new force.

"Open your eyes, Violetta." He growled passionately when she closed them with a sharp inhale. "Look at me."

He could tell it was hard for her. She had to fight her instinct to close her eyes and sink into the oblivion of physical bliss, but he wanted to see her, memorize her, and savor every second of this night. The gods alone knew if there would ever be another chance in this life for them to make love in this life.

"Cassian." She whispered, resting her forehead against his. Her hands gripping his shoulders so she could bear down on his cock, taking him deeper with each stroke. "In Rome…"

"I know, beloved, I know. Let us not speak of it now." He cut off her words then kissed her neck, biting just below her ear to make her moan deliriously.

She nodded and their bodies moved together. Riding faster, he was fighting the building climax so that the moment would not end. Though he meant to be with her more than once that night, perhaps even in the earliest hours of the dawn, there was something especially frantic about this embrace that screamed for the need to be cherished. Cassian could not have explained it to anyone, the need to linger and to draw out every stroke, but it was very real.

He let out a hiss between his teeth when Violetta drew the tips of the tips of her finger up his spine and gripped his shoulders before leaning as far back as his would allow her to. The change in the angle of his penetration, coupled with her aggressive return of each passion filled stroke, was too much for his control. Cassian let go and gave in, to her, to lust and to the will of the gods that brought them this far and would have to be trusted to carry them further.

Their pace was building. Their bodies connecting and colliding at a feverish pace while the sounds of their cries echoed against the stone walls. The candles that he had lit for her pleasure cast their shadows upon the wall, an erotic display of light and dark. Though it was a beautiful site, to watch Violetta move in perfect duplication, in his arms and shadowed on the wall, the woman in his arms, the living beauty, was what captivated him.

Cassian felt her body tighten around him, the shortness of her breath and the sweat dewing on her breast and knew that her release was near. He had to hold on long enough for her to climax first. Her bliss was the most important achievement he could focus upon, this night and all others.

The short, breathy gasps and soft whimpers told him that Violetta was on the very edge of climax. It was up to him to ease her across it or crash into it with all the fervor of a man facing death.

Easing her, carefully, onto her back Cassian kept his eyes locked to hers while he slid her legs over his shoulders and pushed closer until Violetta's knees were against her chest and his body was as deeply locked to hers as it could be. When her jaw dropped in the moment of deepened penetration Cassian renewed his pace. Thundering hard and fast into her body and drowning his own pleasure in the sounds that sang through the night air with fresh fervour.

It was too much, but not enough, and her hands gripping tight around his wrists were frantic in their ecstatic clutching.

Violetta cried out beneath him, calling his name along with other undistinguishable words. She was at her most beautiful when she was like this, impassioned and fully immersed in the moment. Whether it was making love or her work in the infirmary, seeing her lost in passion was becoming his favorite thing.

He wanted to see it again.

Shifting his hips Cassian stroked the head of his cock over the special spot that brought another cry from her lips and sent him over his own edge with a roar. Spent within her and gasping for breath Cassian gently eased himself down to lay beside Violetta. Kissing her shoulder, he gathered her in his arms and held her against his chest.

"This will not be the last night we have together." He murmured softly. "I will be victorious in Rome and Tertius will see to it that you are a permanent part of this house. You will never have to serve the house of Census again, Violetta. You will be safe, and we will be together."

"Will he do it? Do you think that Dominus will keep his word?" Violetta asked him, pressing a soft kiss to the arm encircling her.

"I will give him no rest until he does. I will not fight if he is not fighting to have you at my side."

He meant it. Though he was not sure how he would be able to avoid fighting without suffering an injury Cassian knew that he would not fight again until she was safely away from Census for good.

"I do not want you to suffer because of me." She said softly. "I know how much you love the games and standing in the arena. Do not give that up for me, please."

"You are worth everything I have Violetta. I will make sure that you are safe" He replied, rubbing her arm, and resting his head against hers. The smell of the soap she used in her hair intoxicating him with simple cleanliness.

That was Violetta: clean. She was pure and innocent still, in the way that Romans couldn't take from her. It had nothing to do with soaps or scents and everything to do with her soul. He could only hope that being near her, with her, might have a similar effect on his soul as well. It was the only way he could hope that the gods would see them together in the afterlife.

His redemption would be her reward, not his.

She turned to face him, and he had to fight not to get lost in the dreams of their future that he saw in her eyes.

"Cassian, I mean that. I do not wish to be the cause of your fall. You are now and shall always be the champion of my heart. The actions of the Romans will not change that."

He pressed a kiss to her forehead, smiling when her fingers traced down his stomach to where his cock was hardening again.

"Their actions matter less and less in our lives with each passing day Violetta. Once you are removed from the grasp of the house of Census for good then the whims of those who think themselves our masters will no longer effect us."

"What do you mean?" She asked, distracting him by kissing from his navel down towards his shaft.

"I will show you, when we return from Rome." He said with a grin, shifting to his back and easing Violetta back onto his cock. "Let us not think about that now. This night is for us, for passion."

His beloved priestess nodded and took his hands in hers while she began to ride him again. Their bodies fit together in ways that could only be matched by the ways that their hearts did the same.

"Then let us make the most of it."

They made love over and over that night, filling each moment with as much of each other as they could. Even in rest their touches were as intimate as though they were making love. It would be a night that Cassian would remember for the rest of his days and one that he prayed he lived long enough to recreate with her again.

When, at last, neither or them could summon the energy for more and Violetta lay safe and asleep in his arms Cassian watched the light of the sun begin to rise over the horizon. This was how every dawn should be greeted, with the love of his life in his arms and all the opportunity in the world before them both. The centurion would be here soon, to wake them, steal them from the moment and take them to the wagon that would be dark and crowded with the other gladiators.

They had so few chances to be like this, perfectly happy, he did not want to surrender it. His arms tightened around Violetta instinctively. Even though he was ready to fight he was not ready to risk dying and leaving her alone. Tertius must follow through with his vow to purchase her.

He must.

The silence was disrupted by the faint ringing of the metal gate closing. Lucius was on his way. Even though Cassian knew that he could trust his friend to give him as much time alone with his beloved as was possible the night that had been so beautiful was over. It was time to put away the lover, the husband-to-be and become the gladiator again. He had to become the killer once again.

He had to become the champion.

"Violetta? Beloved? It is time to wake. The centurion is coming. Morning is here." He whispered in her ear then pressed a kiss to her cheek.

He loved watching her wake, even if it were only to answer to the will of the Romans. The slow blink of her inky lashes and the flash of realization in her eyes when she saw him smiling down at her sent his heart soaring.

"It is morning already?" She asked, lifting he head to kiss him. "I thought it was still night, that we still had time together."

"I wish that it was, but we must prepare to depart for Rome." He replied, stroking the hair from her face. "Here is your dress."

"Oh gods." Lucius' voice cut through the comfortable silence. The guard spun to lean his back against the cell door. "I will let you dress, but there is little time. The lanista is not patient."

"Purge your mind of what you saw, Roman, and we will be ready in moments." Cassian joked, trying to ease the embarrassment of them both. Helping Violetta to her feet he then picked up his own garments, dressing as though each peace were armor and not stained linen.

"It is purged, I swear." Julius said, turning to unlock the door. "Let us hurry, the wagon is ready."

"I need to gather my bag from the infirmary, and the tools that Arturo has packed." Violetta said, sliding the straps of her dress over her shoulder and joining Cassian in the hall. "Is he coming with us to Rome? Did the lanista decide?"

"Gather your things, young medicus." The guard said, looking Cassian in the eyes. "For you all take the journey. We can only pray that each of you returns."

Cassian watched Violetta rush to retrieve her things then looked at his guard, his friend, and said with a deadly flat voice.

"I will return, victorious, and champion of the Republic and my cause or not at all."

Continued in "The Champion's Cause."

About the Author

Born in Hardisty, Alberta Monica developed an undeniable love of reading at an early age. Homeschooled during her primary years, her mother not only taught the basics to her five children, but she also read to them at least twice a day. From Anne of Green Gables to Tolkien's Lord of the Rings the stories and the people behind them instilled a love of the written word.

As soon as she could hold a pencil Monica began to write her own stories. Her first complete work was 'Monkey Millionaires' in which a pair of monkeys became millionaires by selling ice cream. While it was a huge hit among the kids in the neighborhood it was just the beginning. After discovering the TV show Spartacus, and full immersion into that fandom, Monica was disappointed to find there was very little fiction to satisfy her desire to indulge a love of Roman era romance. The spark was then lit to write the stories she wanted to read herself.

Despite some eye-opening experiences (it's not as glamorous a profession as the movies would have you believe) she would not change her journey in the slightest. When she is not working or writing, Monica is a single parent to a little girl. Nothing makes her happier than when her daughter tells her that she wants to be a writer, "Just like you, Mommy." So, to keep inspiring a very special little girl, and to bring some elements of romantic Rome and the romance of real life to some not-so-little girls, she is pleased to be writing as M. Francis Lamont and brings you "The Champion's Torment," the second book of her centurion saga, and many more stories to come. She encourages everyone to "Live with Passion. Live with Purpose. And most important of all, Never Lose." Welcome to the beginning of something wonderful.

Book 4 of The Champions, "The Champion's Cause," Coming Soon!